THAT ONE
Moment

*To Garry!
Best Wishes! Wiseman
Patty*

PATTY WISEMAN

BOOKS BY
Patty Wiseman

Velvet Shoe Collection
An Unlikely Arrangement
An Unlikely Beginning
An Unlikely Conclusion
An Unlikely Deception

Success Your Way

A Division of Y&R Enterprises, LLC
PO Box 2283
Lindale, TX 75771

This book is a work of fiction. Therefore, all names, places, characters, and situations are a product of the author's imagination and used fictitiously. Any resemblance to actual persons, living or dead, places, or events is entirely coincidental.

Copyright © 2017 Patty Wiseman

All rights reserved. No part of this book may be used or reproduced in any manner whatsoever. For information address Y&R Publishing Rights Department, PO Box 2283, Lindale, TX 75771.

Interior Book design by Champagne Formats
Printed in the United States of America

Library of Congress Control Number Data
Wiseman, Patty
That One Moment / Patty Wiseman.
Contemporary—Romance—Fiction.2. Suspense—Romance—Fiction.
Fiction. | BISAC: FICTION / Romance / Contemporary. | Fiction / Romance / Suspense.
2017
Library of Congress 2017938946
First Edition.

ISBN: 978-1-940460-90-1

www.pattywiseman.com
www.yandrpublishing.com

PRAISE FOR *THAT ONE MOMENT*

Patty Wiseman's portrayal of beautiful, independent Ricki whose life is almost destroyed by Russ Desmond, a sociopath seeking revenge keeps you turning the pages. Ricki tries to wipe Kory Littleton from her mind, but can she control her heart and withstand his charm and the security he offers? Wiseman adroitly weaves a romantic tale full of suspense that finds Ricki high on a mountain trail fighting for survival. But the reader wonders, what is worse: Ricki's struggle to survive the elements or her struggle to escape Desmond's maniacal plan. Wiseman's story reveals to the reader how easy it is for a self-reliant woman to fall prey to the vulnerabilities of the heart. I recommend this fast-paced page turner.
~Linda Pirtle, author of The Games We Play Series: *The Mah Jongg Murders* and *Deadly Dominoes*.

Two battered hearts daring to love again; a deranged man determined to stop them. In a world of deception and betrayal, can they find the strength and courage to risk it all again, or will the past destroy them? Patty Wiseman weaves a tale of betrayal, heartbreak and rebirth that will keep you turning the pages long past your bedtime.
~Award Winning Author Dana Wayne

Patty Wiseman is an author of immense talent who brings her characters to life. As you turn each page you will find yourself wondering what will happen next? And she continues to keep you wondering until the last page.
~Ruth Ann Buck, Credit Analyst

Dedication

Sometimes you get it wrong, sometimes you get it right. This book is dedicated to my long-suffering husband, Ron. Because of one moment in time, my second chance materialized the day we met. Without him, I could never have accomplished my dream. That one moment changed my life.

CHAPTER *One*

Ricki Sheridan didn't expect to die falling off a mountain ledge.

One misstep, a soft spot on the trail, and her leather hiking boot slipped over the edge, sending a shower of gravel over the jagged cliff.

Unbalanced and top-heavy, her scream echoed across the deep ravine like a wounded loon falling from the sky. She jerked the backpack to the right, dragged her left foot up the ridge, and fell against the rocky cliff gasping for air.

A misty fog wet her face and chilled her fingers while tendrils of fear snaked around every nerve. *Breathe, Ricki, you didn't go over. You're okay.*

She shrugged the pack off her shoulder and eased her already sore body onto the makeshift cushion. The trembling persisted, uncontrolled and violent.

Crap, a little too close for comfort.

Thankful no one witnessed the near disaster, she gulped the crisp mountain air to restore balance and quiet the pounding in her chest. A mixture of grit and sweat slid over one brow and stung her eye. The only thing available to erase the grime and unbidden tears was the sleeve of her faded denim shirt, which she hastily swiped across her face.

The pup tent on top of the pack slid to one side. She stood to re-center it, and mumbled, "This trip might be a bad idea. I should have stayed in Texas."

A devastating betrayal found her on this mountain to help eradicate the pain from her mind. Ricki is a strong woman most times, but the most vulnerable aspect of her personality failed her, again. When it comes to men, she always chooses the wrong one. This time was the last straw, because *this time* it involved her best friend.

Another deep breath diminished the shaking. "Lucky I didn't tumble down on top of the *second* team."

"You all right?"

A deep male voice made her jump and spin around. Off balance again, she teetered to the right and kicked another spray of gravel over the edge.

The man reached out to steady her. "Whoa, let me help you."

He was one of the trail bosses. She saw him at Wolf's Den Lodge, noticed his ink black eyes and quick smile, but chose to hang back and keep her distance. When the group took to the trail, she decided to bring up the rear. As a result, she fell farther behind the others, but it suited her purpose. Her goal was to be alone. She aimed to keep it that way.

"Thanks, I'm fine, just tripped. Pack is a little off balance. I've got it covered."

Her wanna-be rescuer ran a hand through thick, raven hair, assessed her with a glance, and said softly. "You look like you need a break."

Overcome with a sudden awareness of her physical state, her hand went swiftly to her own disheveled mane. She smoothed the windblown tangles as best she could. "I said I could handle it. It's steep here, that's all. I was looking up instead of at the trail. No harm done."

"What's your name?"

She ducked her head. "Ricki Sheridan."

He stretched out his hand. "We didn't get to meet formally. I'm Kory Littleton, Trail Boss."

"I know who you are." The rude retort wasn't natural to her, but necessary to keep the distance she coveted.

"I saw your name on the list. Nice to put a face to it. Ever been on a pack trip before? This is a good mountain to start on."

To her relief, she didn't have a chance to answer. Another group arrived in single file, impatient, and unable to pass.

A short, scruffy man scanned the sky and looked back at Kory. "You gonna stop on this narrow ledge or what, Chief? It'll be nightfall soon."

Shadows darkened the snow tipped peaks, clouds drifted across the late afternoon sky, and a keen breeze cut through Ricki's thin shirt.

She shivered.

Littleton stepped around in front. "Take your troop on ahead. The lady experienced a small set-back. Her ankle's bleeding. I'm gonna doctor it." He lowered his voice. "Watch the trail over there, Steve, it's soft. Don't want anyone to slip off the mountain."

Steve Gorman eyed the edge of the trail and turned back to survey Ricki's injured ankle. He nodded and spit a stream of tobacco juice into the dirt.

She looked down. Blood oozed over the thick, woolen sock onto her low rider boot.

"Next time, try the high-tops. They're safer," Steve said. He brushed by, motioning the others to follow. He and the rest of his band followed him around the bend.

"Sit down, the first aid kit is in my pack," Kory ordered.

Her chin rose in defiance, another chink in her armor—a quick temper. "Thanks, I can bandage it. Take care of the rest of your group."

He grinned good-naturedly and displayed a cheerful salute. "I'm an Eagles Pass Trail Boss, ma'am. We never leave anyone behind. It's our motto. I'm the head guide, gotta set the example." The bulky pack slipped easily off his broad back.

"Head guide, huh? What makes you so special?" Embarrassed about her clumsy mishap, she couldn't resist the urge to goad him.

"Oh, I don't know, probably because I've been around longer—saved a few more lives." The smile flashed again before his teeth ripped through the adhesive bandage. "Now hold still, I've done this a couple of million times, we'll be through in a flash."

She flinched at his touch as a small shock of pain raced through the ankle.

"It's bruised, and it'll be tender, but should be fine," he said.

She watched his face as he worked. The image of trail boss conjured up flannel shirts, knee-high boots, a gruff personality, and five o'clock shadow. *This one is different. Clean shaven, strong white teeth, weathered skin, and he's kind. He's got the red flannel shirt down, though.*

She shivered again, this time from his strong hand holding her ankle so gently. "Look, Mr. Littleton, I appreciate your help. The backpack got the better of me, I admit…packed too heavy. I'll fix it and be right along. Please get back to the others. I'm an experienced back-packer, thanks to my father. I know the mountains."

"The *name* is Kory. Steve is my back up. We need to stick to the rules. I'll help you rearrange your load, and we'll both catch up. We don't leave anyone behind, remember? 'Fraid you're stuck with me. Can you put weight on the ankle?" He slung her pack over one shoulder and heaved his pack over the other arm.

She winced at his reprimand, but eased herself to a stand. "Yes, it's okay."

Taking orders wasn't her strong suit. From the ROTC program in high school and college to a Crime Scene Forensic Investigator in the U.S. Navy, she was used to having the upper hand. But, it was all over now. After her enlistment was up, she turned civilian and applied for the game warden academy. She was assigned to a position in Dallas after graduation. Wildlife suited her more than a stuffy office. She thrived in the outdoors with nothing to confine her but the blue sky.

"Better get a move on, then. There's a wide spot in the trail up ahead. We'll reorganize there." He disappeared around the bend.

She followed slowly, testing the ankle with each step.

Sprawled on a rotten log, he systematically unloaded the first few contents of her pack. The boyish grin flashed, again, as he held up a small journal. "Ah, reading material. Hope you don't plan to keep your nose in a book the whole time. This is a retreat, I know, but don't forget we have nine other people here. Good practice to interact with the other campers."

She snatched it from his hand. "Put it down. It's none of your business. I said *I'll* redo my pack."

Kory drew back his hand—the smile disappeared. "Sorry Ricki, I meant no harm. Chill out, I didn't peek."

She flung the remaining contents on the ground, one a time. "This trip's a big mistake. I'm heading back to the lodge."

His voice changed from jovial to real concern. "Hey, slow down. You'll never make it down the mountain before dark. The weather calls for a storm sometime tomorrow. I can't let you go." He picked up each item she threw at him and organized them according to weight and size.

She stomped her good foot. "You can't stop me. I paid my money. It's on *my* head. I don't want to do this anymore."

To her horror, hot tears trickled down her face. She started to shake.

In one stride, he reached her before she toppled over. "I apologize, Ricki. Sit down. You're exhausted. Six miles is a lot when it's uphill luggin' a pack, especially if you haven't done it in a while. I'm here for a reason, let me do my job."

Suddenly, weakness overcame her in a most disconcerting way. She collapsed against him, sobs wracking her body.

His strong arms encircled her. He wiped two large tears from her cheek with his thumb, and whispered softly, "It's okay, Freckles. We all have our breaking point."

"Don't call me Freckles!" She gulped between sobs, the unpredictable temper blazed hot.

"I'm sorry—again. I can't say anything right, it seems. Too long in the mountains, I guess." He hesitated. "I meant it as a compliment. They're very pretty on you."

"I…I never cry. Never." The temper subsided into annoyance.

He held her a little too tight and whispered a little too softly in her ear, "Maybe it's time to let go."

The sobs stopped abruptly at the intimate encounter. She pulled away and wiped her eyes on one dirty sleeve. "It's over now. It won't happen again."

He turned, grabbed a bedroll, and spread it on the ground. "Sit." His voice left no room for argument.

Never in her memory had she done anything so embarrassing, so out of character. Self-control was one of her strong suits, a source of pride to her. Military training taught her well.

He rearranged each item in her pack, buckled it up, re-cinched the straps, and set it against the dead log. "All finished. Feelin' any better?" He squatted on his heels in front of her. "You're in no shape to hike down the mountain. Let's see if we can sort this out before we rejoin the others."

Her protest withered on quivering lips. Voices echoed in the faded forest. Someone or some*thing* was about to round the bend.

CHAPTER Two

A DISHEVELED CHARACTER APPEARED FROM THE BEND IN the trail. "Everything okay here? Can I help? I came back to check on you, Kory. No time to take a break as I see it. Night's falling fast. We'll be lucky to make base camp before it's dark."

"Hey, Kyle, we're fine. Ankle problem. Takin' a short rest. Nothing to worry about," Kory answered.

Kyle Bennett's tall, skinny body bent slightly under the weight he carried. Long stringy hair framed a thin face. A yellow lodge shirt, the color assigned to new trail hands, indicated this was his first solo run.

Several of his troop peeked over his shoulder to see what caused the commotion.

"Oh, right, Kory, I gotcha." He winked. "I'm on my way, then. See ya on the other side."

Ricki shuddered when Bennett looked her up and down. He

grinned, displaying missing teeth. Disgust roiled in her stomach.

She turned and faced Kory, face flaming. "Sounds like your reputation precedes you, Mr. Littleton. You do this for all the women, right?"

He sighed, sat down, reached for his canteen, and offered it to her.

She ignored the gesture.

He sloshed the liquid in the container until she jerked it out of his hand. "I'm a trail guide; I live here, away from civilization, for a reason. I don't know much about women, we don't get many up here. I know why *I* do this, why don't you tell me why you are here?"

She jerked the canteen out of his hand and took a swig. The cool water soothed her parched throat, and she savored the refreshment, letting her anger dissolve. "Sorry, I know it's your job to help and my problems aren't part of it. These retreats help people step out and make a change in their lives, broaden their horizons. I get it. I signed up because I thought this would be a good change of pace for me. Anyway, I chose the wrong venue for my escape. I should have gone on a long cruise, alone. I'll follow you to the camp and head back in the morning. I know it's a long hike to the lake. I just don't need this."

"Too late, Ricki, the sun's gone. The temperature is dropping. We can't make it to the first camp. We'll have to stay here, catch 'em in the morning. We're twenty minutes from total darkness. Predators come out at night."

The last glow of daylight dipped behind the tallest peak until only a sliver of light remained. Panic gripped her. "We can't stay here tonight. The others will think … well, we need to find them. You have flashlights, don't you? It can't be far." She jumped up and grabbed the pack wincing in pain.

"The others won't make it to the lake before dark, either. We always make camp in a small clearing about two miles from base camp the first night. Tests the camper's mettle *and* the new guides. If they can make it the first night, the rest goes like clockwork. It's all in the plan. You can't maneuver the trail in the dark, though. It's too treacherous, and the fog is rolling in. We're stuck here." He picked up a few dried limbs and gathered a couple of broken logs.

She stared at him, pack in hand. "What are you doing?"

"Building a fire, it gets cold up here. Grab the rotted log over there, it'll burn nicely. The longer you stand there, the longer it will take to build the fire, and believe me; you'll want a fire in about an hour."

She dropped the pack and retrieved the crumbling wood.

In no time, a fire danced within the ring of stones Kory gathered.

Bone tired, she settled against the log.

"Hungry?" he asked. He rummaged in his pack and brought back two foil pouches.

"What are those?"

"Campers MRE's. We use these the first night. The remainder of the trip you rely on your wits, fish, berries, and the like. These are pretty good if you heat them."

He nestled a flat stone in the coals, at the edge of the fire, and placed the pouches on the hot rock. "I'll make some coffee. I've got all we need in my pack."

He went about the business of coffee making and camp building with practiced precision.

She watched, fascinated.

Neither spoke while they waited on the meal. The fire crackled sending sparks into the night, a pleasant companionable sound. They didn't talk, simply sat together staring into the flames.

How did this happen? I simply wanted to get away, forget about what happened. Now, I'm stuck on the side of a mountain with a strange man.

An owl hooted in the distance and shook them out of their reverie.

Kory checked the coffee. "It's about ready. I've got utensils in my pack, can you get them?"

She found the tin cups, metal plates, two spoons, and a ragged, blackened hot pad. The aroma of hot coffee signaled the hunger in her stomach. The smell of cooking meat tickled her nose. "Beef stew?"

"Isn't it amazing? They can do so much with this stuff now. Here, I think it's ready."

She poured the coffee while he ripped open the meals and dumped them in the plates.

They ate in silence, side by side. The darkness heightened the night sounds as the mountain's nocturnal prowlers awakened—eerie and unsettling.

Kory cleaned up and settled beside her, coffee cup in hand. His easy manner told the story of a life in the outdoors. One knee up, the other sprawled out, lazy, and unafraid.

"Would you like to talk about him?"

"Who?"

He kept his head turned toward the fire, the cup relaxed on the top of one knee. "The guy you're running from."

She shrugged. "Nothing to tell. Same old story. *And, I'm not running.*"

"Well then, why are you out here with me?" He faced her and grinned.

She surprised herself and laughed. "Because you forced me. I *would* be back at the lodge, but for your stubbornness."

"You have a pretty laugh. It's good to hear. Why *did* you run?"

A coyote's howl in the distance held her spellbound for a moment. Such a lonely cry. "I *said* I'm not running. I wanted a change of pace, a fresh start, out with the old, in with the new."

"Men can be pigs, can't they? He must be blind."

She continued to stare straight ahead, irritated he persisted with the subject of men.

He picked up a long stick and poked at the coals.

Flames shot up and lit the perimeter of the camp for a brief time until the blaze dwindled, and then, smoldered, much like her emotions.

"I didn't see it coming. You would think I'd learn."

He shot her a look. "It's happened before?"

"I hate to admit it, but yes, once."

"You need new friends, Ricki."

"Yeah, I need a whole new life. Guess it's why I ended up here."

His voice lost any sign of arrogance. "Where are you from?"

"Dallas."

"Dallas? And you came to the Rockies for a retreat?"

She took another sip of coffee. "I suppose I ran back to my roots, the peace of the mountains. Not much calm in the city. Our family loved backpacking, camping, fishing. There's something about the peacefulness of the wild that restores the soul."

"What do you do there?"

She hesitated. "Game Warden. Surprised?"

His laugh was easy. "No, I'm not surprised. Takes guts to do a ten-mile hike, up-hill with a fifty-pound pack on your back." He paused. "The guy. He's a cop?"

She shot him another look. "How did you know?"

"Lucky guess." He scooted away from the fire. "We need to hit the hay, get an early start. You look better after fillin' your stomach, but you need a good rest. Put your sleeping bag in front of the fire. I'll be behind you to block the wind."

"What do you mean? Can't you sleep on the other side?"

He shook his head. "You'll be thankful for my body warmth. We're on an open ridge. The wind's gonna blow hard tonight, and it's damp. Our regular base camp sits in a stand of trees, protected from those gales, but on this ridge, it's wicked. I'm used to it. This is survival, Ricki. You need to put modesty aside."

The wind whipped through the makeshift camp and sent sparks flying into the air.

She nodded.

"The fire is about out. I better stoke it up for the night."

He rose, and in the dim light of the dying embers, she could make out his form loading dead branches in his arms. "Can I help?"

"No, can't take a chance on the ankle in the dark. You can go ahead and turn in. We've got a lot of trail to make up tomorrow."

The cord on the sleeping bag didn't cooperate. Her cold fingers picked at the knot, over and over, while she followed his movements in the dark. "Don't you have a family, Kory?"

"I did."

"I see, man of few words, huh?"

His face hardened, and his voice strained, "We all keep private bits of our lives hidden away. Leave it alone."

"Touché, sorry." Ricki wrenched the knot free. With an angry flip of her wrists, she unrolled the sleeping bag, kicking herself for prying into his private life.

I hit a nerve for sure, but he didn't have to be such a jerk. Oh right, he's a man. Why am I surprised? All men are jerks.

Before she turned her back, he closed the gap between them in two strides, dropped the firewood, his face open, his eyes sorrowful. He grabbed her shoulders. "Freckles, forgive me. It's something I don't talk about. Nothing personal. I guess everyone who knows me understands. Too much pain. Can we change the subject?"

She winced. "You have strong hands." Her voice softened. "And don't call me Freckles."

His grip relaxed, but he didn't release her. "Oh man. I'm sorry. Don't know my own strength sometimes."

The silence of the forest enhanced the tension between them. She wanted to respond to his touch, but her mind resisted, the sound of a steel door closing echoed in her thoughts.

"Ricki, I…" His eyes searched her face, one hand touched a cheek. He leaned in, his kiss soft.

Eyes closed, she savored the salty taste and smoky scent of him. The moment sweet, normal, even comfortable. Her guard lowered.

She almost gave herself to the kiss.

As quickly as it happened, it ended, and he disappeared into the trees like a ghost.

She stood alone—numb and vulnerable. "What's happening?" she whispered to the darkness, shaking, trying to find a sense of equilibrium.

Pine resin popped deep inside the fire. Logs shifted, fiery sparks danced into the sky, and restored her senses. A quick survey of the wilderness around the camp revealed nothing. He simply vanished. The darkness deepened.

"The fire..." She hobbled to where he dropped the wood, gathered it into her arms, and fed the branches one by one into the hungry flames.

Where did he go? What in the world just happened?

Strength in difficult situations was one of her strong suits. Her resolve to finish tough assignments defined her. She carried a gun, self-defense came easy for her, but one thing left her indefensible—her heart. She picked the wrong guy, every time. For her to lean into his kiss and drop her guard scared her more than any gun-toting thief or half-crazed bear. *What was I thinking?*

She returned to the old log by the fire, picked up her coffee cup, and waited, resolved to give him a piece of her mind when he returned.

He'll come back. He wouldn't leave me here, alone.

Another coyote howled, rustling noises sounded behind her, and resoluteness turned into abject fear. Nothing prepared her for a night alone in the middle of nowhere.

Is this their idea of teaching us to survive? Not smart in my book.

Twenty minutes later, a figure emerged from the darkness.

Ricki watched as it drew closer until she made out a man's form and finally, Kory came into focus, hair ruffled, his mouth in a grim line.

Her breathing stopped as she watched him advance, but now, she relaxed and released the piece of wood gripped tightly in her hand.

He dropped hard on the log in front of the fire and watched the flames, silent.

She waited.

"I'm sorry," he said. "I shouldn't have kissed you. It's unprofessional, and I apologize. I'm alone out here, most of the time. The mountains work on a man's mind. Can we forget it happened?"

For an odd moment, her heart dropped. She hadn't expected an apology, didn't know what she expected. The kiss stirred an unwelcome hunger in her, the need for a male touch, a connection. She *almost* savored that one moment, but once again, she pushed it aside as a sign of weakness. *No good comes from physical desire. At least, not for me.*

She nodded, curtly. "Of course, no need to apologize. We'll forget it. I'm bushed, think I'll turn in."

"Yeah, me too. We'll have a hard day tomorrow. Better get some sleep. I'll make sure our fire makes it through the night. Good night, Ricki."

The fire blazed, the stars twinkled, and she snuggled inside her downy sleeping bag; a corduroy jacket her pillow.

Kory secured the camp, packs between the fire and their bedrolls for protection from night predators. Coyotes roamed the hills at night, raccoons scavenged the forest.

A hammer echoed in the dusky night.

She poked her head out of the bag. "What are you doing now?"

"Settin' up a lean-to for windbreak. I always carry a small tarp."

The plastic crackled and whipped in the breeze, secured by ropes, one end almost to the ground.

He's very efficient.

In a semi-sleepy state, she noticed the chill on her backside disappear a few minutes later. He lay next to her.

"Good night, Ricki. Sleep well," he whispered.

Her eyes closed, secure in a cocoon of warmth for the first time in two years. "Good night, Kory."

CHAPTER Three

Ricki wasn't sure what woke her. The dying embers of the fire greeted her unfocused eyes.

The fire is almost gone. He must be dead tired to have forgotten it.

She struggled out of the sleeping bag, grabbed a jacket and boots, and sat down on the dead log.

Let him sleep. I can build up the fire.

One by one, she tightened the rawhide bootlaces, but with a strap in each hand, froze at a low growl from the edge of the woods. Afraid to move, she listened for the sound again and cringed. "Coyote."

A quick glance at Kory's sleeping bag sent a shiver down her back. It was empty.

Slowly, she moved to face the threat. *Stay calm, girl.*

Two yellow eyes glowed at the edge of the darkness.

Before she could decide a course of action, a voice hissed out an order, "Sit still, don't move."

The voice sounded familiar, but it wasn't Kory's. Whoever it belonged to stood behind her.

"Where's Kory?" she whispered.

"Shhh…"

Something whizzed by one ear, followed by a thump, and a yelp. The golden eyes disappeared into the abyss of the night.

"He wanted what's in the pack, not you. Lookin' for food. He won't bother you now."

The male voice moved around her. "Steve!" She looked into his pock-marked face. "Why are you here? Where's Kory?"

He tucked the slingshot into his back pocket, added an armful of wood to the puny fire, and helped himself to what remained of the coffee. "An emergency. Appendicitis we think. Poor woman. A lot of pain. Kory's the only one who can negotiate the trail in the dark. He's taking her to the lodge where they can call for a helicopter to pick her up. I carried her here. He took the rest of the jaunt. Told me to let you sleep, but our coyote friend decided different. I've gathered enough wood to make it until morning. Go back to sleep, I'll stand guard. Four more hours before daylight."

The hollow in her stomach increased. "Gone? He'll be back, right?"

"No, not possible. By the time he gets down the mountain he'll be exhausted and need rest for the next week's group coming through. I'm afraid we've seen the last of him on this trip. You're stuck with me." His mouth split open to reveal chipped, yellowed teeth.

The security and warmth of the evening evaporated. She wished she was back in Dallas. *Why did I think this was a good idea?*

For one evening, the painful break up disappeared. Long forgotten emotions surfaced in a small camp, deep in the forest with an attractive man. Now he was gone. *Fool. I probably imagined the whole thing anyway.*

She didn't want to be stuck with Steve—didn't like the way he looked at her.

"I can get myself down the mountain and back to the lodge tomorrow, can't I?" she asked.

"I'm afraid not. There's only Kyle and me now. Need two guides, at all times. You'll have to finish the trip." He positioned himself on a tree stump near the trees, but still close to the fire.

Ricki slid back into the sleeping bag to wait for morning, but sleep didn't come. An hour later, she heard Steve wriggle into Kory's bag and cringed at the uncomfortable proximity. His unwashed body odor drifted through the air.

She pulled the bag over her nose and closed her eyes, resigned. *Bad timing. Wrong place, wrong man. Finish what you started, girl. Kory won't be here to distract you and get you off-track. You wanted this new adventure, so focus.*

"Get up sleepyhead, time to move."

Steve's voice jolted her awake.

A large, black spot lay where a cheerful fire danced the night before. Steve cleaned up the last of the debris, held out an unappetizing square of hardtack and a canteen.

She grabbed the meager breakfast and put on her boots. After testing her weight on the ankle, she hurried after him, hoping the injury wouldn't hinder her. The pace he set brutalized her back and legs. The ankle was tender, but didn't slow her down.

Determination drove her on. Intent on proving her worth; she kept up, thankful to focus on the trail and not Kory.

An hour later, he stopped and dropped the pack. "We'll stop here for a bite to eat. We have another hour, maybe two before we reach base camp. How's the ankle? Can you make it?"

She removed her own load and ignored the pain in one shoulder, jaw set. "I can make it. The ankle is taped up good. Don't worry about me."

A grin crossed his face.

Grin all you want, Steve. I'll make it.

The beef jerky and hardtack chased by a swig of water did little to satisfy the gnawing hunger. Her mind wandered back to what Kory told her of the week the group would endure in the wild. *Fish and berries? Trout cooked over an open fire sounds like a feast right about now.*

Steve didn't talk much. She passed the time comparing his looks to Kory's. They couldn't differ more. Steve had an unruly dark beard and dirty blond shoulder-length hair. She couldn't determine the color of his eyes because he never took off his aviator shades.

Not half the man his boss is.

"What's the story on Kory? Is he married?" she asked.

"No, he's not married. Not now anyway. He was."

"So, what happened?"

Steve adjusted a strap on his pack and shrugged it back onto bony shoulders. "Ask him. He's a private person. Not up to me to give out his information. Better get going."

"Just passing the time, Steve. And by the way, I did ask him. No luck."

They trudged up the trail in silence for the next two grueling hours.

An empty camp greeted them.

"Where is everyone?" she asked.

"Out finding their supper I imagine. Better get your camp set up and join them if you want a place to sleep and dinner in your belly. I'll get you started, but the rest of the week, it's up to you. You can team up or go it alone. Your choice. Most everyone has a partner by now, though."

He found a spot at the outer edge of the camp and gave instructions to set up. "Meet me in the clearing when you're finished."

She didn't like the closeness of their tents, but knew the options were slim. Thirty minutes later her tent stood proud.

Thankful her dad taught the basics; she set about finding a spot to cast her line.

"Guess it's just you and me, doll," Steve said. "Come sit next to me. I'll show ya the ropes."

"I've got this. No worries," she answered. His comment made her uneasy.

Finally, one by one, the others straggled back into camp. She relaxed a little. A few came down to the water to try their luck.

Steve explained the best places to put in. He handed her a small can of salmon eggs. "I always carry some with me. They work pretty good up here."

While she baited the hook, a new energy emerged. *Maybe this is what I need, after all. I can do this. Survival of the fittest. This isn't so bad.*

For a fleeting minute, she wondered where Kory ended up—and the woman he helped. There was something about the rugged trail boss. He stirred up emotions she didn't know she had, a rush of *something* not even her recent relationship brought to the surface. Her thoughts kept going back to the kiss on the mountain. The warmth of his lips, the giddiness, the fire in her groin left her breathless—and wanting more.

But, she forced the reflections from her mind. *Never mind, Ricki. He's right, I need new friends.*

About two yards away, a young woman slipped into the water when her pole jerked abruptly.

May as well start now. She moved closer. "Need some help over there?"

"I think I've got it, thanks. Hi, my name's Rebecca Blair." She swung the dangling fish onto the shore. "Aren't you the lady who hurt her ankle? Where's the good-looking guide?" She stepped back on dry ground, juggling her pole. She flashed a smile before she turned her attention back to her catch.

Ricki walked by Steve and held out her hand to Rebecca.

"I'm Ricki Sheridan. What do you mean where's Kory? Didn't they tell you he took someone back to the lodge? Appendicitis or something."

"No, I didn't hear about anyone being sick. I don't know everyone, yet. Who was it?" Rebecca asked.

"I don't know." She pointed to the trail boss. "Steve told me about it. He came back and helped lead me here this morning. Said Mr. Littleton left in the middle of the night."

"Too bad. Hope she's okay, but I wouldn't mind being carried out by him."

One by one, trout bit Ricki's line. It brought back memories of childhood as she hauled them to the shore. She and Rebecca fell into a friendly competition, enjoying the sport of it.

They passed the time in comfortable companionship. At closer inspection, Rebecca looked like an outdoorsy girl. Short, curly brown hair, slender build, and a determined confidence showed on her face with each fish caught. Ricki tried to guess what this novice fisherwoman did for a living.

Rebecca finally pulled her line in. "Hey, I gotta get my fire started for dinner. Want some help with yours? Looks like we both have quite a mess of fish. Where's your tent?"

"Over there, by Steve's," Ricki said.

Rebecca's nose crinkled. "Ouch, how did you end up over there? He gives me the creeps. We can move it later, if you want. You can camp by mine. I think we'll get along really good."

She stared at Steve's tent, feeling queasy. "I might take you up on your offer."

The uneventful evening meal behind her, she joined her new friend for a game of cards. She met a few of the others, but the bond between her and Rebecca was growing stronger.

"Are you going to move your tent tomorrow? I hate to think of you by Steve, all alone. Wish your Mr. Littleton had stayed around. Him I could get used to," Rebecca chided.

"Sure. We'll try to find some time tomorrow. I think its raft building day. Like it or not, Kory is gone. It's Steve or nothing. He's more in tune with the bears, I guess. At least he smells a lot more like them." She laughed.

Rebecca snickered.

Ricki rose to leave. "I'm bushed. It's been a busy day. I'll catch up with you tomorrow."

She unzipped her tent door, switched on the flashlight, and yelped.

Steve stood by the corner of her tent.

He put up his hands, defensive. "No need to be skittish. I just came to visit. No harm done."

Rebecca came up behind her flashing a light in his eyes. "Steve, what are you doing over here?"

"I was worried about her after the night on the trail." Steve backed toward his tent. "You don't have to sneak around. I'm just doing my job."

"Go on back to your own tent. She can take care of herself," Rebecca ordered.

"Sure, sure, uppity women, I meant no harm," he mumbled.

"I came by to suggest you bunk with me tonight. Glad I did. Get your cot and sleeping bag," Rebecca said.

Ricki didn't argue.

CHAPTER Four

KORY WATCHED THE HELICOPTER UNTIL IT DISAPPEARED into the night, thankful the sick lady was in good hands. It wasn't the first time a medical emergency disrupted the plan, but this time was different. The last thing he wanted to do was leave Ricki on the mountain. The connection between them sparked an emotion long buried. "Man, I've been in the wilderness too long," he said, softly.

Alone on the steps of the lodge, he looked up. Only a few stars peeked out as the clouds moved slowly across the night sky, signs of the coming storm. "Ricki's on the mountain. I want to go back."

When Steve arrived with the woman, true to his training, he knew not to cause alarm for the others. He gently poked Kory and motioned him to the edge of the camp where the woman leaned against a tree, pale and in obvious pain. A light sleeper, he eased out of his sleeping bag with a finger to his lips and a nod toward Ricki.

He wanted to wake Ricki to tell her where he was going and why, but she slept deep, her head buried in the sleeping bag. No need to disturb her.

He assessed the woman's condition and determined she needed medical attention. The pain in her abdomen worried him. Time to get her off the mountain. It was a long hike down, but he had no choice.

The hike was difficult, but he could see the trail with his headlamp. He talked to the woman all the way down to keep her awake, asking her name, where she was from, any children, anything to keep her mind off the pain. Sometimes, he carried her so she could rest, sometimes, she put her arm around his neck and half walked with him. They made good time with no pack to worry about.

He did what he was trained for, she was on her way to the hospital, and he was relieved and satisfied.

"Okay, sport, this job is over. Best get some rest." Everything in him screamed to get back to Ricki. It wasn't desire, but a sense of concern. Of what, he had no idea, but intuition told him to get back to his original camp. The notion gripped him, wouldn't let him go.

Suddenly, his mind was made up. "Enough! I'm going back." He went inside to inform the boss of his intention to return to the mountain as soon as the sun rose.

Lodge owner and Kory's boss, Wolf Kelley, a six-foot four, two hundred fifty-pound bear of a man, earned his name in legendary fashion fighting off wolves bare-handed, back in the day. Born and raised in the backcountry of the Rockies, he was the undisputed authority in surviving the wild. The harsh winters forced him to slow down as he aged, but only his gray beard gave it away. He was still as gruff and intimidating as when he was younger.

Kory stated his case about going back up the mountain. "It's my decision. I'm going."

Wolf didn't look up from the ledger in front of him. "Exactly right, Kory, but not to your old troop. Steve and Kyle have them under control. We have two late comers who want to join the group on the ridge a few miles away. This is the next to the last event for the season and the last one is already full—so I let them in. Get an early start in the morning; you have quite a trek ahead of you."

Kory held the title of Head Trail Boss and was the ultimate authority on the mountain, but at the lodge, Wolf called the shots. The relationship between them stood the test of time. Ten years ago, he found his mentor in Wolf and never looked back.

Kory knew better than to argue, but his plan just took a detour. "You out of trail hands? I was sort of looking forward to my original group. They're quite a spunky lot."

Wolf looked up and scowled.

"Right," Kory whispered, and headed up the stairs to his room.

His plan to get back to Ricki fell apart. Instead, he had to take another group of greenhorns up the ridge to the higher lake.

While he went through the motions of showering, he couldn't get her face out of his mind. His head bowed under the force of the water. He leaned against the shower wall and let the water course down his chin. "I missed my chance. She slipped right through my fingers. I've got to find a way to see her again. Been a long time since I looked at a woman in that way."

Towel dried and warmed from the steamy shower, his head hit the pillow with visions of the freckled faced beauty standing on the ridge, short auburn curls blowing in the breeze. And the kiss.

While he gulped hot coffee at the breakfast bar the next morning, two men approached.

"You Kory Littleton?"

He turned and surveyed the men. "The one and only. You the ones who want to attempt the higher lake?" He glanced from one to the other. *Hmm, not the city slickers I imagined, but not rugged either.*

The one who spoke first extended his hand. "Russ Desmond, this is Miles Parsons, my partner."

Russ was big: his biceps looked as though they would burst out of his khaki shirt, his brown eyes brightened as he flashed a disarming smile. Miles was a little taller, but slender and his blue denim shirt looked a bit deflated next to his friend. His smile wasn't as quick; he sported a five o'clock shadow, not too noticeable because of his light-colored hair. It wasn't lost on Kory there were perfect creases in their shirt sleeves and jeans. Each wore a survival watch on their wrists.

Fancy city dudes. Those watches must have set them back a couple hundred dollars. We'll see how long those creases last on the mountain.

Kory shook hands all around. "Glad to have you aboard. Daylight's burning, we need to get going. Your packs all ready?"

"We're good to go. Can't wait," Russ said. "Thanks for taking us on."

"No problem. We should reach the ridge before dark. It's a steep uphill climb. Hope your legs are in shape." Kory grinned.

"Lead the way!"

The familiar weight of the pack and the open trail always gave him a thrill. He headed toward the edge of the clearing and let the trees enfold him into their warm embrace. He glanced back to make sure the two men followed.

Every step he took carried him away from Ricki. *It's not the way I wanted to leave it. I broke the trail boss cardinal rule and let desire lead me. I totally blew it. Now, I'll never see her again; never get a chance to explain.*

He stopped just inside the woods.

A doe and two fawns crossed the path ahead, paused to evaluate the intruders, and bounded away to safety. The wonders of nature always made him smile. The mountain wild was home and the small family of deer struck a cord in his heart. He always wanted a family of his own. As much as he loved the solitude of the mountains, he missed the connection of a permanent relationship.

He shook off the gloomy mood, but memories of his first wife surfaced despite himself. *No one to blame but yourself, Littleton. The mountain is a jealous lover. If only I'd been there when Laila fell, it might be different. The fall broke her leg and destroyed our love. Can I ever consider subjecting another woman to this way of life?*

The attraction toward Ricki was real, like a beacon of light in the darkness. For the first time since his divorce he was compelled to share his story with another woman. He wanted to explain about his ex-wife… how he'd made a mistake, how he shut off all emotion, refused to feel anything, and lost himself in his work. Something pulled at him now, a weight lifted, and Ricki's face floated into his mind.

It's time to feel again, take a chance. If I can only get back to her somehow.

Thunder rolled in the distance. *There's a storm coming. By the look of those clouds, a big one.*

He set a brisk pace and hoped the men could keep up. Nothing worse than getting caught in a storm on the mountain.

Ricki looked forward to the next step in the program on the second day of camp. Rebecca's friendship helped dispel the growing dislike for Steve and the unsettling episode by her tent. She slept well, sharing a tent with her new friend. *I like her! She's a spunky lady. So glad she's on this trip. I've made a new friend, someone not a cop! A smart, outgoing nurse from Philly.*

Thanks to her father's fishing instruction; she enjoyed a steaming plate of charbroiled trout for last night's meal. Even better, her tent now stood beside Rebecca's and away from Steve's.

Raft building was the order for today.

"You're really getting into this, aren't you?" Rebecca laughed. "I'm glad you're my raft partner. You're making me look good."

On the north side of the lake they found the smaller logs needed to assemble the craft, and Ricki relished the task. Armed with rope and gloves, she lost herself in the work, stopping only to wipe a damp brow. Her outrigger design should keep them steady out on the lake. "I never thought I would like this so much. I almost quit and went home."

"Let me guess. Kory Littleton?"

"Not exactly, but it *has* been a while since a man acted interested in me. It's not why I stayed though."

Rebecca laughed. "The way you've thrown yourself into the camp thing, I figured either you are trying to *forget* a man, or you're attracted to one. I'll bet on the latter, considering the look in Mr. Littleton's eyes back on the trail."

She glared at Rebecca. "What *look*? You didn't see any look. You're teasing me."

"Oh, he gave you a look all right."

Damn this complexion! I know my face must be red as a chili pepper. She tried to redeem herself. "I'm through with this conversation."

She turned her back on the other woman and forced the rope around the ends of the logs, angry, and embarrassed.

Rebecca touched her shoulder. "Hey, I didn't mean anything by it. It looks like I hit a nerve. Ease off a little. You're wearing your feelings on your sleeve. It's a dead giveaway."

Ricki's shoulders sagged. "I'm sorry. I came up here to *un*complicate my life and instead almost got distracted by another handsome face. It's not your fault. You're calling it like you see it." She sighed. "Let's get back to the raft building part."

"I'm here whenever you want to talk about it. Sounds like you had a pretty rough time."

"Thanks, how about later tonight? Right now, all I want to do is finish this raft."

CHAPTER
Five

———•⤳ℯ•———

KORY HEARD THE HEAVY BREATHING OF THE MEN BEHIND him. His pace was steady, but for those not used to the ascent, he knew he'd have to slow down, soon. For now, the two men stayed close behind.

Meanwhile, he tried to figure a way to get back to Ricki's camp. Wolf always sent two experienced trail bosses up to highest lake. There were only two the boss would send besides himself, Buck or Mack.

If I see they have the camp in hand, I can hike around the ridge and meet up with Troop Ten. I gotta try.

Right now, however, he needed to make sure he didn't kill his charges by pushing them too hard. "Let's stop here for a drink and a bite. There's room enough for the three of us to sit and catch our breath."

Neither man answered, just dropped their packs and flopped

down on the ground, gulping for air.

"How you holding up? Pretty steep trail. Don't want to push you too hard."

Russ fished out his canteen and took a swig. When his breathing slowed, he said, "I thought I was tough, in shape, but you're kickin' my ass right now."

Kory laughed and pulled a protein bar from his gear.

Russ and Miles followed suit.

"It's the steady uphill and the thin air. You two must work outdoors or something to keep in such good shape. You keep up better than most. What do you do back home?"

Russ glanced at Miles. "We're business partners—sporting goods. We work out together, but this is certainly out of our comfort zone."

Kory made short work of the snack and gulped water from the canteen. "Find us on the internet? Or did someone tell you about us?"

Russ and Miles exchanged looks again. "A friend told us. Said it was a beautiful place. They weren't wrong."

"Huh, I might have been their guide. What's the name?"

A large gust of wind kicked up reminding him of the impending storm; tree tops and branches swayed overhead. They still had several miles to go and it looked like rain.

He didn't wait for more conversation. "We need to hit the trail. Need to make it to camp before the rain hits. You ready to go?"

The men scrambled to their feet, adjusted their packs, and followed him up the steep path. No one spoke the rest of the way. It took too much energy, and they needed every ounce to make it to camp.

Kory's thoughts stayed on Ricki and how he could get back to her.

The rest of the trek continued without incident. Just before nightfall, they broke into the clearing by the lake. Tents dotted the area, fires burned, and the smell of fresh cooked fish filled the air.

"Hello the camp," Kory shouted.

"Hey, Littleton, what are you doing here? I thought you were with Troop Ten. Needed more excitement, huh?"

Buck was a tough, weathered man with a scruffy red beard and a knit cap squashed on his head and looked like it hadn't seen the inside of a washing machine in years. Intimidating at first glance, but when his mouth split open in a grin all menace dissolved. The total opposite of Wolf, who got his kicks out of instilling fear in his employees, Buck had a jovial face and kind, twinkly eyes when he smiled. Excluding the lodge owner, Buck had the most experience among the trail bosses.

"Hey Buck. One of mine got sick. Had to carry her down the mountain and get her on the helicopter. Wolf sent me right back up with these guys. Late-comers wanting to get their adventure in before the season ends."

Buck looked the men over. "Good, two more strong backs. I'm Buck. There's a storm coming, we'll need all hands to secure the tents. Park your gear over there, fellas, and get set up. There's a mess of fish cooked up if you're hungry. Kory can show you the ropes."

Miles sniffed the air. "Oh God, we're starving. It smells so good."

Kory made quick introductions. "This starving greenhorn is Miles and this one is Russ."

Buck clapped Miles on the shoulder. "Glad to have you aboard. Let's get crackin.'"

It didn't take long for the two men to eat and set up their tents. Kory was pleased to see them go around the camp offering help, but something about Russ bothered him. A disarming smile, a swagger of self-confidence when he walked, a tough edge to the set of his jaw. *He's polite, respectful, ready to work, but still…there's something about him.*

They sat around the campfire enjoying the night air, swigging down black coffee, and telling exaggerated tales of their exploits.

Thunder boomed in the distance.

Kory directed a question to Russ. "Ever been in a storm on the mountains before?"

"Can't say I have."

Kory poked a stick into the fire and watched the embers sizzle. "It can get rough. Let any of us know if you need anything."

Russ stood and poked Miles in the shoulder. "I'm hitting the hay. Goodnight."

Miles followed, leaving Kory and Buck by the fire.

"Wore out your greenhorns, Kory?" Buck moved closer to the fire.

"Guess so. Where's Mack? I haven't seen him. Didn't he come with you?"

"Not this trip. Went to see his mother. She's in a bad way. Just me this time. But now you're here, I don't feel so lonely!" Buck laughed.

"Look…Buck. I need a favor."

"Sure, Pal, what is it? Anything for you, kid."

"I need to get back to Troop Ten. There's a situation. Do you think you can handle this one alone?"

"Aw sure, I got this. And with those two strong backs you brought along, well, I'll be just fine. You ain't leavin' in the dark are ya? The storm might be on us sooner than we think."

He checked the night sky. "I don't see the storm hitting until sometime tomorrow. Troop Ten is only a few miles down the mountain, and there's a clear path between the two camps. Got my headlamp and my knife. I'll be fine."

Buck tossed the last of the fish bones into the fire. "She must be mighty special for you to take a chance like this. She gotta a name?"

Kory stood up. "Don't know what you're talking about. Just don't like leaving my troop."

"They've got Kyle and Steve."

"Steve I trust, but Kyle's a trainee. Storm's coming. Want to be sure everyone is okay, is all."

Buck snorted, but kept silent.

After a readjustment to his tent and pack, he turned to Buck. "Thanks for the fish. I'll try to check back this way if all is well."

The moon floated in and out of view, obscured by the clouds. Only a few stars managed to peek through the sailing shadows as he set out. The trail was a little tricky at night, but he'd hiked it a thousand times. He could wait until morning, but he felt compelled to go now. All he wanted was a chance to explain to Ricki, to find out if there was a connection between them. He wanted the moment—that one moment.

CHAPTER
Six

———•~~~•———

Ricki invited Rebecca to play cards and shoot the breeze before calling it a night. Guilt niggled at her conscience after the brush off when Kory's name was mentioned earlier. *She was kind enough to let me bunk in her tent last night. I wouldn't have slept a wink with Steve lurking around.*

Rebecca slid a candy bar out of her pack, split it in two and threw half on the makeshift table. "Stashed it inside my pack in case I got tired of berries and fish. I know it's cheating, but I couldn't help myself."

Ricki laughed and gladly took half. "I feel like a kid with my hand in the cookie jar."

"I know. Isn't it fun? I'll bet the others have their stash, too. I hate to think I was the only one."

While Ricki dealt the cards, Rebecca sat cross-legged on the tent floor. "Feel like talking about it? The guy I mean."

"It's a long boring story. Not worth listening to and certainly not worth telling."

Rebecca persisted, "If it's any consolation, I'm coming off a break up, too. Ten years of marriage. His secretary. His excuse? I work too much, he says. I'm simply not fun anymore."

She stopped with the pack of cards in mid-air. "Ten years of marriage. Wow, that's gotta be rough. Do you have kids?"

"No, we decided to wait, put money away so I could quit working when the child came. Now my best years are behind me. I doubt I'll ever have children." She pulled off her jacket and used it as a cushion. "Men and their fun."

"Isn't it the truth," Ricki resumed dealing with a little more force.

"What's your story? Were you married?"

"No. Dated almost two years. Thought everything was set up for the next step. He and my best friend hooked up behind my back. Made a complete fool of me. I bolted and well…here I am."

"Ouch. Best friend, huh? I don't know what's worse. In the end, it's all the same. They get tired of us."

"I guess so. I answered the survival trip ad on a whim. Start a new life I told myself. Go on an adventure." She heaved a sigh. "But, I was wrong. Think I'll go back to Dallas and try to get a transfer to another city. I've worked too hard to get where I am. Stupid to throw it all away over a man."

"Let's enjoy this little adventure and forget about men. Of course, if Kory Littleton showed up, you might change your mind." She giggled.

Ricki shot her a look. "I'm through with men. Now play, it's your turn."

They played cards late into the night, talked non-stop, and Ricki relaxed knowing she had an ally among the group.

The next morning, the women cleaned up their breakfast and hurried down to the lake, eager to finish the raft.

The other campers were way behind in the raft building process.

Ricki watched Steve's impatience with a few of them. Kyle said very little, just walked up and down the shore grunting instructions.

"Those two don't fit the character of a trail boss, in my opinion. They don't seem to like what they're doing," Ricki said.

"I agree. I'm so glad you're my partner. At least, they stay away from us. Of course, it's too bad Kory couldn't be here. Now there's a man who enjoys his job."

"Stop talking about Kory, Rebecca."

"Well, you better get used to it, he's here." Rebecca pointed to the clearing.

Kory breathed a sigh of relief at the sight of Ricki at work. The clearing made a perfect vantage point. He watched her, amused.

She skillfully wound the sturdy rope over the ends of each log lashing the timbers together at a furious pace.

This isn't a race, why is she in such a hurry?

Ricki spun around at something the other woman said, and his heart raced. The unchecked expression told him all he needed to know—wide eyes with an open smile. Whether she would admit it or not, she was glad to see him. Unsure how to approach her, he waited and wondered if she would make the first move.

But, he couldn't wait. He had to know, so he walked toward her.

Ricki spoke first. "Steve said you wouldn't be back."

He took another step and stopped in front of her. "There's a storm coming. Steve and Kyle will need my help, but it isn't the reason I'm here. I wanted to see you—to explain. Health issues don't wait up here. The woman was seriously ill. We couldn't risk it. I'm sorry, I should have told you myself."

Ricki averted her gaze. "How is she?"

"Who?" Distracted by her auburn curls dancing in the breeze, her cheeks pink from exertion, and those freckles, he didn't hear the question. *Those damn freckles!*

"The woman you carried out of the woods."

"Oh, yes, Mary. I got her to the helicopter. I think she'll be fine. She's in good hands."

He reached and closed his fingers around her gloved hand. "I couldn't get you out of my mind. I needed to see you again, to explain what happened on the trail. And there's something else…"

Her hand wiggled out of his grasp.

"You don't owe me an explanation, Kory. It's your job." She stepped back and looked away.

"I'd like nothing better than to share a meal and talk. What do you say?" he asked.

She smiled.

His hopes soared.

"Sorry, Rebecca's my partner. I'll eat with her. I'm glad you're back, Kory. I need to get this barge sea worthy, if you'll excuse me." She turned back to the raft.

He looked at Rebecca.

The nurse shrugged, shook her head, and moved in to help Ricki.

Steve broke out of the trees behind him, arms full of firewood. "Hey man! What did you come back for? You had a few days to chill out in the lodge. I sure didn't expect to see you, again."

"You know I get antsy surrounded by four walls, Steve. Thought I'd see how you handled your first big guide trip." Kory continued to watch Ricki.

"I'm handling it fine. Got some fine trout cooked up at camp. Hungry?" Steve asked.

He looked at Ricki bent over the raft. She didn't turn around. "Yeah, I'm hungry. Let's go."

Steve's camp sat about a half of a football field length away from Ricki's 'boat landing'. They sat on two stools, honed from the ravages of the forest, and watched, amazed, at Ricki's determination.

"You come back for *her*?" Steve pointed his fork toward the women.

He avoided the question. "Have you noticed the dark clouds? You and Kyle will need my help if the storm gets out of hand."

Steve grinned at his boss. "You don't fool me. It's written all over your face. You're interested, for sure. Besides, Kyle and I aren't exactly greenhorns."

"How has she been up here? The ankle okay?"

"Ankle seems fine. Hardest working person out here. I don't know what happened between you two. She tried to ask questions about you." Steve picked the bones of the trout clean and tossed the skeleton in the fire.

"She did? Like what?" Kory followed suit and grabbed another trout.

"Are you married, have a family? Those kinds of questions."

Before the fresh kill reached his lips, Kory stopped in midair. "She asked if I was married? What did you tell her?"

Steve worked on his third fish. "Nuthin'. Not my style."

Kory watched her in the morning light. "Thanks, pal. She's giving me mixed signals though. If she is interested in me why the brush off?"

"You probably upset her by leaving. I'd say she's running scared. Did you get that take on her?"

He mumbled under his breath, "Yeah… yeah I did."

⁘∽℮⸱

Ricki avoided him all day. All he wanted was one chance to bridge the gap between them, make a connection, wanted a chance with her, one chance. He stood in the doorway of his tent and watched the women finish what they could. The darkness settled like a cloak around the camp ending any opportunity to finish the raft. He had no doubt Ricki would have it seaworthy first thing in the morning.

Ricki and Rebecca gathered their gear and started toward the tents. It was good to see her smiling. The two women hit it off, he could tell. Maybe after a few days, she'd relax and talk to him. He couldn't push her. She needed trust. He'd give it more time.

Fifteen minutes later, he was outside her tent. The storm was moving faster. The wind whipped through the trees. He needed to make sure the tents were secure. "Ricki, Rebecca, you need to anchor your tents down. The storm's going to hit before morning."

Ricki drew back the tent flap and stepped out, flashlight in hand. "I heard the thunder, figured it would hit in the morning. Come on, Rebecca; let's tie these old tents down."

He reached out. "Can I help you, Ricki?"

"No thanks. We're on it. Go help someone else."

The first large drops of rain hit the canvas tent.

"Ricki…"

"I said we've got it." She rounded the back side of the canopy.

A loud crack of thunder made him duck. The storm wasted no time—the deluge came fast, hard, and cold. He hurried to help the others, pounding extra stakes into the ground, lashing more rope to hold down the lightweight tents. There was no time to think about Ricki.

The fury of rain and lightning waged for several hours. Water from the lake rose and threatened to swamp the tents closest to its shore. He hunkered down in Steve's tent.

"You look like you've lost your last friend, buddy. We'll be fine. Everyone's anchored down." Steve nudged his boss.

"I'm sure of everyone except Ricki. She wouldn't let me help. At least you and Kyle checked their tents, right? Why is she being so stubborn?"

Steve's brow wrinkled. "Man, I thought she was the first one you checked on. Kyle and I left her tent to you. Don't worry. It's like she has to prove something. Wonder who she's proving it to, you?"

Kory ignored the last question. "Okay, I thought one of you

would check it out. I'm going out there. They might be in trouble."

"You can't go out…" Steve attempted.

The tent door zipped open; he flew into the night, and ran through ankle deep water to where Ricki's tent stood. "Ricki!" He called. Rain lashed his face, the wind whipped his clothes.

A faint voice called in the night. "She went to save the raft. I tried to stop her."

Rebecca peeked out of the tent door holding a flashlight.

Frantic, he called her name, fighting through flying debris to the water's edge, unable to see past the shoreline. "Ricki, where are you?"

Still nothing. He ran back to Steve's tent.

"Get Kyle and your lights. We'll spread out, Ricki's missing. She went to save the raft."

They tramped up and down the shoreline calling her name, the rain pelting them, wind whipping their clothing, Mother Nature showing her force.

After an hour searching, the storm abated, the winds calmed, and the rain diminished to a drizzle. Darkness was their only enemy, now.

Steve turned the flashlight on Kory. "It'll have to wait 'til morning. We can't see out here. I need to check on the others."

"No, she could be in the lake. I gotta find her."

Kory struck out alone while Kyle and Steve checked each tent and did a head count.

He continued around to the opposite side of the lake, climbing over downed trees and branches, water filling his boots.

"Ricki, Ricki, can you hear me?" he shouted.

A lull in the wind caused him to stop and listen. He heard a faint sound, a moan. "Ricki? Are you there?"

The dim morning light illuminated the darkness and bathed the lake in an eerie glow. The water lapped the shore, and Kory's eyes adjusted enough to see something bobbing in the shallows, a body crumpled like a rag doll on one end.

CHAPTER Seven

THE BATTERED RAFT, TWISTED AND BROKEN, PERCHED HALF in and half out of the water, was wedged between two cottonwood trees.

Kory slogged through the debris to reach her. "Oh God, Ricki."

Her head raised slightly, her voice hoarse and feeble answered, "Help me."

"I'm coming." He cradled her against his chest, gently making sure all bones were intact. Satisfied she was in one piece, he lifted her into his arms and trekked back to camp, her head lolling against his shoulder, in and out of consciousness.

He whispered close to her ear, hoping she felt the erratic beat of his heart, sensed his fear and relief. "What were you thinking, Freckles? It was only a raft, not worth your life. Thank God, you weren't killed."

An hour later, Ricki sat cross-legged in her tent, sipped hot coffee, and tried to explain how she ended up across the lake, on a pile of logs, half drowned.

Kory and Rebecca sat across from her, their faces lined with concern, eyes hollow from lack of sleep.

"Stupid, I know, but I worked so hard on the raft. I tried to anchor it, flopped down across the end of it to find the lead rope. The wind and rain beat me up. I couldn't see, couldn't find the rope. It broke free and floated into the water. The wind pushed it out into the lake. I was so cold…it's all I remember."

Kory shook his head, his voice stern. "Why didn't you let me help you? You could have died out there."

She ducked her head. "I'm sorry. I suppose I wanted to prove to myself I didn't need anyone. Especially you. You took care of everything the night on the ridge. I wanted to show you I could take care of *myself*."

The softness returned to his eyes, his voice lowered to a whisper, "You're a stubborn woman. This might not be the proper time, but I'm going to say it anyway. Could be its time to explore a new strategy in life. I could teach you. I bent the rules to make sure I got back to this camp because I believe we connected. I know you felt it, too. I'm not asking you to jump into a relationship so soon after your break-up, but how about we take the time to explore this new friendship between us?"

Rebecca stood up and squeezed Ricki's hand. "I'm so glad you are safe, Ricki. I'm gonna get out of here and let you two talk. I'll be down at the lake catching lunch."

Ricki smiled. "Thanks for the coffee and the support, Rebecca."

The tent door zipped shut as she left.

She turned back to Kory, searched his face, wanted so much to believe in him. "It's a lovely offer, but your wife…your career?"

"My wife—it's what I wanted to tell you, before. I made a mistake, never considered what *she* needed. She went on a pack trip with me, but I went ahead to scout the trail with the other guide. I left her with the others. She slipped off a ledge, broke her leg. She blamed me. This life never suited her; I didn't want to see it. I tried to force her into my life style. The relationship was doomed from the beginning. You're different, strong, determined—your own woman." He glanced around the tent as if searching for the right words. "Look, I have an idea. You need a change of pace, I need another pack partner. It's a good job, nice money, all the freedom in the world. How about it? You told me you wanted to change your life. This could be the avenue you're looking for."

The warmth in her soul wasn't from the coffee. Secretly, she yearned to hear those words from him. Fantasized about the moment he said it out loud. But, she hesitated. "You mean you'd give me a job after all the stupid mistakes I made?"

He smiled. "Yes, there's a couple's retreat held at the lodge. They need new directors; a couple, or at least, a man and a woman. There's time for you to train, time for us to see if we can work together."

"You mean stay on the mountain? Snowed in? All winter?"

His laugh had a deep tone, genuine and carefree. "All the guides stay, Ricki. Plenty of provisions for the long-haul. You can have a room in the lodge. You and I can start over. Get to know each other in a proper manner. *This* time I'll try to make a better impression. Want to take a chance, really start over?"

She set the coffee cup on the mat beside her. Every fiber of her being wanted to say yes, her heart leapt at the chance for a new beginning, and if it meant being near Kory, well—. But, it was the old Ricki. Never again would she gamble on a man she barely knew. She needed to let the fetters of her old, predictable life fall away before she could step out on an emotional ledge. This time, she wanted to really think it through.

She shook her head and stood. "I can't accept your offer, Kory. I'm gonna take the advice you gave me on the trail the first day. Slow down, get new friends, find out who I am. Sorry, but I'm going back to Dallas when this trip is over, restart my life there, and try to get it right. It's no good to run away. I'll transfer to another city, start all over. I gotta follow my training and face my demons." She took his hand gently. "Thank you for saving my life. I was foolish not to listen to you last night. I'll always be grateful."

He stared at her for a long moment.

She saw the hurt in his eyes and almost let those molten chocolate pools draw her in.

He squeezed her hand and let it go. "There's something between us, Ricki. You can't deny it. Maybe I've jumped the gun, but I'm not giving up."

Sunlight streamed through the open tent door, one flap moving with the breeze as he left.

His presence had filled the tent, now the space was hollow, desolate.

"I did the right thing, I know I did," she whispered.

Exhausted from exposure, she slept the day away, rose at dinner time, and accepted the fish Rebecca brought her.

"Gotta get your strength back, Ricki. We have almost a week left. You don't want to miss the fun, do you?"

Within minutes, sleep claimed her again, allowing her to escape the emotional upheaval warring within. How she wanted to accept Kory's offer, but she also wanted to prove she could go back to Dallas and finish the job she'd taken on there. Kory's idea of staying in the mountains, learning something new with him tempted her, sorely. He was right. There was a connection between them, but she had to make sure, not jump the gun. They'd only known each other for a couple of days. *Love doesn't happen so fast, does it?*

Tossing and turning the rest of the night, she thought about what to do. The city represented so many obstacles. *Can I blow it off and* *work around a sorry excuse for a boyfriend like nothing happened? I need to face him, show him I don't care anymore, hold my head up high, and be done with him, once and for all. And what of <u>her</u>, my so-called best friend? The traitorous witch didn't deserve even the tiniest consideration. But still, I must face the unforgiveable insult head on. Show them they don't matter anymore.*

She fell into fitful sleep thinking, *Yes, I made the right decision. I have to face my enemies and destroy them.*

The next morning, she woke to the chatter of birds in the trees and voices buzzing outside her tent. Fully rested and restored, the new day brought a new perspective to her initial decision—doubt. *Maybe, I <u>should</u> just walk away, start over, rid myself of the demons in the fresh mountain air. I have nothing to prove to him. I did nothing wrong. He's the jerk and doesn't deserve to see how much he hurt me. Maybe I should take Kory up on his…*

The noise outside escalated. Something was going on. Curious, she dressed hastily and emerged into the morning sun, blinking, trying to take in the chaotic scene. "What's the racket out here? It looks like everyone is breaking camp."

Rebecca walked over and put an arm around her shoulder. "They want us to move camp, join up with the troop higher on the mountain. Said the lake is too full of debris here, makes it hard to fish. We'll try our luck up there."

"But…where is…?" Ricki glanced around.

"Kory and Steve went on ahead to check out the trail. Kyle's gonna guide us. Better get busy, girl. Can't lollygag around all day," Rebecca teased. "Seriously, though. I'm so glad Kory found you last night. You had us all terrified."

To hide the disappointment, she flashed a quick smile, turned toward camp without a reply, and set about taking down her tent."

It came down easily, and the rest of her gear fit neatly in the backpack. Breakfast consisted of a dry piece of hardtack and a swig of water from the canteen.

One by one, the campers drifted toward the center of camp, each packed and ready to go. Ricki took one last look around camp and joined Rebecca.

They trudged up the trail single file with Kyle in the lead, his tin cup banging a steady rhythm against a metal fry pan dangling from his pack. A simple trick to ward off bears.

After two hours of hard climbing, the battered band of hikers broke through a clearing and into the new camp. Miraculously, the damage from the overnight storm was minimal here. Tents dotted the edge of the woods, a few smoldering campfires sent small tendrils of smoke skyward, but the camp was empty.

Several of her group poked around the campsite. A tall man with a long scraggly beard, she thought his name was Ben, asked, "Where is everybody? The tents are here, but it looks deserted."

Kyle brushed the comment aside. "Probably scoutin' the lake for the best fishing area. We gotta eat. Set up camp. They'll be along soon. Let's try the clearing over there."

Kory's absence worried her at first, but Kyle made sense. His job consisted of looking out for the troop. The unusual circumstances of the storm didn't change anything.

Her mood lightened; convinced the other guides would appear before the noon meal. *"Nothing like hard work to clear your head."* She joined the others and glanced around for a suitable spot for camp.

"You know, we might want to slow down on the raft building this time. We might want to fish more off the shore, instead." Rebecca tossed her pack onto a grassy area. "This looks like a good place for the tents."

A secret desire to camp near Kory almost overtook her, but she shrugged it off. She didn't have time to look for his tent.

"You can if you want, but I think I'll try my hand at the raft again." She dropped her pack beside Rebecca's. "This is a perfect spot, good eye girl."

The nurse turned around and surveyed the water. "Have you

looked at this lake? It's beautiful, more scenic than the last one. The trees are taller and closer together. See how they reflect off the water? I really like it here."

Ricki searched the opposite side of the lake hoping Kory would break through the thick stand of trees. When he didn't, she looked up at the sky. "Well, it looks like more rain. We better get set up and catch some fish if we're going to eat."

Rebecca nodded. "Let's get busy."

Darkness fell fast in the mountains, no time to worry about situations out of her control.

They unrolled the tents and worked together. Side by side, they raised them, driving the stakes securely into the ground, and making sure the ropes were taut.

Rebecca stood back to admire their handiwork. "We're getting good at this. Look how fast we got these up."

They slapped their hands together in a triumphant high five.

Ricki grabbed a fishing pole. "Now for supper."

The lake was surrounded by trees, but close by the other camp a sort of clearing opened. The shouts came from there. Several campers ran toward the edge of the trees as a small group broke into the clearing led by a burly looking character with a stocking cap on his head.

The women followed the rest of the group to greet them.

A small man with wire rimmed glasses stepped ahead of the small band, "Hello the camp! Look, we've got company."

A large hulk of a man with a long, red, bushy beard shrugged his pack off and came toward her. He snatched off the stocking hat and spoke with a deep southern drawl, "Name's Buck, leader of this ragged group behind me. You must be the ones Kory told us about. Glad to have you on board."

She strained to see around Buck. "Where is he?"

Buck looked confused. "Who?"

"Kory. You said he told you we were coming. Where is he?"

"Oh, right. Out with a scoutin' party. We need more wood. He's also looking for signs of bears. It's almost winter; they'll be trying to store up before they hibernate. We don't want it to be us they decide to munch on." He surveyed their handiwork. "Looks like you're all set up. Good work."

"Bears?" Rebecca asked.

"Yeah, for some reason they like this lake more than the others. Have to be very cautious. We'll put on extra patrol at night to keep everyone safe." Buck turned to his group. "Okay, everyone grab your poles, time to snag some supper. Those of you lucky enough to find some berries, separate them into equal portions for the rest. We share out here. It's the rule."

Ricki stopped Buck when he turned away. "Are the berries close by? I wouldn't mind picking some after I fish a bit."

Buck smiled. "The bears scavenged most of them. You have to go out quite a way to find any. There won't be any near camp. What you *won't* do is go out alone. We go in groups of four or more for safety. We'll organize a new group tomorrow for the berry brigade. For now, you need to fish."

Ricki returned his good-natured smile. "Sounds good. I'd like to go on the brigade."

He gave a friendly wink, and said, "You'll be the first one I call on."

Buck smacked the hat back on his head. "Well, better get to securing camp. I'm hungry and dark falls fast around here. Glad to see you are all set up. I'll be around later to give you an update. Soon as I get a report from Kory."

The girls walked slowly back to their tents.

Rebecca jabbed an elbow to her in the ribs. "Wow, you got it bad, girl,"

"What are you talking about?"

"You only mention Kory's name every other word. What did you and he talk about last night?"

"Oh, never mind. Let's get dinner."

Shouts drifted across another point of the lake and all eyes turned toward the excited cries.

Buck stood as two men stumbled into the sunshine.

Ricki strained to see, trying to spot Kory. "He's not with them."

Rebecca chimed in, "Doesn't look like it."

"Why are they running?"

Rebecca grabbed her arm. "Wait, there he is. Behind them."

All three men hurried toward Buck, gesturing toward the woods.

She couldn't hear the conversation, but she saw Buck point toward their camp, waving excitedly.

Kory glanced in her direction and broke into a run.

Her pulse beat strongly as she watched him; excitement mixed with fear. Something was wrong, but it didn't matter, because all she could focus on was Kory. She held her breath and blinked twice. When she focused again, she saw something else.

Another man, striding toward her.

She knew the walk.

CHAPTER
Eight

"OH GOD, NO, RUSS!"

He reached out. "Ricki, I found you. Darling, I'm so relieved."

She recoiled. "Wha…What are you doing here?"

"Why looking for you, what else? I tried to find you after our little misunderstanding, but you left town without a word. If it hadn't been for Leila I never would have found you." He moved closer.

She stepped back. "Leila? How could she possibly know where I went? She was in your bed when I got to your house."

"Oh, she *didn't* know, but she had your spare key, remember? The one you wouldn't give to me." The light left his eyes for a moment, his jaw tensed. "When I got to your apartment, I found the brochure for this place in your night stand. I'm a detective, after all. It's what I do."

Her mind reeled at the knowledge he went through her apartment like a common thief. She didn't miss the arrogance on his face, the challenge he issued with just one look, chin up, an unnatural shimmer in his gaze.

The ability to breath left her as if she was gut punched. Rage swept through her filling every empty space in her mind. The quick temper washing over her like a flash flood. She growled in disbelief, "You broke into my apartment?"

"Broke in? Of course, not. I had the key you gave Leila for emergencies. *This* was an emergency." The light in his eyes dimmed and any trace of a smile disappeared.

She balled her fist and raised it to strike.

Kory stepped around between them. "Whoa, wait a minute here. What's going on?"

Russ kept his eyes trained on her, but spat. "This is between me and my fiancée, trail boy. Butt out." His hand dropped to his belt as if to grab a gun.

Kory blocked her, but she lunged forward anyway. "I'm not your fiancée. We have nothing to talk about. You're a liar, a cheat, and now a common burglar. I want nothing to do with you." She trembled and fought back tears. Self-control ebbed away.

Rebecca pushed in front of Kory and Ricki. "You heard her. Get out of here. Leave her alone."

Kory glanced between Russ and Ricki. "So, this is the guy you told me about?"

Russ turned, chest out, fist clenched. "I said this was none of your business."

A few campers gathered behind Kory, necks' craning to see what was going on. Some grumbled, a few asked Kory if he needed help, but most just watched.

Buck broke through the crowd. "Break it up. I don't know what's going on here, but this is my camp and we got no time for personal feuds. Got more important problems to worry about. Like a rogue bear coming too close to this camp. We need to get a plan in place. Everyone back to their own tents. Kory, you, Steve, and Kyle come with me." He pointed to Russ. "You come along, too. Whatever is going on is over."

Kory looked at Ricki. "Are you okay?"

"Yes, go. Rebecca will stay with me."

He nodded, looked at Russ and said, "Let's go."

Russ hesitated, but unclenched his fists.

Miles, who watched from afar, stepped closer and clapped a hand on Russ's shoulder. "Come on, the bear is close. First things first."

Russ looked over his shoulder at her. "This isn't over."

Kory hung back until Russ and Miles followed Buck.

She watched them go, heart pounding.

Rebecca urged her toward the tent. "Come on. Let's go inside and sit down. You're still shaking."

Inside, she reached for the canteen and took a big gulp. When it didn't help, she took several deep breaths.

Rebecca sat cross-legged on a corner of the sleeping bag and motioned for her to sit. "I take it you never expected to see him up *here*, right?"

"Not in a million years. I thought it was the one place he wouldn't find me." She searched her friend's face. "What am I gonna do? I can't stay here with him in the same camp."

"I don't know. Maybe Kory will figure something out."

"Kory, oh God. Russ might have hit him, he has an ugly temper. If he even suspects Kory has feelings for me, he'll pulverize him."

Rebecca laughed. "You don't think Kory can take care of himself?"

"Of course, he can, but you don't know Russ."

"Who's the guy with him?"

"Miles? He's Russ's side kick. More like a shadow. He's harmless."

"Is he a cop, too?"

Ricki's chuckled. "No, Miles owns a golf course. He and Russ have been friends since grade school. Miles is a tough guy wannabe."

"Well, your color is back, at least. You're not shaking. Almost got it under control?"

She took another deep breath. "Yeah, I think so. It was such a shock to see him. I'm glad Kory and Buck are here. I hope they'll keep him away from me."

"Well, one thing is for sure. We better bunk together. Russ will try to corner you again if he came all this way to find you. He'd have a harder time fighting both of us."

Footsteps sounded outside the tent door.

The girls stared at the door, barely breathing.

Ricki held one finger to her lips and grabbed her walking stick.

Rebecca chose the flashlight sitting by the door.

They raised their weapons, ready to pounce.

"Miss Ricki? It's me, Buzz. I brought you some fish. With all the ruckus, Buck didn't know if you had time to catch dinner. Got several good-sized ones for ya."

Ricki looked at Rebecca and mouthed, *Buzz?* "Just a moment." She slid toward the door and unzipped the flap, walking stick held tightly in her grip.

The small man with wire-rimmed glasses pushed a stringer of fish toward her with a kindly smile on his face.

"Oh, Buzz. I didn't know your name. I do remember you." She reached for the fish. "How very kind, but are you sure you can spare these?"

He blushed. "Oh yes, ma'am. Everyone contributed. It's the way we do things around here. Share and share alike. Buck wanted to be sure you and your friend had a full belly." He nodded toward Rebecca.

"Oh, I am sorry. Have you met Rebecca?"

His blush appeared, again. "Nice to meet you. Better get those cookin' and clean up the camp. It's liable to be a long night."

"What do you mean a long night?"

"They're sortin' it out now. Who's gonna stand watch. First shift, second shift, and so on. There'll be noise, maybe even the ole' bear will wander in. Gotta sleep light and be ready to go."

"I see. Shouldn't we take our turns, too? We're part of the group."

"Well, they might ask ya, but right now I think we have enough men to get us through the night. Buck will co-ordinate all of it. He'll call if he needs you." He turned to go.

"Wait, I want to thank you again, Buzz. It was a very nice thing to do."

Rebecca chimed in, "Yes, thank you Buzz!"

His glasses had slipped down his nose. He adjusted them, gave a little salute, and said, "It's nothin', ladies. It's what we do up here in the mountains. Y'all have a good night."

Ricki stood holding the fish and watched him head for the other camp.

The shock of Russ's appearance ebbed a little. Clarity returned as she gazed at the other camps. Separated in groups of three, each group formed a semi-circle around the small inlet at the end of the lake. Bucks camp was in the middle. His campers arranged their tents in a circle like pioneers in a wagon train. The other two groups did the same. They were nearby, but separate. She wasn't sure of Kory's location. She hoped it was near her. She did recognize Steve's tent to the right of hers, close, but not too close.

Russ and Miles must be on the other side of Buck's people. Good, the farther away, the better.

"You gonna stand there all night with our dinner? I'm starving." Rebecca tugged at her pant leg.

"Oh, right. Dinner."

While the women prepared the fish, and started the camp fire, Ricki remained silent. Her stomach growled as the fish sizzled. "I'll feel better after I eat."

"What did you say, Ricki?"

"Did I say it out loud? I said I'd feel better after I eat. I didn't realize I was so hungry."

Rebecca poked the fire with a small stick, and then, pointed it toward Buck's camp. "Looks like a big pow wow going on over there.

Do you see Russ or Kory?"

"No, I don't want to look over there. Afraid I'll lose my appetite. These are ready, let's eat." She pulled out the tin plates and tossed one to her friend.

"Nothing like fresh-caught fish over a camp fire," Rebecca remarked.

"You're right about that."

"Looks like the pow wow is over. Two of them are coming this way."

Ricki couldn't tell in the dimming light who was walking toward them, at first, but as they got closer, she recognized Kory.

Buck accompanied the trail boss and spoke first, "Everything under control, ladies?"

"Yes, just finished our dinner. Thanks to the camp for sharing the fish." She tried not to look at Kory, but her eyes had a mind of their own.

"Great," Buck continued, "Want to give you an update on what to expect tonight. We got a rogue bear wandering around these parts. Gonna put two men on watch in shifts all night. They'll be moving around camp, mostly behind the tents, to catch any unusual movements in the woods. Didn't want you to be alarmed. There will be three shifts. A whistle will sound if the bear is too near the camp. Keep your fire going, keep your own whistles around your neck. The other men are assigned tents to check on if the bear is close. You might not get much sleep, but I can't take a chance on someone getting hurt."

"But, shouldn't Rebecca and I help with guard duty?"

"Not this time. You don't have enough experience. I leave situations like this to the experienced personnel. It's enough for you to keep your fire going for the guards and stay in your tents. Secure any food, don't leave scraps out. We don't want to give the bear an engraved invitation. Any questions?"

"No. Keep the fire going and stay close to the tent, got it. Thank you."

"Gotta tell everyone else." Buck trudged toward the next tent. Kory hung back.

Rebecca retreated inside the tent.

"Ricki…I," Kory stopped.

"Look Kory, I'm sorry you had to find out this way. I had no idea Russ would show up here. What am I supposed to do now? I don't want to spend the rest of this trip dodging him."

"I can take you down the mountain tomorrow. *If* it's what you want."

"It *is* what I want. Thank you." He stepped closer and whispered, "Are you really done with him?"

She fought back tears. "Yes, I'm totally done."

"I'll see you in the morning, then." He turned.

"Wait."

"Yes?"

"I didn't properly thank you."

"For what?"

She grabbed his hand. "For everything. You've been patient and kind. I really do appreciate all your help, saving my life, offering me a job. You're a good man. I wish the timing was different. I might…" Quickly, she planted a soft kiss on his cheek and whispered, "Thank you."

His arm snaked around her waist. He pulled her close. "I'd do it all again for that one kiss."

Their lips met and Ricki melted into the kiss, savoring the physical touch, his strong arms. *I could get lost in these arms and never want to leave.*

She lingered, pressing into him, breathing in the smoky fragrance of his shirt, his hair, losing what little resolve was left.

He pulled her closer.

She didn't resist, but yielded to his desire wrapped in his strong arms.

A loud crack on the edge of the campsite jerked them apart.

Kory pushed her behind him.

She grabbed the back of his shirt, fear rippling up and down her spine. "Is it the bear?"

"I don't know."

A shadow, a glint of light, and whatever lurked in the darkness, faded into the woods.

CHAPTER *Nine*

KORY REACHED FOR HIS WHISTLE.
Ricki continued to clutch his shirt as she strained to see into the darkness.

He whispered, "I saw a flash of something. Maybe eyes reflecting from the moonlight, but more like light reflecting off the barrel of a gun. At any rate, I've got to alert the rest of the camp, check on the rest of the sentries."

She let go of his shirt and stepped back. "Of course, I'll tell Rebecca."

He turned toward the other campers, but stopped. "Ricki, the kiss…it was…"

"Go, Kory. We'll talk later."

He nodded. "Steve's tent is next to Rebecca's. Do you have your whistle?"

"Yes."

"Good. You and Rebecca stay together, stoke your fire, don't venture out until we give the all clear. I'll be right back."

She watched him hurry to Buck's camp, aware of the emptiness of her arms and longing to have the moment back. Her pulse raced, perhaps from fear of the bear or the excitement of the kiss, she wasn't sure. The fire popped and drew her attention back to the glowing goals. Addressing the fire, she said, "What am I doing? Falling for a guy I barely know. Dammit. I made a decision. I've got to stick to it. I've got to get back home and restart my life." She turned away.

"Rebecca," she called. "Rebecca!"

Her friend emerged from the tent. "What is it? What's wrong?"

"We think the bear is just beyond the tree line. We heard something and saw a flash of light, maybe its eyes."

"Oh no, too close for comfort. What should we do?"

"Just do what they told us. Kory's gone to alert the rest. They'll whistle if there's any danger."

They stood by the fire gazing at the sizzling embers, casting furtive glances toward the darkened woods.

"Look, Rebecca, I know what they told us. Stay in the tent, just come out to stoke the fire, but really, I think we need to do our own watch. How about we take shifts sleeping? One stay up by the fire, the other get some sleep. Maybe two hours on, two hours off. I don't feel safe with both of us inside."

Rebecca grabbed a stick and poked at the flames, sending embers into the air. "Good idea. Looks like we have enough firewood gathered to last the night. The bigger log will smolder for a while. Just need to keep a flame going." She stretched her back. "I'll take the first shift. You need some sleep after all the drama. Get rested. I'll wake you when it's your turn."

She yawned. "Think I'll take you up on the offer. I'm exhausted. Kory said he'd take me down the mountain in the morning, get me out of here before Russ can start any trouble. I need sleep if I'm gonna make the hike."

"You're leaving? Crap, Ricki. I'll have to find another fishing buddy."

She drew a deep, ragged breath. "I'm sorry, but I just can't stay here. Russ will eventually try to corner me. I've got to get back to Texas, get my feet on the ground, and deal with what's happened. Start over. I'm a mess. For once, I'm going to face all this."

"Why can't Buck ask *them* to leave? Seems like they're the ones who upset the apple cart."

She saw the disturbed look on her friend's face, knew she was disappointed. They had really bonded as friends, but she reminded herself she didn't come here to make new friends, but to set her world back on its axis, take control, make better decisions. Part of the process was to stick to the plan she made. Go back, transfer to a different city, and continue in the profession she'd trained so hard to achieve. Rebecca and she could write, maybe go on another adventure together somewhere, but too many times she made a snap decision and lived to regret it. Time to make a change.

"I have to go back. I've been running away and it's time to stop." She gave her friend a bright smile. "Besides, you're a lot more outgoing than I am. I'm sure you'll find a new fishing buddy right away."

Ricki waited for a reply; it didn't come. She turned and headed for the tent.

"What about Kory?" Rebecca's reply was barely audible, but still packed a punch to her gut.

She stopped, but didn't turn around. "Kory and I can't happen." With a flip of her wrist, she unzipped the tent door and hurried inside, but heard Rebecca's reply.

"I think you are *still* running away. From Kory."

The flames cast shadows on the tent wall. She saw her friend's silhouette slowly sit down on the log in front of the fire, her head bowed.

She curled up on the sleeping bag like a scared child, emotions bouncing off the walls of her brain. She wanted Kory, couldn't deny the attraction. Wanted to see what could come of a relationship with him, but Russ and his deceit changed everything. She couldn't trust her own instincts anymore. *Everything is upside down. All my plans obliterated because of Russ. How could I have been so blind about him? Now, I don't trust any decision I make. It's why I must go.*

She drifted off into an uneasy sleep watching shadows from the campfire dance across the canvass walls.

Someone pushed at her shoulder and called her name, but she rolled over, not wanting to face consciousness.

Another shove, the voice a little louder, "Ricki, come on girl, it's your shift. I gotta get some shuteye myself. Ricki! Wake up!"

Her eyes flew open as memory came back. "How long have I been asleep?"

"Three hours. I gave you another hour. You were actually snoring. I'm beat. Can you take your shift or shall we just go ahead and take our chances?"

She rolled to a sitting position and rubbed her eyes. "No, I'm good. Thanks for letting me sleep. I can handle it now. Go ahead and crawl in."

"Man, I hated to wake you. I did put some coffee on, maybe it will help. Wake me in two hours."

Ricki zipped the tent door closed, stepped to the fire, and rubbed her hands. It was cool out and the fire felt good. She bent to pour a cup of coffee, sat down on the old log, and glanced around the lake.

Campfires dotted the shoreline, each tent harboring their own fire, a good deterrent for any stray bears. She squinted into the night, trying to spot any of the sentries. If they were there it wasn't apparent, but she was confident they manned their posts as Buck instructed. *No one would have the courage to go against Buck!*

She relaxed and enjoyed the hot coffee, listening for any sounds of an approaching bear. The night noises intrigued her, the constant chirp of crickets, the croak of bullfrogs near the water, the hoot of an owl, and the lone cry of a wolf. Her thoughts turned to the hike down the mountain at daybreak, and she began to worry. *How in the world* am I going to get away without Russ knowing? He's stubborn, he'll follow me. Maybe get into it with Kory. I know he'll come looking for me at first light. We can't take a chance on leaving in the dark if the bear is out there.

The first hour passed quietly and gave her time to think about her departure. *I'll just have to stand my ground. Russ will insist on leaving with me. I'll just tell him either he can leave or I will, but we aren't leaving together. It's over. I'll just make sure he knows I run my own life now.*

As the night wore on, she relaxed, confident she could stand up to him. She decided to take Rebecca's shift, let her rest since she would shoulder the rest of the trip without her support. The night air invigorated her, bolstered her resolve. She let worry roll off her back in a new-found confidence.

Maybe the bear decided to forage elsewhere with all these campfires blazing. Speaking of which, I need a bigger log to keep ours going until morning.

Most of the stacked wood was toward the back of the camp, out of the arc of light from the small pop up lantern. There was one particular log she wanted to grab. It would burn good while.

She glanced at Steve's tent, his fire burned low and his tent was dark. *He might be on patrol. I'll put another log on his fire, too.*

Glad to have something to do, she stepped around the back of the tent, alert, but confident someone would sound an alarm if the bear was near. Police training kicked in. *Proceed with caution, never cause panic.*

The darkness obscured anything recognizable. She stopped to listen. Nothing unusual. She stooped to pick up two small logs.

It happened so fast, she had no time to react. A strong arm grabbed her around the waist, a hand clamped over her mouth. She reacted; wriggling to get free, but whoever it was, held her fast.

She couldn't scream, couldn't breathe. She fought, but was no match for the intruder as he dragged her farther away from camp and into the dense trees.

CHAPTER Ten

K ORY STRETCHED, WORKING OUT THE KINKS IN HIS BACK. Time for my shift. I'll bet Steve is ready to get some sleep.

The coffee smelled good as he stoked the fire and prepared to pour a cup. The urge to glance over at Ricki's tent got the better of him, and he stole a quick look. The fire was at a medium height, a small lantern shone in front of the tent, but there was no sign of her or Rebecca.

Good, she's getting some rest. She'll need it for the hike out of here.

While he sipped from the tin cup, he recalled the kiss they shared. It was everything he imagined and more. She pressed into him. He heard the tiny gasp as they sealed the kiss and felt her body yield.

Right or wrong, it makes no difference now. She's leaving. Wants to go home. Can one kiss get her to change her mind?

Russ weighed on his mind. *He must really love her to come all this way to find her. But, there's something about the guy...*

Steve emerged from the trees on the south side of the lake and Kory watched him walk toward the camp. He waved.

Kory kept his voice low, almost to a whisper as Steve entered camp. "You look beat. Any sign of the bear?"

Steve plopped down beside him. "Nah, it's all pretty quiet out there. Wish I'd heard something to keep my mind occupied. Would have made it easier to stay awake. There's a stump just inside the tree line. It's where I set up for my shift. I think we're all evenly spread out." He reached for the coffee. "I shouldn't drink this before I hit the hay, but it smells so good. Maybe just a sip."

"You look tired enough to sleep through any caffeine spike. I don't think one drink will affect you." He pointed in the direction of Ricki's tent. "I think the girls are sacked out. Haven't seen any movement there. I think Kyle is out behind their tent. Go get some rest. You'll have to take over some of my duties tomorrow."

Steve glanced sideways at him. "I will? You plan to sleep all day?"

"No, I'm taking Ricki back down the mountain. She refuses to stay with Russ up here."

"Ah, what's up with all drama, anyway? I saw the little fracas. Seemed you were right in the middle of it."

"I was breaking it up. A bit of a disagreement."

Steve stood and rubbed his eyes. "Last thing we need up here is more drama. I'm too tired to care. See ya when you get back."

Kory watched him head back to his camp, stoke up his fire, and disappear into his tent. *Well, time to get out there and scout some bear.*

One by one, he surveyed each tent as he made his way to the sentry post. Everything looked secure. The fires all burned brightly. The bullfrogs continued to croak. If a bear approached, the sound would stop.

He found the stump Steve told him about and settled down to listen and watch. The only bad thing about this lonely sentinel was he had plenty of time to think about Ricki and her plan to leave the mountain, to go home and start life over. *I don't want to lose her before we've explored what we feel. The kiss proved it. I've got to make her stay.*

Ricki's squirming slowed as the breath left her body to the point of unconsciousness. As blackness overtook her, the grip on her mouth and chest suddenly released.

She gasped for air.

"Ricki, breath deep, relax. You're gonna be fine. I'm here."

Air filtered back in her lungs and the cloudiness in her brain cleared. "Who…who—?"

"It's me, darling. Russ. We need to talk."

She struggled for balance and scooted away as quickly as she could, still gulping in the night air, trying to talk, to shout, but she was too weak.

Russ sat on a log and watched her. "I know I shouldn't have sneaked up on you, but you left me no choice. If you will give me a chance to explain everything we can put this behind us."

She blinked at him, unable to comprehend what he was talking about. As the fog lifted from her brain, she clutched at the whistle around her neck. It was gone.

A whisper was all she could manage, but she made it count. "You bastard!"

He reached her in a split second and put a hand over her mouth again. "Now, sweetheart. We don't have to alert the whole camp. This is between you and me. I took the whistle because I knew you'd try to use it. Come on. Can't we have a civil conversation? I just want to explain. You didn't give me the chance back home. You just disappeared."

She shook her head vigorously, fear beating an erratic rhythm in her ears.

His grip softened. "Look, I'll let you go if you just promise to sit down and give me a chance to tell my side. If you don't like my explanation, I'll leave and you can go back to camp. I'm a reasonable man. What do you say?"

This might be the only chance I have to get away from this lunatic. She nodded.

He kept his hand over her mouth. "Do you promise?"

She nodded again.

Slowly he removed his hand, but gripped her arm. "Okay, good. Much better."

Her breath remained ragged, but her heart rate slowed a bit. *He's lost his mind!*

As she tried to calm down, his hand relaxed its grip until it released completely.

He handed her a canteen. "This will help. Take a swig."

The water slid down her parched throat restoring her voice. "Why are you doing this? You could have come to my tent and asked to talk to me."

"Really, Ricki? First of all, you were pretty worked up. Second, your lady friend looked as though she wanted to clobber me. And last, but not least, trail boy was a little too eager to come to your defense. With the whistle around your neck, I would have been surrounded in a split second with one blow. This was the best way."

She shook her head. "No, this is kidnapping."

The scowl returned to his face. He reached for the canteen and jerked it back. "Cut it out, Ricki. I didn't kidnap you. You're free to go, if you want. But, you did promise to talk to me."

"And you promised never to cheat on me. So, who is the bad guy now?"

Silence followed her declaration.

It was interesting to watch the change on his face. He could go from angry to puppy dog in a split second. She wondered if it was a sign of a sociopath.

"Okay, I get it. You were mad because you found Leila and me in bed together." He sighed. "It wasn't what it looked like. A funny thing happened. We ran into each other at the coffee shop, I invited her to have a cup. You were on your shift. We talked. She's an artist, as you well know. Said she had done some drawings of you and me together. I wanted to see them. We went to her apartment, had a glass of wine while we looked at the artwork. Before I knew it, she had me between the sheets."

He stood, opened his arms wide as if encompassing the forest. "It wasn't my fault. She got me drunk and seduced me." He turned to face her. "You really should pick better friends, Ricki."

There it is! Making it my fault. I've been so blind. He does it every time. Next comes the charming smile.

He knelt on one knee, a lopsided, sappy grin on his face. "Ricki, darling, you know you are the only one for me. I barely remember the encounter with Leila. It meant nothing. Are you going to throw away the last two years over a silly encounter conjured up by your so-called best friend?"

The seductive mask Russ wore disappeared before her eyes. She saw him for what he really was—a master manipulator, so full of himself, so enthralled with his ability to play women like marionettes, pulling their strings until they believed every word he said. It was a drug to him.

If she answered negatively he might become angry again. "The truth is Russ, I've thought about my future with you for a while. I don't think we're a match made in heaven. I want to go back to my hometown and bolster the law enforcement agency there. Dallas is too big for me. I want to move on. So, you see, it's not only the incident with Leila. I've been unhappy for a while. It's why I came up here. To sort it out. I want to go back home."

She studied his face, watching for any sign he might erupt again. "You want to leave me?"

Now was a good time to try her negotiating skills. "Leave you?"

she said in a soft voice. "I think it's the other way around. You've felt me pull away. Maybe it's why you ended up in Leila's bed. Maybe *you* were leaving me."

A light appeared in his eyes. He smiled, nodded, ran his hand through his hair. "Me leave you? Well—maybe this relationship *has* run its course. I've been struggling with how to tell you."

Her heart did a flip. *He is such a narcissist. I merely suggest breaking up was his idea and he's ready to let me go.*

She stood, her strength fully renewed. "Seems to me, it's a mutual agreement, don't you?"

His eyes darkened. "Well, let's not rush it. We have to get back to home, make sure everyone knows this is my idea."

My God! He really is a sicko. "Sure, Russ. I'm good with the decision. It's time for you to be with a woman worthy of you."

He stood straighter, smiled broadly, a slight gleam pierced through the cloudy look. "Yes, I'm afraid you're right. You are a wonderful woman, Ricki, but I need a different type. One more suited to my needs. It's great of you to understand."

"Good. I need to get back to camp before Rebecca misses me. It's almost time for her shift. Aren't you supposed to be patrolling?"

He blinked twice. "Shift?" He looked around. "Yes, the bear. My shift is over. I need to get back, let Miles take the next shift."

"Miles? You're going to let Miles patrol the woods?"

He frowned and she was afraid she'd blown it.

"Miles is fine. He can handle anything. Just because you don't like him, doesn't make him a pansy."

"I didn't mean he's a pansy. He's never been in this situation before. He's not a cop like you, Russ. Bears are way out of his element. I just want him to be okay."

"He'll be fine," anger rising in his voice. "I need to get back."

He walked toward the clearing and disappeared, leaving her alone.

She called after him, softly, "Wait, my whistle."

He didn't turn around.

Not worth going after it. If he's off my trail the better for me. I can do without a whistle.

Relief flowed through her as she headed back. *This could have ended so badly.*

Before she left the wooded area, she looked around hoping to see someone, anyone, to assure her safety. The only person was Russ heading back to camp. If he figured out she'd played him, he might come back after her. She hurried back to the campfire.

It was time to wake Rebecca. *I need to find Kory and start down the mountain before daybreak. The sooner I get away from Russ the better.*

CHAPTER
Eleven

KORY WAS SATISFIED THE BEAR HAD MOVED ON, BUT STAYED vigilant for the safety of the camp and the possibility of other predators. One more shift, and it would be daylight. He could take Ricki down the mountain, have time to talk, find out how she felt about the kiss. He might even convince her to stay at the lodge until he could finish this assignment.

Everyone told him he needed to start socializing again, find a new woman. *Easy for them to say. I'm a natural born loner. At home in the mountains. Ricki's a city girl. Use to the fast pace. Could we really make it together?*

It was a bad habit of his, arguing with himself. *I must be what they call a pessimist. Always seeing the worst-case scenario. Prepare for the worst. It's my motto.*

He foraged a bit of beef jerky out of his small pack and chewed thoughtfully, watching the sky, listening. A silhouette emerged from the trees illuminated by firelight from the camps; a long shadow danced grotesquely in the dim light.

He squinted.

A man! At first, he thought it was Kyle, but the stocky build didn't match. A few steps more, and he realized it was Russ. His heart beat faster. *What's he doing by Ricki's tent? He's supposed to be across the lake.*

Fearful for her safety, he jumped to his feet. Russ reached his tent and went inside. He started forward, his focus on her campsite. Russ could wait.

Before he could take a step, he stopped dead in his tracks and his heart dropped. Ricki stepped into the light from the side of her tent. He knew it was her, the slender build, the short auburn hair gleaming in the lantern's glow.

He watched her stoke the fire, rub her arms against the night chill, and then slip into the tent.

They were together.

The reality stunned him. He stared at the empty campsite trying to comprehend what he just witnessed. *Our kiss meant nothing to her.*

Buck's tent was close. *I need to wake him. Tell him about Russ.* Instead, he plopped down on the stump again. His head bowed, eyes closed, as he wrestled to make a decision. *It's not my business, but Buck should know Russ left his post. The campers are priority. Whatever stupid choice Ricki makes is her own.*

His fist clenched, he pounded it on his knee. *Damn!*

A soft voice called his name, "Kory."

He looked up to see her standing right in front of him, auburn curls bobbing around her face in the breeze, her curves accentuated by the back light of the campfires. Joy soared to the surface, but took a nose dive the very next second. *God, I love her, but she isn't mine.*

"I need to talk to you."

He stood, tried to wipe any sign of emotion from his face, and turned away to pick up his pack. "No need. I *saw* all I need to know. I'll get Kyle to take you down the mountain. I imagine Russ is going with you."

She grabbed his shoulder and tried to spin him around. "What are you talking about? He abducted me! I want to go now, while he's asleep. Please," her voice cracked.In an instant, he whirled and seized her shoulders, his heart breaking at the tears running down her cheeks. "What do you mean? Are you hurt?"

"No, I'm okay now, but he frightened me. I have to get out of here." She leaned into him.

"It's dark, treacherous in the daytime, let alone at night. I gotta alert Buck. We can't let a lunatic run around this camp."

"No, please. He can't know I'm leaving now. I promised him we'd leave together. But I can't…"

"My God, what did he do to you?" He wrapped his arms around her and held her close.

She looked up. "No time to tell you now. Can't we just leave? I've told Rebecca. I'm packed up. We have our headlamps, please. I have to get out of here."

"I can't just leave without telling Buck. He has to know."

He took her pack and led her a few feet into the woods, found a downed log, and gently eased her onto it. "Stay here. He won't see you in this thicket. There's been no evidence the bear is close, tonight. Use your whistle if you need to alert anyone. Do you have your bear spray? I'll be right back."

"Kory."

"What?"

"He took my whistle."

"He what? Never mind, here's mine." He pulled the cord over his head and handed it to her. "I'll grab my stuff, tell Buck, and we'll head out. Buck will corral him until we're down the mountain. We can call the authorities at the lodge."

She nodded.

He went straight to Buck's tent. "Buck, get up old man. We've got a situation."

The head trail boss was a light sleeper with cat like reflexes. It's what made him such a good leader. Always ready to take charge, he popped out of the tent door. "What's up? The bear?"

"No, it's Russ. He left his post. Went after Ricki. She had to make some sort of agreement with him. He's back in his tent for now. I'm taking her down the mountain before he wakes up. She's terrified of him."

"The bastard."

"Sorry to leave you with this mess, old man, but I gotta make sure she's safe."

"I've got it handled. I'll post a guard at his tent. We'll hold him until you've had time to get her to the lodge. I'll send two men to escort him down and get him away from the rest of the campers. You gonna call the cops?"

"Yes, as soon as we reach the lodge. I'll make sure Ricki is out of sight. Look, I gotta go. I left her in the trees over there."

They shook hands.

"Be safe, Kory."

"Thanks, Buck."

He grabbed a small knapsack from his tent and hurried back to hidden log.

"Let's go, Ricki."

CHAPTER Twelve

RICKI'S HEART BEAT SO FAST EACH BREATH WAS A SHORT gasp as the forest swallowed them up. All she wanted to do was put as much distance between her and Russ as possible. Her training in law enforcement taught her how to control fear, an emotion she didn't indulge in, but this time, it was personal. The fight to rein it in took enormous effort.

Her headlamp kept Kory in sight, giving her comfort, in the pitch blackness of the trees. The prospect of stumbling upon a bear crossed her mind, but Kory's experience reassured her. Right now, bears didn't take precedence.

He glanced back at her, occasionally. She gave him the thumbs up, even though her chest burned from lack of air. Fear nipped at her heels and pushed her faster.

Thirty minutes passed before he slowed the pace.

It was still dark, but the trees thinned out and a small clearing appeared in her headlamp.

He motioned her to follow him to the edge of the trees.

"We can rest here for a few minutes, but we need to stay out of sight."

All she could do was nod as she fought for breath.

Side by side, sitting on their packs, they drank from the canteens, silent but wary of their surroundings.

"I'm sorry I pushed so hard, Ricki. We needed to cover ground before daybreak, didn't want to risk Russ discovering we were gone. We can take it slower, now."

Her head shook vigorously. "No, it's fine. You did exactly what I wanted. The faster I get down this mountain, the better. I say we keep going at the same pace; Russ is sneaky. He could easily extract himself from any guards they put on him. We need to move fast."

"It's your call. Just want to make sure you're able to keep up."

She stood and grabbed her pack. "I'm more than able to keep up. Let's get going."

"Whatever you say."

By daylight, they should be half way to the lodge. The hike down was always faster than going up. She looked forward to sunshine and the ability to see more of the trail ahead.

The sky lightened through the misty clouds and revealed more of the landscape. They took another break, shut off their lamps, and allowed themselves a breakfast of hardtack and water.

Anxious, she urged him forward.

"We're way ahead now. You need to breathe and rest for a few minutes. This altitude will play havoc with you. Slow down. I'm not going to let anything or anyone get to you."

Reluctantly, she agreed.

Kory took advantage of a downed log to sprawl out on his back.

She used her pack as a cushion.

"You gonna call the cops when we get to the lodge?" His eyes remained closed, but his voice took a hard tone.

"I promised him I wouldn't," she whispered. "Told him I'd go back so he could tell everyone he broke up with me."

He sat up and looked at her. "You're going to let him off the hook? Ricki, he's a psychopath. He'll kill you if he doesn't get his way."

"Maybe."

"So, he gets away with kidnapping you and putting a knife to your throat?"

"I just want out of here. I'll figure it out when I get back to Dallas." She snatched her pack and shrugged it onto her shoulders.

"Ricki…"

A series of short high-pitched whistles interrupted him.

Their heads jerked toward the sound simultaneously.

"Oh God, it's Russ!" She ran toward the trail to escape.

"Wait, it's a signal for a bear sighting. Someone's in trouble."

"A bear?"

"Yes, I have to go back. The bear could kill whoever it is. You can stay here, or come with me, but I'm going."

"But, it might be Russ. We'd be running right toward him. It might be a trap."

Kory shook his head, slipped on his pack, and headed up the trail from where they came. "Can't help it. I won't let anyone die up here, not even him."

She hesitated, heart pounding, but turned and followed him.

Another series of whistles pierced the air.

"Give me the whistle. I need to let them know help is on the way."

She pulled the whistle cord over her head and handed it to him.

He answered the distress call with three short spurts of his own.

Before she heard an answer, Kory was sprinting ahead.

Three more short bursts.

The sound was close, now.

They reached a small cleft of rocks just off the trail. Large boulders scattered the terrain at the bottom of a steep drop off.

She saw Russ cowering between a large rock and the wall of the quarry, the whistle in his teeth, a stick clutched in his hand, and a large black bear below him.

Kory motioned for her to stay back.

The bear looked up at its prey. It growled and swiped a paw, but Russ poked the stick into the air and blew the whistle.

"I'm here, Russ. Hold on," Kory shouted.

"For God's sake, do something. It's climbing closer," Russ yelled.

Kory blew his whistle. Loud and long.

The bear's attention wavered. He slowly turned toward the new intruder, stood on his hind legs, and roared.

Kory knew the bear felt doubly threatened now and would attack without reservation. He drew out the bear spray.

"Russ, when I have his full attention, slip behind the rock and make your way back to the trail. Wait until I say go. I've got to get him close enough to use this spray."

The bear fell to all fours and lumbered quickly toward him.

Russ didn't wait for Kory's signal, but ran full tilt toward the trail, distracting the bear again. It stopped and looked toward Russ.

"Dammit Russ, stop! Don't run!"

Russ hollered over his shoulder. "He's all yours. I'm out of here!"

Kory blew the whistle again. The enraged bear swung its large head around and ran full speed toward him. Sixty feet, now thirty. At about twenty feet, Kory let go with the spray, aimed directly at his eyes.

The bear shook his head.

Kory blew the whistle again. Loud and long.

The bear must have had enough because he turned and ran away.

Ricki didn't realize she was holding her breath. "Kory, you might have been killed!"

He hurried back to the trail. "It's not over yet. Pepper spray won't hold him off for long, and now, he's mad. We need to get out of his territory." He looked around. "Where's Russ?"

"I'm right here." Russ stepped from behind a tree.

Kory shook his head. "I told you not to run. It's the worst thing you can do. You put us all in danger."

"I don't give a damn about you, trail boy. I came for Ricki." He turned toward her. "Why are you running from me? I thought we had a deal. Or was it a lie to put me off?"

Ricki stumbled. "I...just want to go home. This trip is a disaster. It's not for me."

Kory stepped forward. "Leave her alone, Russ. She's a grown woman and can make her own decisions."

Russ lunged forward and twisted Kory's arm behind his back in a quick and practiced move. "She's not your concern, boy. I'll take her down the mountain. We're leaving together."

"No, Russ! Stop!"

He pulled a pair of cuffs out of his vest and clapped them on Kory's hands. "There ya go. Try to get out of that." He turned to her. "He's gonna be our bear bait. You and I are going down this mountain together, just like we said."

"Russ, you can't. You don't want murder on your record, do you? You're a top cop. Don't ruin it now," she begged.

"Too late, darling. Besides, they'll never find him once the bear is through with him." He pushed Kory to the tree line and pushed him down.

"Please, Russ, don't do this."

"You're kind of sweet on him, aren't ya? Well, say goodbye, because you aren't going to see him again." He pulled a couple of zip tie cuffs from his pocket and looped them through the metal cuffs and fastened them around a low tree branch. "There. He's all snug."

She lurched forward, but Russ was too strong for her. "Oh no, baby. You're all done with this one. We're going down the mountain and taking your car. I need to leave mine for Miles. You're gonna tell the story the way I want it told." He pushed her forward. "Let's go. The bear will be back soon and I want to be long gone."

"Russ, please—."

"I said, let's go." He shoved her again.

She looked back at Kory, trying to figure out how to help him, but Russ's hand in her back left her no choice. *I'll have to outsmart him and double back. I can lose him in the woods if the right opportunity comes up.*

Russ kept shoving her forward until she couldn't see Kory anymore.

"Why did you come after me, Russ. I thought we were through. Why do you care if I leave or not?"

"You lied to me, Ricki. You said we were doing this together. I'm not stupid. You wanted to get to the lodge first and call the cops on me. Well, it ain't going to happen."

"But, they had guards—."

He laughed. "Really, babe. They posted guards in the front of the tent, not the back. How stupid do you think I am? Your friend was very forth coming as to your whereabouts after I applied a little pressure."

"My friend?"

"Yes, what's her name? Rebecca?"

Her heart skipped a beat. "Tell me you didn't hurt her."

This time his laugh was evil. "Let's just say she's a well put together woman."

"You didn't..."

"Shut up, Ricki. You need to worry about yourself. They'll find her, and when they do, they'll get an eye full."

Her stomach clinched, bile rose in her throat. *I've put everyone in danger. Even Rebecca. Oh, my God! What have I done?*

CHAPTER Thirteen

K ORY STRUGGLED AGAINST THE TREE, TRYING WITH BRUTE strength to break the zip tie. "I have no chance against the bear if I don't get loose from this tree." He rubbed the tie against the bark, hoping to cut through it. "The bear didn't go far. It's just a matter of time before he comes back. Now, Ricki is in danger and it's my fault."

He wriggled around to get a better view of the small cliff. The bear would come up the steep ravine when he got the pepper spray out of his nose. *And he'll be mad as hell.*

Every nerve in his body was alert, waiting for the lumbering sound of his killer. He worked his way around the back of the tree hoping the angry bruin wouldn't see him as he crested the hill, but he knew its sense of smell was better than its eye sight.

Ten minutes passed. Ricki might already be dead. *What would stop Russ from killing her and dumping her body in some deep canyon.*

He'd escape and his buddy Miles would make up some story to get him off. If I'm dead as well, he leaves no witnesses. Except...the handcuffs. If they find any part of my body and the cuffs are on, maybe they will know it wasn't the bear, but murder. He sighed. *Small consolation, but it's nice to see Russ made a mistake. He assumes the bear will eat me. No evidence.*

Another five minutes passed. Time was against him. Each minute might be his last.

A sound caught his attention. Branches breaking. *Here he comes!*

More movement, gravel tumbling, rocks careening down the hill. His heart beat hard in his throat. He closed his eyes, but opened them again. *No, if I'm going to die, I'm not going to die like a coward. Come on bear. I'm ready for ya.*

"Tell us what happened, Rebecca."

Still shaken from the ordeal, she swallowed hard and tried to put a coherent sentence together.

Buck urged her again, "It might be the difference between finding them alive or not."

She nodded. "I was in my tent, thinking about what Ricki told me. I never dreamed I would be a target, because the maniac was after her, not me. They were gone about an hour when Russ unzipped my tent door and barged in. He demanded to know where Ricki was. I put him off, hedged. I didn't want to tell him."

Buck's voice softened, "I know this is hard. Please, what happened next."

"He grabbed me, forced my arms behind my back, and before I knew it, had my hands bound with some kind of rope. Then, he said, 'We can do this the hard way or the easy way. I want to know when she left and what her plan is.' I was terrified. He had such a crazy look in his eyes. I shook my head." She looked down. "He slapped me—hard."

"Then what, Rebecca?"

"He...touched me. My breasts. Said if I didn't co-operate, I'd be sorry. I shook my head, again. He ripped my shirt open." She sobbed. "I'm so sorry. I...I told him."

"Is that all he did? I mean..." He stopped in mid-sentence.

She hung her head. "Wasn't it bad enough?"

"Of course, dear. What did he do after—?"

"He left, just as fast as he came. I sat on the floor shaking until Buzz found me an hour later."

Buzz stood next to Buck, but ducked his head as she turned toward him.

"Thank you, Buzz," she said, softly.

He blushed. "Just glad I came to check on ya, ma'am. I was worried after all the commotion in camp."

Buck clapped a hand on Buzz's shoulder. "We're all glad you did."

Rebecca regained a bit of her composure. "How did he get out? Ricki said you had guards on him."

"My fault. Didn't post one at the back of the tent. He cut his way out. Guess he saw the shadows of Kyle and Steve standing guard." He attempted a smile. "Glad you're safe. We've got a group going after them. Steve will stay to finish the tour. Anyone who wants to go back to the lodge is free to go with a guide. This isn't how I wanted to end the season."

"Do you think he'll harm her? Ricki, I mean."

"Don't know. Right now, I figure they're all in danger. You need someone to sit with you, Rebecca?"

Buzz stepped forward. "I'll stay with her. She needs a good breakfast. I got fish. Once she has a good meal and some hot coffee in her she'll feel better."

Rebecca smiled. "Why thank you, Buzz. What a kind thing to do. I sure could use some coffee." *An unusual champion, but I could use a knight in shining armor right now.*

Buck snapped tree branches in his way with a vengeance as the group he put together made their way down the mountain. *In all these years, I've never had an incident like this. Now, my best guide and a client are in danger. All on my watch.*

Earlier, Buzz ran headlong into his tent to inform him of Russ's escape and Rebecca's ordeal. *At least Rebecca wasn't physically hurt. I only hope the others are safe.*

"Buck, bear tracks." One of the men shouted.

He moved to where the man pointed. "Sure is. Big one looks like."

The prints drove home the urgency to find Kory and Ricki. Not only were they in danger with Russ on the loose, but the bear posed a serious threat to them all.

"Keep moving, but keep your eyes peeled. We've got to find them."

Kory tensed in anticipation of the attack. "Maybe if I play dead, he'll leave me alone. It's all I can do tied to this tree. God, I hope it's quick."

More rocks fell down the hill, but something else made him sit up straight. Voices. He waited. *Could be Russ coming back to make sure I'm dead.*

He heard several voices, all male. He shouted. "Over here! I'm over here!"

Buck's head popped over the ridge. Kory almost wept with relief. "Oh, my God. I'm so glad to see you!"

Buck hurried over. "What the hell? Handcuffs? Doesn't he know there's a bear prowling around?"

"The guy has lost it. He's got Ricki. We've got to stop him. Get me out of these."

Buck cut the zip ties with his knife, but scratched his head at the handcuffs. "A knife isn't going to get you out of these, Kory."

Kyle popped over the ridge and hurried toward the two men. "What happened to you? Where's the cop?"

"No time to explain. He's got her and is headed down the mountain. We've gotta go after them."

"You can't go like this, Kory. I'll send a man back to camp with you, maybe they can figure out how to get you out of those."

"No way! I'm going with you, even if I have to travel with my hands behind my back."

"Hold on a minute." Kyle fished in his pocket. "I can get you out of those in a jiffy."

He pulled out a wire pick and went to work.

In a matter of minutes, the handcuffs fell off and Kory was free.

Buck stared at Kyle. "Where did you learn how to do pick locks?"

Kyle grinned. "Maybe you don't want to know, Buck."

He rubbed his wrists. "Let's go! We're wasting time."

The rest of the men gathered around.

Buck took charge again. "We've got to spread out. I'm not sure Russ will stick to the trail. He's got to know we're after him. All kinds of games trails wind around the main trail where they find the berries and small game. We need to have a few men follow those. But, it's dangerous. You might run smack into a bear. Everyone got their whistles and pepper spray?"

Everyone nodded.

"You two head down the lower trail. The rest of you to the right. Kory, you're coming with me. I'm not letting you out of my sight."

"The hell I am. I know these woods better than you. I saw where he was headed. I'm going this way. You can follow me or not."

CHAPTER Fourteen

"Russ, slow down. I can't catch my breath." Ricki stumbled as her captor pushed her hard from behind.

"No way are we slowing down. I know your game. Those delay tactics won't work on me, sweetheart. Just keep moving."

Another shove, she fought to keep her balance.

The trail narrowed at the switchback. Ricki remembered the exact spot.

Maybe I can make something happen there, catch him off guard. It's my only chance.

They crashed through the woods, stumbling over rocks and tree roots, but she stayed focused on how she might distract him.

She looked ahead, searching for the spot they camped the night she hurt her ankle, but all hope disappeared in an instant when he grabbed the collar of her flannel shirt and jerked her backwards.

"This way," he barked.

Her footing faltered at the sudden jolt. "What are you doing?"

"We're taking the game trail. Have to get off the regular path in case someone follows us. They don't think I know these woods, but I'm smart enough to know the game up here follow the river. It might be the long way, but they won't expect it. Now get going." He shoved her again.

Panic set in. "But you don't know what's down there. More bears, something worse. Russ, don't be foolish. We don't know the terrain."

"It's a chance I'll take. I don't know how long before they find Kory's body, but it should be long enough for us to get out of here."

Branches slashed her face as he pushed her forward on the unbroken trail. She didn't feel the sting, instead, her heart pounded so hard it almost jumped out of her chest. *Please God, don't let Kory die that way.* Every few seconds she glanced from side to side, hoping to find a way to escape. The woods only closed in tighter around them, sealing them against the main trail.

Suddenly, a tree root in the path snagged on the toe of her boot. She stumbled and fell. "Russ, I can't breathe, please I need to rest."

Beads of sweat peppered his forehead and sweat marks spread under his armpits, ruining his expensive shirt. He gulped air trying to infuse oxygen into his body.

He's exhausted, he can't go much farther. I must do something.

"Get up," he spat. "We're not stopping."

She rose to her feet and thought about bolting into the trees, but decided it was too risky. *He's not in as good of shape as he pretends. I need to keep him moving. Not let him rest. My chance will come.* Her chest burned for air, her feet and legs screamed with pain, but she knew her physical stamina was stronger.

I have the advantage. Fear is driving him, now. He's not used to being the prey. The mountain is out of his element, far outside of his comfort zone.

Instead of taking time to assess the environment, he careened forward on a frantic hike toward whatever fate awaited them.

God help us.

―❦―

Kory rushed forward, taking the lead, determined to catch up to Russ and Ricki.

Buck cursed under his breath, but followed, motioning to the others to head toward the areas he assigned them. "Hang on, you stubborn cuss. I'm coming." Under his breath, he mumbled, "Somebody has to keep their head on straight, might as well be me."

"What did you say?" Kory glanced back at his friend.

"Nothin', just talkin' to myself," Buck answered.

Kory's focus centered on how to catch up to Ricki. When Buck caught up he barked out his plan. "I figure they got about an hour's head start. If we do double time, we can catch up pretty fast. Ricki's tired already from our trek this morning. She'll try to get him to rest, try to give someone a chance to catch up. Her training will help with handling Russ. She'll stall, get him off track."

Buck wheezed beside him, but kept pace. "You've got to consider the idea he went off-trail. He's not stupid. He's a cop, he knows how this works. Don't you think he's figured out we've discovered his escape by now? He could be anywhere on the mountain." He tried to pull Kory's arm to slow him down. "Listen. We need a plan. I propose we head straight back to the lodge, get a search party. We can't find him alone."

He jerked his arm from Buck's grasp and pushed forward. "No way will I waste time to form a search party. He could kill her, dump her somewhere. We'd never find her. You go if you want, Buck, but I'm staying on his trail."

They travelled in silence for twenty minutes, neither man slowed down. Kory didn't know what Buck would do if they found evidence Russ went off-trail, but he couldn't worry about it.

He knew the bend in the trail was just ahead—the place he and

Ricki camped the first night. It's what he worried about the most. *It's so steep there. If they scuffle or if he panics, he could shove her off the cliff. I pray she's alive.*

As he hurried forward, he recognized the path was recently travelled—the boot prints, the smashed leaves and broken twigs, but suddenly, water was standing in the leaves and all signs of prints disappeared.

I missed something. I've lost the trail.

"Buck, they've left the trail. Look." He pointed to the leaf-covered trail.

"Yep, no one has been on this part of the trail for a while. We didn't overshoot it by much though, let's re-track."

The two men scoured the path they'd already searched, eyes glued to the forest floor.

"Here, this is where they left the trail. Looks like they scuffled here." Kory looked up toward the thick trees. "There's a game trail and I see boot prints. I'm taking it. This is where we part ways, Buck."

"Oh hell no. I ain't about to leave you out here alone, unarmed, with a madman. You're stuck with me."

He gave Buck a quick nod and plunged into the thick trees.

Together, they battled vines and branches and watched the trail for signs of Russ and Ricki.

Forty-five minutes passed. Still no sign.

"I think we're off base Kory. We should be catching up to them by now. We need to go back."

"No, I still see prints. They're on this trail all right. I'm going on. You can turn back if you want."

"Damn stubborn, cuss. But if we run into a bear, I ain't savin' you this time."

"Fair enough."

Ricki stopped and turned. "Russ, there's a split here, a fork in the trail. Which way do you want to go?"

He pushed past her and studied the ground. "We'll go right, follow the trail down. It'll head toward the streams."

"Game will be there too, most likely the bears. Are you sure you want to chance it?"

"I'll deal with it when we get there. Get moving."

The brush was thick, but she refused to look down or close her eyes, instead, grabbed the branches and broke them as she went along.

It isn't much, but maybe Kory will notice, anything to leave a trail.

A quick glance behind her revealed how the trees swallowed them up, leaving very little in the way of clues.

But the guides know this mountain, surely, they will see our tracks.

After a while, the trees thinned and opened into a meadow. A small river glistened on the other side. Her knees ached, she was covered in grime, and the water looked so inviting. "There's the river."

For a moment, they stood side by side gazing across the meadow, but his voice turned gruff. "Stick to the tree line, we'll meet up with the river farther down."

It was obvious he didn't want to strut across the open meadow in plain sight, but it would take them another half an hour to get to the water.

This time, he took her arm and she stumbled beside him.

The rush of water became a muted roar as they approached and Ricki whimpered, desperately yearning for the cool water.

Finally, the water's edge appeared, but relief was short-lived. A small water-fall careened down a ragged cliff offering no easy way down. To make matters worse, a large black bear fished off a large boulder in the pooling water at the bottom of the falls. Thankfully, the wind was in their favor and he didn't look up.

Russ pulled her toward a clump of trees and hunkered down. "We'll watch what he does. Maybe he'll move on after he gets his fill."

"If he sees us, we're goners. We've got no protection. I told you it wasn't a good idea to go off-trail, Russ."

"Shut up. If we're smart, he won't bother us. Especially if he gets his fill of fish."

They waited, barely breathing, staring at the huge bear.

The fish-eating shaggy beast took his time pulling one fish after another out of the water, devouring each one with gusto. The systematic progression carried him farther downstream.

"He's moving away. We can follow at a safe distance. Keep him downwind of us," Russ whispered.

"Are you crazy? One tumbling rock or the snap of a branch will give us away. He's not far enough away. Besides, there's probably others. It's almost time for them to hibernate. They'll fill their bellies for the winter. I don't want to confront a hungry bear."

"You don't have a choice. We have to keep distance between us and the camp leader, Buck. Can't take the chance they'll catch up. Now, get ready, cause we're going down the falls."

"No, I won't …"

"Let her go, Russ," Kory called from the edge of the clearing.

"Damn. He's alive," Russ swore.

Ricki stood and waved her arms in warning. "Go back. Bear." She tried not to shout, kept her voice low hoping they got her meaning.

Russ yanked her viciously to the ground. "You bitch. I'll show you!"

He dragged her toward the water. "We're going down the falls and we're going now.

Kory and Buck ran toward them.

Russ looked back and pulled her harder.

Frantic, she fought back. "No! The bear. He'll attack if he sees us."

"Got no choice now, thanks to you."

Going over the falls was a death sentence. If the sheer drop didn't kill them, the bear surely would. She kicked his groin, bit his hand, grabbed his hair, and pulled until a hunk came out in her hand. One more hard kick and she was free.

Relief turned to horror as she watched him lose his balance and careen over the edge.

CHAPTER
Fifteen

REBECCA SAT BESIDE BUZZ IN FRONT OF THE FIRE. THE charbroiled aroma of fish made her stomach growl. "I didn't realize I was so hungry. It's good of you to share this with me."

"Ain't no big thing, Miss Rebecca. A person's gotta eat. Besides, I like providin'." He handed her a cup of coffee.

The steam warmed her face as she looked sideways at her unlikely companion, studying the scruffy beard and twinkling eyes. *He's the real deal. A kind, caring man. Why couldn't I have found one like him before?*

Hurried footsteps interrupted their companionship. "What's all the commotion in camp? Where's Russ? I can't find him." Miles Parsons stood awkwardly at the perimeter of the camp fire.

Buzz bent over and reached for the coffee pot. "You don't know? We don't cotton to your kind up here in the mountains, Mr. Parsons.

Abductin' women and scaring them half to death doesn't sit well with us." Buzz poured the coffee, slowly, staring into the fire. He let his words sink in, then stood as if preparing for a confrontation.

"What in the hell are you talking about? What women? Who abducted who? Where's Russ?"

"Miss Rebecca was terrorized by your buddy this morning. Russ escaped the tent where we was holdin' him. He's gone after Ricki after she accused him of kidnapping. You can't tell me you didn't know about his plans. I suggest you gather your gear and head on down the mountain."

Parsons shook his head. "I have no idea what you're talking about. I had a case of the stomach flu last night, went to bed early. Are you saying he kidnapped Ricki?"

Buzz nodded. "Late last night. She convinced him to release her, but she turned him in and left the mountain with Kory. Russ escaped, came over here and forced Rebecca to tell him where she'd gone. He's an animal. I hope they catch him before he does any more harm."

She studied the ground as Buzz recounted the events, unwilling to look at Parsons face.

"Rebecca, did he hurt you?"

She didn't look up. "No, just my dignity. You need to pick better friends, Mr. Parsons."

"He's always been a hot head. I'm truly sorry." Parsons turned away, then back. "Is there anyone who can get me down the mountain? I'm sure all of you would like me to disappear."

"We can't spare any men. Much as I'd like to send you out on your own, it wouldn't be proper. You're going to have to wait it out like the rest of us, until we have news. They're searching now." Buzz said. "Stay close to your tent."

Parsons walked toward his camp without another word.

She cut her eyes toward the retreating man and continued to watch until he ducked inside his tent. "He's a city boy, Buzz. He's probably out of food, if he had any to begin with. I'm sure he doesn't know which end of the pole to cast in the water. Probably hungry."

Buzz stayed silent, staring into the fire.

She waited.

He got up, forked a trout out of the pan, plopped it on a plate, and turned to her. "You got a good heart, Miss Rebecca. After what his pal did to ya, not sure I would be as charitable. Could you hand me some hardtack and a cup of coffee?"

She smiled and watched as he waited outside Parson's tent, handed the meal inside and headed back toward her camp.

He sat down on the log and continued his own meal.

"You're a good man, Buzz."

"Hrrmmph," is all she got in return.

"Buzz, what if they don't catch him? What if he hurts Ricki? I can't live with myself if something bad happens."

"Buck and Kory are the best around. Them and the others will find him before he can hurt her. They're natural trackers. Don't you worry none."

"I came out here to get away from violence and stress. Trying to start my life over, get a new lease on life. Where can anyone go to truly get away?"

"Seems to me you found a true friend in Miss Ricki. Those are hard to come by nowadays. It's why I come to the woods. I'm not much on people, but I can spot the good ones pretty quick. Like you, Miss Rebecca. I knew the minute I laid eyes on you. Despite what happened you can't throw away a friendship like what you got with Miss Ricki. So, you see, something good came from all this, after all."

"And you, Buzz."

"Me? What do you mean?"

"I found you. Seems to me we've got a pretty good friendship going, as well."

Buzz blushed.

Rebecca smiled and reached for his hand.

Frozen with fear, all Rikki could do was stare at Russ's still body.

Kory ran up behind her, grabbed her around the waist, and pulled her away from the edge. "My God, you could have gone over with him."

She struggled against his grip. "Is he…is he dead?"

Buck caught up and peeked over the side. "He's movin', Kory. We have to go down and get him."

"No. There's a bear down there. He'll kill all of you." She turned to look at Kory. "Please, don't go down there. You're no match for him."

"I can't just leave him down there, Ricki. It would be a brutal death. I have to try to save him."

Buck pulled out a bowie knife. "Kory's right. We can't condemn a man to such a gruesome end."

"You're going to leave me up here to watch you all die?"

"Look, there's two of us. Buck and I have fought bear before. We'll work him between us." He looked at his partner. "First, we find a way down. We don't have much time. He can reach Russ faster than you can spit, Buck. Let's go."

She looked on, helpless.

They peered over the side, stopped to look at each other, and stepped back.

Kory turned to her. "He's gone."

"What do you mean, he's gone? The bear?"

"No, look for yourself. Russ is gone. He's not there. The bear is headed downstream, but where the hell did Russ go?"

She ventured toward the edge of the falls and looked down. "Oh, my God, he's still alive. Where is he?"

"We're going to find out. Come on, Buck."

"Wait, the bear is on the move. Can we chance leaving Ricki up here by herself? There might be another bear or this one might double back." He pointed toward the stream. "She's defenseless up here."

Kory stopped. "What can we do? It's no good to face a bear alone. And we can't take her with us."

"The hell you can't. Have you forgotten I'm a game warden? I'm going with you no matter what you say. Besides, we shouldn't split up right now."

"All right, all right. We're wasting time. Russ is probably hurt from the fall. If he's bleeding, the bear will find him soon."

Without a climbing rope, the descent presented a huge problem. They'd have to rely on each other to make it down safely.

Kory went first. He tested the footholds, scoped out any handholds. After a few feet, he motioned for her to follow. "Step exactly where I did. Hold on where I did. Take it slow."

Inch by inch, she duplicated his steps. Moss covered rocks made each step slippery. A few scrub trees served as handholds, but she retained her balance and reached Kory. She looked up at Buck. "Your turn."

One by one, they descended the jagged slope until they reached the boulder where Russ landed.

"There's blood. He's hurt." Kory glanced around. "Looks like he went into the trees. He's dragging one leg, probably broke it when he fell."

Buck agreed. "He can't be far."

The ground was rocky, but the trail led into the woods where the forest floor smoothed out.

"I'll hang back, keep an eye on the bear. He's gone downstream, around the bend, maybe he won't find us," Buck said.

"Okay, but don't stay long. I might need your help with Russ. He's strong, he'll want to fight."

Buck nodded.

"Let's go, Ricki."

Together, they reached the tree line and cautiously stepped into the woods.

Kory whispered, "He might be thinking of an ambush, so keep your eyes peeled."

Ricki searched for signs. It was a clear path. Russ's bum leg made it very easy to follow.

Kory called out, "Come on, Russ. You're hurt. Give it up. There's a bear close by. You don't have a chance without our help. We're not leaving you."

Silence. Even the birds were quiet.

Ricki tried. "Russ, this is out of control. We need to get you to a doctor. You might have internal bleeding. Come out before you bleed to death."

A moan several yards away alerted them at the same time.

Kory pointed. "Over there."

A downed tree lay on the forest floor, almost hidden in the jungle-like tangle of vines. Russ lay beside it, barely conscious.

Kory knelt beside him. "Russ, you gotta stay awake. Don't pass out on me. We need to carry you out of here."

In a strangled voice, Russ spat, "Get away from me."

Ricki took his pulse. "His heart's beating all over the place. He's going into shock."

He ripped off his flannel shirt and wrapped it around Russ.

Buck hurried toward them. "The bear is coming back this way. We gotta move."

"He's in shock, Buck, I need your shirt."

Buck ripped off his flannel and handed it to Kory.

Kory found the gash in his leg and secured it with the shirt. He motioned for Buck to grab hold and together they lifted him to a standing position. He was dead weight, but it wasn't impossible.

"Ricki, can you grab the gear? We've got our hands full with him."

She quickly gathered the emergency packs and looked at the men. "Which way, Kory?"

Buck answered, "We can't go back to the water, the bear is moving upstream now."

Kory nodded. "We've only got one way to go. We've got to skirt the stream until we can connect to it again without the bear."

Slowly, they made their way through the underbrush. Russ moaned, tried to speak, but mostly stayed in and out of consciousness.

They didn't talk, saving their energy for the trek ahead.

Every few yards, they gently lowered Russ to the ground, made sure he was conscious and breathing.

An hour passed, the routine repeated over and over.

A clearing came into view.

"Over here," Kory called over his shoulder. "We should be able to get to the stream through this clearing."

At the water's edge, Ricki nervously looked around for bear.

Kory scouted a bit upstream while the others rested.

"We need to keep moving. If we follow the stream, we should come to the old bridge. It crosses the ravine. It'll be easier going from there."

Ricki smiled at Kory. "I'm so glad you know these woods. Not sure I could have found my way out of here."

Once again, the two men hoisted Russ up and picked their way through the rocky terrain, staying close to the river.

Ricki followed closely.

Fifteen minutes later, Kory stopped. "Listen."

Everyone stood still.

"Voices," Ricki whispered.

Buck agreed, "Must be the others. Thank God. We can transfer him much faster with more people."

Kory whistled and waited for an answer. None came.

Instead, a low, guttural snarl at the edge of the woods made Ricki's blood run cold.

CHAPTER Sixteen

R**ICKI'S TRAINING TAUGHT HER TO KEEP CALM, BUT SHE HAD** her back to the bear and couldn't judge the distance between them. She looked at Kory.

He twisted around to face the bear, still hanging tight to Russ.

Buck whispered, "Stand your ground. Nobody move."

She wanted to turn, to face the threat of death from this fierce animal, but understood the need to remain still.

The bear didn't approach, but she could hear its huge paws flinging dirt every time he moved from one foot to the other. His breathing came in grunts, anxious and alarming.

Kory looked at Buck. "He's at least four hundred yards away. We need a distraction. Something to get him to move away from here, but what?"

"I think he's confused with so many scents, plus there are four of us. He might be hesitating because of it. I can hike off in the opposite direction, use the bear spray on him when he gets close enough, blow the whistle. Maybe he'll take off. Let's lower Russ to the ground. You can't hold him up alone."

Kory disagreed. "I can't let you do it. He needs food for hibernation. He'll attack."

Buck shook his head. "I don't see we have much choice. If we don't do something quick, he'll attack anyway."

Kory nodded.

They lowered Russ to the ground, slowly.

Russ snarled at them. "You cowards, leaving me here for bear bait. I'll kill all of you."

"No one is leaving you, Russ. Kory and Buck are going to distract the bear *away* from us," Ricki spat, "Now shut up."

Buck eased away from the others, downstream, slow and silent.

The bear watched him while his rocking motion increased, but he didn't move toward him.

Kory followed Buck. "Don't make eye contact. Stand tall, don't crouch down. Bears don't see well, so if he detects we're moving, he might forget about Ricki and Russ."

Buck moved farther downstream.

Kory stayed closer to Ricki and Russ.

She could hear the bear continue to rock back and forth.

Ricki's muscles ached with tension. *What if this doesn't work. What if he attacks anyway?*

Buck drew his whistle out of his shirt and put it to his lips.

Just as he was about to blow, voices broke through the silence on the other side of the river.

"Hey, Kory! Buck! Gosh, we've been looking all over for ya!"

Ricki panicked. *The bear!*

Kory waved his arms, pointed to the bear. "Stop! Bear."

Buck blew the whistle. The bear turned and disappeared into the woods.

"Good God, it's a good thing we showed up when we did."

Kyle shouted.

Buck hurried back to the others. "We won't have much time. He'll be back."

Kyle's group hurried down the hill and joined them at the river. "I see ya found the scumbag. What's the plan?"

"Let's get the others down here. There's eight men, so we can transport him much faster. Four on, four off, change out every few miles. Get the guys down here quick, before the bear comes back," Buck ordered.

Ricki gathered the gear as the others scrambled to organize the transport. She turned to Kory. "Who's going to watch for the bear? I can hang back, keep a look out."

"We'll hang back together. When it's my turn to carry, we'll swap out."

Ricki watched as the men carried Russ, glad to have Kory by her side. "We sure dodged a bullet, this time. Do you think the bear will return?"

"It's hard to say. They don't like people as a rule. Our numbers are in our favor. He'll probably circle around for a bit, but when he sees we're leaving his territory, he should back off."

"He ate a bunch of fish, so maybe he wasn't hungry enough to chase us."

They laughed together.

"Are you okay, Ricki? We haven't had a chance to talk. Did Russ hurt you?"

She shook her head. "No, he didn't hurt me. He pushed through the woods pretty hard, but other than being winded, I survived okay. What about you, Kory?" A sob escaped. "My God, I thought you were torn apart by a bear, tied to the tree with no way to escape. I couldn't stand the thought of it." She clamped her hand over her mouth to stifle another sob. When she gained control, she asked. "Not knowing tore me apart. How did you get free?"

"I didn't. Buck and the others found me. I had no way of getting out of those handcuffs. Fortunately, Kyle was with him. Did you know he did time in prison? Petty theft. He carries a wire pick with him everywhere he goes. One of his throwback habits, I guess. Lucky for me. He got me out in no time."

"It's funny. Something about Kyle always bothered me, but right now, I'm glad he was around."

"So, you missed me, huh?" Kory smiled.

"Well, my God. Russ handcuffed you to a tree. *Wanted* a bear to eat you. Anyone would be concerned." Her face flushed hot and she looked away.

"Well, it's nice to know you were concerned. Hungry?" He handed her a strip of beef jerky.

"I'm starving. Thank you. Russ would barely let me get water."

The smoked meat made her salivate, and her stomach clenched as she devoured the tasty snack.

"Russ is going to prison. How do you feel about it?"

The sinewy tidbit kept her mouth busy as she contemplated on how to answer. It was clear he wanted to understand her feelings toward Russ and whether she was completely over him after these horrific events. *She* knew all feelings for Russ were erased. But, what of Kory?

How could I be so wrong about Russ? How can I trust what I think I feel for Kory? How do I tell him I need time to figure it all out?

She faced him, squared her shoulders and plunged in. "I'm booking the first flight home. I don't care what happens to Russ. He can rot in jail for all I care. I'm a mess. I doubt my own judgement, right now."

His jaw tightened, but he stayed silent.

Her voice quivered, "I have to go back and face my demons before I can move on with my life." She fought back tears. "Please, try to understand."

He didn't look at her, didn't speak, but kept his eyes on the trail ahead of them. The look of sadness on his face wrenched her heart.

He'll push his emotions down, tuck them inside, maybe never dare to love again. But, I am a train wreck. I can't commit to another man until I sort this all out.

He didn't speak again as they hiked along. When it came time for the swap, he took his turn lugging Russ without another word.

She was stuck with Kyle. The last person she wanted to be near.

"Glad we found ya, Miss Ricki. Russ is one messed up dude," he said."

"Yes, I'm glad you found me, too. Thank you. Glad you got to Kory in time."

Conversation wasn't on her agenda. Too many emotions whirled around in her mind as she watched Kory's muscles ripple with the weight of his load.

"Miss Rebecca's okay, too.

"Oh, my God, I almost forgot about her. What happened? Russ didn't hurt her, did he?"

"Well, not physically, but she was shook up. Thank goodness for Buzz."

Kyle recounted how Russ terrorized Rebecca and how Buzz found her.

Ricki couldn't hold back the tears. "It's all my fault. She was in the situation because I put her there. How can she ever forgive me?"

Her tears appeared to fluster him. "Now, now. You can't be blamed for someone else's crazy. This ain't your fault." He jabbed a finger toward Russ. "It's his. He's the one causing all the havoc. Don't you blame yourself. Miss Rebecca is a tough cookie. And Buzz is watching over her real close."

"Buzz?"

"Yeah, I think he's sweet on her."

She wiped a tear from her cheek. "Sweet on her? You mean…?"

"Yep. He's got a big crush. By the looks of it, she's got one, too."

A smile replaced the tears. *Well, at least someone found what they were looking for. I'll have to keep in touch with her. I've just got to let her know she did the right thing and I don't blame her for telling Russ where I went.*

"They'll all be comin' down the mountain tomorrow, at first light. Too much craziness to continue this trip. Besides, the police will want to question everyone, her especially."

"I don't want to wait until tomorrow. I have to get out of here." Kyle was right, of course, she couldn't leave. But, how long would she have to stay?

He spit alongside the trail. "Nah, with something like this the coppers want to talk to everyone. Especially you and Rebecca. You won't be able to leave."

A lump rose in her throat, tears threatened to spill over again. "I...I can't."

"You ain't got a choice."

CHAPTER
Seventeen

RICKI DIDN'T SPEAK TO ANYONE FOR THE REST OF THE TRIP, or rather, no one spoke to her, not even Kory. A knot of apprehension grew in the pit of her stomach. *I must get away from this mountain right away! I can't stay around Kory. Not like this. Damn Russ Desmond! Why did he have to come after me?*

Instead of joining her at the back of the pack when he was relieved, Kory headed to the front of the line and conversed with Buck. He wouldn't even look at her.

I've hurt him. He's upset and won't talk to me. Well, isn't it what I wanted? For him to stay away so I can get my mind straight. It's for the best. We need to end this, right now.

The trail widened suddenly and she knew the lodge was over the next rise.

I'll forget all about Kory Littleton, bury myself in my work back home. I don't need a man to be happy.

She repeated the phrase over and over in her mind, hoping it would take hold.

The lodge came into view and her heart leapt. *I need to get to a room, fast. But how?*

Relief came quickly when she saw Kory and Buck take hold of Russ and firmly escort him to the entrance to the lodge.

She held back.

The rest of the group followed them in.

Still, she held back.

It would take time to get the police out here. Russ would, no doubt, be held in a room somewhere until they arrived. Her timing had to be perfect.

Once she assumed enough time passed, she went inside. Wolf wasn't at the desk, another young man stood smiling at her.

"I've got a room for you, miss." he said. "Mr. Wolf said all campers had to stay until the police finished their questioning. You're the last one, but I held a good one for you."

"Lovely. Can I go up now? I'm exhausted."

"Yes, ma'am. Do you have bags in your car? I figure you want a change of clothes."

She glanced around. The longer she stood out here, the more likely Kory would show up. *Fresh clothes would be so nice, but I can't risk running into him.*

"I'd be happy to get them for you. Which car is yours? Give me the keys and I'll put them right outside the door for you. So, you can go ahead and take a shower," the boy offered.

She smiled at the nice young man. "Wonderful. Not sure my legs would hold out if I tried to lug them."

"No problem. I'm here to help." He grabbed a room key from the board. "201. All the way down the hall in the corner."

She fished out her car keys and tossed them to him. "Dark green SUV. I parked near the back of the lot."

He smiled a toothy grin and headed out the door.

His lanky frame and gangly walk suggested he wasn't much older than a teenager. But, he was a nice young man and she was grateful to make a quick escape.

Room 201 was tucked back in the alcove of the long hall way. Completely private. Just the way she liked it. *I can stay in my room. Maybe I can have a meal brought up. Surely, the police won't keep me long.*

She glanced around for a room telephone and found it on the desk by the bed. *I forgot to ask the young man his name. Maybe I can catch him when he brings the bag up. He's eager to help, I'm sure he'll scrounge me up a meal.*

It didn't take long before she heard the thud of the bag being dropped at her door. She rushed over and flung it open.

"Oh good, I caught you. What's your name, by the way?"

"Byron." He grinned.

"Byron, what a relief. I was afraid you were going to say Coyote or something. Seems everyone has a fierce animal name around here. Buck, Wolf, etc."

He blushed. "Well, they do call me by my nickname, Beaver, sometimes."

She laughed. "Why Beaver?"

"I make Beaver hats. Trap 'em, skin 'em, and sell 'em. Tourists go crazy for them."

"Well, good for you."

He turned to go.

"Wait. Do you think you could scrounge me up a meal? I'm starving."

He looked surprised. "Supper will be served in the dining hall in about an hour. Good hot food. Everyone will be down there."

She flashed a quick smile. "Look, *Beaver*. I'm exhausted. Please? Can you bring a tray up here for me? I'd be happy to pay extra."

"Well…"

She gave him her best pitiful look. "Please? Just this once?"

He shuffled his feet. "I'll see what I can do, but the police said everyone should meet in the dining room at dinner time."

"The police are here?"

"Yep, they're pretty quick around here. Something like this threatens the livelihood of people who work around here. Tourists won't come back if they think there's danger or a lunatic running around."

"Look, ask if they can come up here to question me. I'll answer everything. I simply need some peace and quiet."

The young man looked sympathetic and nodded. "Okay, I'll do my best."

"Thank you so much."

The door closed quietly. She glanced around, unsure of what to do next. A shower certainly beckoned to her, but she wasn't sure how long Byron would take with the meal. She decided to take the risk.

While the hot water washed away some of the twisted events of the past couple of days, her mind wandered back to Kory.

I don't want to see him, again. If I do, I might lose my resolve to leave right away. I must avoid him, at any cost. I hope Byron can persuade the police to talk to me privately.

Reluctant to leave the soothing warmth of the shower, she lingered, let the water pound her head, her back, her legs. Her scattered thoughts drifted together again, forming a cohesive platform once again. The fractures Russ caused melded seamlessly together and rational thought returned.

A white fluffy robe hung on the peg behind the bathroom door. She donned it gratefully, wrapped a towel around her wet hair, and stepped into the bedroom just as a loud knock sounded on the door.

Hunger took over. She flung the door open. "Oh Byron, you are …"

"Roast beef sandwich on rye. Best we could do. Hope it's to your satisfaction."

It wasn't Byron standing in the doorway holding a tray, but Kory with a pinched look on his face and a policeman standing behind him.

CHAPTER Eighteen

The last face Ricki wanted to see was Kory Littleton's. She clutched the robe at her throat and stifled the scream trapped inside her. "I—I was expecting Bea…I mean Byron. He said he would explain…"

"Yes, Miss Sheridan, he did explain. It's why we're here." The law enforcement officer stood slightly taller than Kory, an imposing figure with full uniform and a shiny gold badge on his shirt.

She noticed the embroidered emblem on his sleeve. Lakeview PD. "Of course. Look, I'm not dressed. Could you give me a few minutes?" Rattled, she stifled the rising panic.

"Yes, we'll wait in the hall."

Kory shoved the tray at her. "Better take this."

"Thank you," she mumbled, avoiding his eyes.

The bag from the SUV still sat on the bed. She found a clean pair of jeans and a denim shirt, and hastily pulled them on. The towel fell from her wet hair. The curls were damp and tousled, but decided a quick run through with her fingers was good enough.

In less than five minutes, dressed and presentable, she opened the door.

"Please, come in."

Kory and the officer entered the room.

"My name is Officer Kemp. I'll be conducting the investigation. You know Mr. Littleton."

"Wolf sent me." Kory still stood in the doorway, his face pinched, jaw set.

"Now, Miss Sheridan. If you'll sit down, we'll begin."

For the next thirty minutes, the officer asked her to go over the events leading up to her abduction. Between bites of the sandwich, she recounted everything she could remember.

"You intend to press charges?" Kemp asked.

She stopped in mid-bite. "What? Of course, I want to press charges." She pointed to Kory. "He tried to kill him, too. He needs to be put away."

"Mr. Desmond gives quite a different account, Miss Sheridan. He says you were in on the whole thing. Claims Mr. Littleton came on to you, forced you to spend the night with him, wouldn't leave you alone. Mr. Desmond told us you contacted him and asked for his help to get 'rid' of Mr. Littleton."

The sandwich dropped from her hand. "How absurd! I slipped and injured my ankle. We spent the night on the trail because I couldn't put weight on it to carry the pack."

"So, you admit you spent the night on the trail with Mr. Littleton?"

Anger flushed her face. Her body shook at the realization Russ would do anything to save his own neck. "You have no right…"

"Ricki, settle down. Rebecca will be here in the morning. She'll give her account. You need to rest." Kory reached for her hand.

"I want to go home, now. I feel better after the shower. I can leave, right? I gave my account."

"I'm afraid not, Miss Sheridan. Everyone is required to stay until the others arrive in the morning." The officer moved to the door. "We'll leave you, for now."

Kemp tipped his hat and left.

Kory stepped into the room. "Wolf sent me up here, afraid you'd lose your temper when you heard the garbage Russ was telling the police. We'll sort this out. Rebecca can back up your story. We have Buck and the others, too. This is a stall tactic on Russ's part. Thinks he can get the law on his side."

The need for Kory's arms around her proved too hard to resist. She leaned into him and sobbed on his shoulder, needing the comfort of his embrace.

But, she pulled away after a few seconds, fighting the desire to give her heart to him. "You need to leave. Russ isn't finished trying to mess up my life. Russ might even get away with this. He's cop. He knows people."

His hands dropped to his side. "I'll go, but I won't forget. You and I both know we had that one moment. It was real, it was meant to be. Deny it all you want, but we belong together. I'll do everything in my power to make sure Russ gets what he deserves. Maybe you can't believe in yourself, right now, but you won't have to worry about looking over your shoulder. I'll make sure of it."

She turned away, afraid she'd lose her nerve.

Kory whispered, "See you downstairs in the morning. Rest well."

After he left, she fell across the bed and sobbed into the pillow. More doubt flooded her mind. *How could I have been so blind. Russ is an animal and I didn't see it until it was too late.*

The sobs lessened and eventually subsided. Sleep overcame her, a fitful sleep with visions of a dark specter looming above her.

At six a.m., she woke with sunlight filtering through the slightly parted curtains. Her clothes were rumpled, her hair plastered to one side of her face, her mouth as dry as cotton.

She sat up and groaned to the empty room. "Need another shower. Can't face anyone like this."

The water soothed the pain in her heart as it cascaded over her body and her resolve to leave after breakfast faded. *I can't let Rebecca go through this alone. She went through hell because of my relationship with Russ. It's only right I support her.*

The half-eaten sandwich on the table triggered hunger. *I'll feel better after I've had breakfast.*

It took only moments to run her fingers through her curly hair, don a fresh pair of jeans and flannel shirt.

Aloud she said, "Okay, Ricki, you can do this. Let's go downstairs."

She hoped the others weren't down yet. *Maybe I can eat and get back to my room before I have to deal with anyone.*

The door to the dining hall swung open. Her world stopped.

Russ Desmond sat at a table with a plate of scrambled eggs and bacon in front of him. "Hello, darlin'. Glad to see you survived this horrible situation. You look wonderful. Don't worry, we'll get that bastard Littleton behind bars."

CHAPTER
Nineteen

Ricki's stomach lurched as Russ stuffed a forkful of eggs into his mouth and chewed with a crooked smile and a wink.

Nothing else registered in her brain until the clank of metal across the table.

Officer Kemp, shackled to Desmond, spoke quickly, "Miss Sheridan, I'm so sorry. It was my intent to leave before you came down."

Her voice shook, "Why is he down here, at all?"

Kemp's voice remained steady. "We didn't have a secure room. He said he was hungry." He turned to his charge. "You're done, let's go."

She spun around and headed for the sunroom. Alone, she fought to control her breathing. The smirk on Russ's face soured her stomach, shook every fiber in her body.

Will I ever be free of him? Can he wiggle his way out of this?

Her eyes squeezed shut trying to push the images out of her head.

"Miss, are you alright?"

It was Byron. His soft voice soothed her jangled nerves.

Through tears, she looked up at him. "I'm better now. Thanks."

"They told me what happened in the dining room. I thought you might need this."

The pungent aroma of bacon combined with the sweet smell of maple syrup and pancakes restored a bit of warmth to her battered soul. "You're a life saver, Byron. Thank you."

He placed the meal on a small table near the window. "It's warm over here where the sun comes through. Would you like a hot cup of coffee? Or juice?"

"Coffee would be wonderful."

"Be right back."

It did feel better in the sun. She sat down and toyed with her food, then ventured a bite. The warm, sticky cakes triggered her appetite and before long, half of the stack and a piece of bacon disappeared.

Byron returned with a steaming cup and placed it near her plate. "Cream or sugar?"

"Black, thanks."

He turned to go.

"Wait. Sit with me. I could use a little company this morning."

"Okay, Wolf sent me out here with breakfast for you, so I'm sure he won't mind if I hang for a while." He sat across from her.

"Good. Why do you work here? Aren't you in school?"

He chuckled. "Wolf gave me this job. 'Fraid I'd drop out of school. My folks tried to get me to stay in, but it wasn't for me. Doing my numbers was okay, but I couldn't take all the English, history and such. I gotta work with my hands."

"So, where does Wolf come in?"

"Wolf mentors everyone. I high-tailed it up here to see if he'd talk to my folks. Convince them to let me out of school."

"Wolf encourages kids to drop out? Doesn't seem like it's any of his business." "Oh no, he doesn't encourage anyone to drop out of school. In fact, he has certain conditions if we come work for him. Hold on."

He got up and went to a vending machine across the room. When he returned, he popped open the soda and took a long drink.

The coffee slid down her throat in a warm, healing relief. "What conditions?"

"Well, for me, it was finishing school online. Had to get my diploma one way or the other. In the afternoon, he sets me in his office at his computer to do my lessons. I'm on the last section." His face beamed.

She sat up straight and took a good look at the young man across from her. "My, my. Wolf is a surprise at every turn. So, he expects high standards from his employees. Good deal. When do you work on your beaver hats?"

"Only on the weekends. Work and school come first during the week. I'm getting good grades, too. Don't know why I do better this way than sitting in a classroom all day, but it works. My parents are happy." He stopped and looked squarely at her. "Enough about me. You haven't told me anything about you. What do you do and where are you from?"

She laughed. "Fair enough. I hail from Dallas, Texas. I'm a game warden. I totally identify with your aversion to a classroom. An office isn't for me. Four walls? Nope. I wanted to be out in the wide-open spaces with nature. I did have to finish school in a classroom and the academy, of course, but it was a means to an end."

"Wow, a woman game warden. Cool. Tell me about …"

"What's going on out here?"

"Oh, Mr. Kory, I was just keeping Miss Ricki company. She's having breakfast out here. It's okay 'because Wolf sent me."

Kory smiled. "He told me. I thought I'd make sure everything was okay."

Byron looked at Ricki. "I best be gettin' back. I'm supposed to man the front desk in fifteen minutes. Nice talkin' to you, Miss Ricki."

"Same here, Byron. See you later. Thanks for breakfast."

He nodded and brushed past Kory.

"Didn't mean to disturb you. Byron can be a bit chatty. I really came to tell you Officer Kemp just drove off with Russ in his squad car. He'll be in the Lakeview jail until this is sorted out. The others should arrive by noon. Maybe we can put this behind us. Enjoy your breakfast." He turned to go.

"Wait. Don't leave."

Kory stopped, but didn't turn around.

"Can we talk a minute?"

He turned to face her. "You've made up your mind to head back. *I* want you to stay. Doesn't seem like there's much to say." He headed for the door again. "I've others duties. Excuse me. When the others get here, we can set the police straight about Desmond and you can head back home."

She watched him go. Tears stung her eyes at the rebuff. *Am I doing the right thing? Should I stay or is it too late?*

The lodge still housed a handful of guests. The tourist season was winding down because of the heavy snow expected. A few people relaxed by the fire in the great room. Some packed their cars, ready to leave. Normally, it was a peaceful place to get away from the rat race of the city.

She was torn. The facility was beautiful with its rustic décor of hand hewn wood and rock fireplaces. It was cozy, comfortable, a place to renew your soul. Half of her wanted to stay, but the other half yearned to get away, leave behind the last couple of days and seek the peace she needed so desperately. How could she heal when Russ's face leered back at her at every turn?

A couple wandered into the room, older, with weathered faces and white hair. They held hands, smiled at each other. They didn't notice her, at all, but sat down by a small fountain gurgling in the corner.

She sat still and watched them. *What is it like to have a relationship like theirs?*

A twinge of guilt pricked her conscience as she observed the two talking in low whispers, enjoying each other's company. She turned away.

If I leave now, they'll see me. I don't want to break their spell.

Byron rushed in. "They're back. They made it down the mountain in record time. Left before daylight. I thought you'd like to know."

The loving couple looked up at her and smiled. The spell was broken.

CHAPTER
Twenty

Ricki followed Byron into the great hall. From where she stood, Rebecca's small frame stood out against the larger men. The pack on her back bobbed up and down in cadence with her steps.

She couldn't see her expression, but noted the weariness in how she walked, head down, legs pumping slowly. Her first instinct was to rush out and greet her, but she waited. *Give her space. Let her recover, first.*

As Kory walked out to greet them, her heart skipped a beat. Every time she saw him, she remembered the moment he kissed her on the side of the mountain. Caught off guard, it was hard to process at the time. He apologized, but she shut out the yearning it exposed. Back and forth, wanting him—pushing him away, his desire, then his stoic resolve to shut *her* out. A bewildering dance between two people guarding their feelings to the point of destruction. His pain, her doubt. And now—the door closed. She made up her mind. *Go back to Dallas and leave all this on the mountain.*

Rebecca greeted Kory. Ricki watched the interchange. The half-smile she gave him, the nod of the head. Kory must have asked a question given the head shaking. Finally, everyone continued to the lodge.

Ricki stood to one side as they entered the main door and waited.

Rebecca came in ahead of Kory. "Ricki. You're okay." She rushed toward her dropping her pack on the floor. "I was so afraid he hurt you or worse."

The women embraced briefly.

"I'm fine. I'm so glad to see you. I can't even begin to tell you how sorry I am for what he did to you. It's all my fault…"

"Stop, right now. It's no one's fault but Russ Desmond's. I won't have you blaming yourself." She turned. "Buzz took excellent care of me."

The unlikely hero stood behind Rebecca. Scruffy, tired eyes, a pleasant smile, and a light in his eyes when he looked at Rebecca, left no doubt how he felt about her.

"Buzz, what you did—well, how can I ever thank you?"

"No need, ma'am. Anyone would have done the same." He cut a look her way, then looked away with a shy smile. "She's a special gal."

"Indeed, she is. Well, you all are exhausted and hungry. Get some rest. When you feel like it, we'll talk."

Rebecca nodded. "I need a shower and some food. Want to meet downstairs in about an hour? I slept well last night. I'll rest later."

She looked at Kory who hung back by the door. "Is it okay if Rebecca and I talk before the police get here to question everyone?"

His tone was cool. "Wolf is about to call them. He'll find out when they'll be here. I don't see why you two can't visit until they arrive. I need to check on the others." He left the three of them in the great hall. The others drifted off to the dining room.

"What's going on with you and Kory? There was a pretty big

iceberg between you two."

"There's nothing going on. No iceberg. Just a mutual understanding."

"Well, I'm too tired to argue with you. We'll talk after I shower. See you in a few."

Ricki watched her friend climb the stairs to her room.

Buzz headed to the dining hall mumbling something about coffee.

Not sure what to do, she chose an overstuffed chair by the fire and sank into it, enjoying the warmth of the flames. As she relaxed, scenes of the last few days travelled through her mind like a movie. *When I get home, hard work will clean these images out of my mind.*

Several members of the troop filtered out of the dining hall and made their way to their respective rooms. Kory walked out talking to Steve. He stopped when he saw her, but glanced away and continued his conversation while they left by the side entrance.

The fire crackled and a large log slipped off the sizzling pile. The sound brought her back to the present and a deep breath cleansed the ever-present doubt. *It's my doing. Kory wants nothing to do with me. I've pushed him away so many times. One time too many, I'm guessing. Well, it's for the best. Everything will come into perspective once I get home.*

"I want to apologize to you, Ricki." Rebecca reached across the table to take her hand. "I shouldn't have told Russ where you were. He was like a crazed animal. How in God's name could you hook up with someone like him?"

Byron came by and swept the dishes from the table next to them. "You ladies need anything else?"

Rebecca shook her head and he gave a nod.

She waited until he finished.

"I ask myself the same question every day. I'm a game warden, I carry a gun. I'm supposed to be tough, a no-nonsense gal. It's my mantra. When it comes to matters of the heart I'm completely blind. The fact is, I just didn't see it. I've read about women like me, too trusting, unable to see a wolf in sheep's clothing. The answer is I don't have an answer." She withdrew her hand and sat back with a sigh. "I'm leaving in the morning."

"What about Kory?" Rebecca asked.

"What about him? I've made it clear I don't trust myself when it comes to men. He's backed off. We're done."

"I don't believe it. I see the way he looks at you."

"Look, all I'm concerned about is your well-being. What Russ did was horrible. Hopefully, the police will see the real story when you and the others give your accounts of the situation. I want Russ locked up forever."

Rebecca looked at the door. "Looks like we won't have to wait long. Here they are."

Officer Kemp tipped his hat to Ricki. "Good afternoon, Miss Sheridan. I hope you're feeling better."

She stood, pushing the chair behind her. "I'm fine, officer."

"Good, I have a few questions for Miss Blair. I'd like to question her privately, if you don't mind."

"Certainly. I'll be in my room." With a quick hug, she squeezed Rebecca's hand and left the dining room.

"I'll be glad when all this trouble is over. Gives the lodge a bad name." Wolf leaned over the counter, resting one elbow on the surface.

Kory sat on a barstool stirring a cup of black coffee. "They'll all be gone tomorrow. We can shut the place down for the winter after the next group."

"I've already cancelled the next group. Weather is moving in, no sense in borrowing trouble. What are you going to do?"

"Well, I was going to lead the last group. But since you shut it down, I'll just stay on and winter here. Lots to be done."

Wolf removed his elbow from the bar and stood up straight. "Thought you planned on doing the couples training. You and Miss Ricki."

"Nope. It fell through. She'll be headin' back to Dallas." He stared into his coffee.

"Shame. From what Steve told me, you two were an item. Is it how the kids say it today?" His deep, rumbling laugh filled the room.

"We've got too many matchmakers around here. She's great, but thinks she belongs in Dallas."

"Well, take it as a sign, Kory. You can't be chasing a woman from state to state. When the time is right, she'll show up."

Kory jerked his head up. "Who?"

"The right woman, dunderhead." Wolf wiped the counter with the bar cloth and went to check his stock.

He stirred his coffee and watched Wolf leave for the stockroom. "I thought she *was* the right woman." The words echoed in the large room with no one to hear them.

CHAPTER Twenty-One

RICKI SPENT THE NEXT FIFTEEN MINUTES STUFFING HER clothes into a duffle bag. She couldn't wait to hear the SUV roaring through the mountain pass headed home. The only thing left to do was verify the police believed Russ was the perpetrator and make sure he stayed locked up.

She rolled the last flannel shirt and crammed it in her bag. The walls closed, each second ticked by so slowly, a scream threatened to escape. She paced to keep anxiety at bay. *Get home. It's all I want.* She glanced at the clock, the hands weren't moving fast enough.

A knock on the door quickened her heartbeat. *Maybe the police are finished with Rebecca.*

It was Byron.

"The police want to see you downstairs, Miss Sheridan."

"Again? Well, okay. I'm coming."

She hurried down and entered the dining room.

Officer Kemp greeted her, "Thanks for coming. We've wrapped up the questioning. I wanted to let you know your story checks out. Everyone corroborates the sequence of events. The D.A. has been notified. Mr. Desmond will be incarcerated until a trial date has been set. You may be asked to return and give your testimony, as will the others."

The air left her lungs as relief washed over her. "You mean I can go home?"

"Yes, we won't need anything else for now."

"Thank you." She headed for the door.

"Ma'am?"

She turned. "Yes?"

The officer gave a half smile. "Don't worry, we'll put this guy away for a long time."

Ricki crossed the room and held out her hand. "Thank you, officer. It's a huge relief to me."

His grip tightened. "The truth always comes out, Miss Sheridan. Mr. Desmond can be very convincing. But, it's all straightened out now. I hope you can get back to a normal life."

The great room was empty when she entered. She really wanted to see Rebecca before she left. Wolf was at the desk, so she went to ask him.

"She and Buzz are in the sunroom. They wanted a private place to talk."

"Thanks."

"Before you leave, I have one thing to say."

"Okay, what is it?"

"You had a good one in Kory. He's a great guy all the way through. If I were you, I'd take some time to think about it before you leave." He didn't look at her, just delivered the statement and went back to his work.

For most of her life, people told her what to do. Overbearing parents, ROTC in high school. The Navy, and even the training for her position of game warden. Sometimes, it grated on her nerves so much she muttered under her breath. The Navy captain caught her, once. One hundred push-ups. Not girl style either. Most times, she could control the urge to supersede authority, but not today.

The familiar flash of temper reared its head. "I'll thank you to keep your opinions to yourself, Mr. Wolf. I didn't ask your advice and you have no right to give it. None of this is your business." She whirled to go, face flaming.

She reached the door.

"Oh, but I do have a right," Wolf's voice simmered with controlled anger.

She lifted her chin and spun around, hands clenched. "Oh really? Well, why don't you enlighten me?"

He threw the towel on the bar with a slap. "My lodge, my employee. I make sure the people who work for me are happy. I can't afford to have them distracted. One slip, one mistake could cost a life. This ain't no picnic up here. I don't coddle the greenhorns who want to have a taste of the wild. My trail bosses gotta be one hundred percent focused and not day dreaming about a woman. This business with Desmond puts a black smear on my reputation. Kidnapping? Attempted murder? Not on my watch. So yes, Miss Sheridan, it *is* my business."

She stared at him. "I…I don't…"

His voice softened, "Look, you look like a tough lady. Kory said you were a game warden or something. I get it. You came to prove yourself. Fine. But, trouble followed you. Sure, sure, the guy is locked up, but because of all this, Kory's messed up. I can't put him out on the trail again until I know he's mentally back to normal. He told me there was talk of you two doing the couples training together this winter, but you backed out. Going home. Well, fine. Do what you gotta do. In the meantime, *I* gotta make sure Kory can come back as a trail boss in the spring. Thankfully, we have the winter to sort it out. I don't mean no disrespect. He's got it bad and it ain't good. I need him focused."

One slow step at a time, she found herself in front of the desk again, the temper flare-up gone like wind from a sail. "Mr. Wolf, I'm sorry. I did bring the trouble here, but not intentionally. I was running from a very bad mistake. Normally, I face adversity head on. When it comes to matters of the heart, I'm lost." She shrugged. "Can't seem to get it right. I don't want to hurt Kory, but I have demons to face back in Dallas. I'm not sure how I feel about him. I do know I will never figure it out unless I clean up the mess I left behind. Can you understand?"

Wolf's face softened, he cleared his throat as if uncomfortable. "I suppose I do. The thing is, Kory is like a son to me. I don't want to see him hurt. This lodge is my life. I protect those close to me. I like you. Somehow, you seem right for him. I just wanted you to know how he feels about you. You go home. Get your head on straight. No hard feelin's."

A nod was sufficient. She turned to go.

"One more thing." Wolf called after her.

"Yes?"

"Drop the Mr., it's just Wolf."

CHAPTER
Twenty-Two

Rebecca and Buzz held hands across the little table by the fountain in the sunroom, heads bent together, deep in conversation.

Ricki hated to interrupt, but the need to head home overruled good manners.

"Excuse me, Rebecca." She turned and pointed toward the door. "The police are finished with their questions. I'm anxious to get on the road."

"Right. Buzz and I were talking about leaving too. You can't go without giving me your phone number and address. We simply *must* stay in touch."

"It's why I came to find you. Here, I've written my information down."

Rebecca took the note and looked around. "I didn't bring any paper with me."

Buzz reached in his pocket. "I've got this little notebook. I'll tear out a page."

"Always prepared. I like that in a man." Rebecca said.

Ricki slipped the paper into her pocket and hugged her friend. "I better hear from you."

"You will. I promise to write or call as soon as I get home."

"Buzz, I want tell to you how much I appreciate what you did for Rebecca. I hope we see each other again."

"Likewise, safe journey home."

She sighed and left her friends alone.

Upstairs, she glanced over the room, hoisted her pack on one shoulder, and headed for the front desk. She wanted to say good bye to Byron and wish him luck.

No one was there. *I could look for him, but daylight is burning. The longer I hang around here, the later it will be when I get home.*

She decided to just go.

The engine roared to life and tears burned at the back of her eyes. *I came here to find a new beginning. Instead, my world turned upside down, again. You can't run from your troubles, they always follow you.*

Before she pulled onto the blacktop road, she checked the rearview mirror one more time. The snow-covered lodge stood beautifully against the mountain backdrop, a serene site, which invoked a sense of tranquility. *Certainly not what I got from all this.*

Something caught her eye. The lodge door stood open. The light from within illuminated a figure standing in the doorway. A man. She'd know his build anywhere, the way he stood, leaned against the doorjamb, one foot crossed over the other.

Kory.

Every fiber of her being wanted to turn the car around, hold him in her arms, and tell him she'd stay. Instead she gripped the steering wheel tighter. *Impulse is what got me into this mess.* She glanced again. *Why didn't he find me to say goodbye?*

But, she knew why.

She tilted the mirror higher to block out the view and continued down the road.

Miles passed and the sound of the tires on the pavement lulled her into a sense of peacefulness. The more distance she put between her and Kory, the better perspective she could gain on the whole situation.

For a while, she fantasized he might come after her, decide he can't live without her. Maybe days would pass, weeks, perhaps even months, but he'd come for her. She laughed out loud at the wishful thinking. *Let it go, girl. He's not that kind.*

As the terrain changed, so did her mindset. The first thing she wanted to do was tell the boss what happened. The second—she wanted transfer.

Secondly, she'd confront Leila.

She needed to get out of her lease and look at which cities had openings. *I can do this. I can start over.*

The city closed in around her in an oppressive way, a far cry from the open, star-filled sky of the mountains. She sat in the front of her apartment unable to open the door of the SUV and get out. The thought of spending the night there sent shivers up and down her spine. Russ violated her in more ways than she could imagine. Her home. He'd gone through her bureau drawers. There was no way she could stay in there, now.

She put the car in gear and headed into town. A hotel was the only option, now. *Maybe I can get a transfer right away and find a new place to live.*

The accommodations she chose offered a spa, a work-out room, a sports oriented boutique, and anonymity. Armed with a few new sweats and t-shirts, she went through a rigorous work-out, showered, and headed for the spa for some pampering. For a while, she relaxed and let her mind clear.

She ordered room service and enjoyed a lovely grilled chicken salad and a glass of wine.

The next morning, she was ready to face the boss and tell her story.

He greeted her with a frown on his face.

"So, you know."

Captain Riley's voice was soft, "Yes, I was informed by the Lakeview police."

"All right, where do we go from here?"

Riley was a big guy, had twenty-five years on the force, didn't have time for nonsense, but he was fair. "Look, I had my doubts when you started dating Russ. It wasn't my business, so I kept quiet. He's a womanizer, plain and simple. It's time he got caught." He stood up and looked her square in the eyes. "This looks bad for the department, the scandal and all, but my money is on you. After we …"

She interrupted with a wave of her hand. "I want a transfer. I'm not here to go all feminist on you and play the victim card. I simply can't work here anymore. Move me to a small town and into obscurity, I don't care. Just get me out of here."

He sighed and sat down. "Ricki, none of this is your fault. Everyone knows you aren't the type to play victim. You're a good game warden. One of the toughest. I don't want to lose you, but since you asked, an online memo came across yesterday. Lakeview PD posted a job for a game warden in the area."

"Lakeview? But, it's just a few miles from the lodge. I don't think…"

"No, it's a small burg called Murphy about seventy-five miles south of Lakeview. It's hard for those small towns to keep wardens. They put out a feeler, but if you're not interested, well…"

"No, wait. Seventy-five miles? It might be far enough away."

"Far enough away from what?"

"It's not important. Did you print it out?"

He handed her the paper.

Murphy was losing their warden because of retirement, leaving them without a one.

"It's perfect. I'll contact them. I hate to leave Texas, but this will give me the exact atmosphere to get my life back on track." She grabbed his hand and shook it vigorously. "Thanks, Captain."

Flushed, he stammered, "Well, you're welcome, I guess. Are you sure you want to leave your friends and family? You could use their support."

"You and a couple of the others are the only friends I have left here. My family are all half a state away. I need a new beginning."

He tapped a pencil on the desk. "I totally understand. Sometimes this big city gets the better of me, as well." He looked up and smiled. "Whatever you need, Ricki. Letter of recommendation, references. I'll do everything I can to help you get the job."

All her life obstacles presented themselves and, one by one, she knocked them down. She was capable, strong, independent, goal oriented, but there was one thing she hadn't mastered. Love. The opportunity she held in her hand would give her the chance to start over, to examine why she didn't see what kind of a man Russ was, why she so misjudged him. His only redeeming quality was his charm and it was all a lie, a cover-up. *But, what did I actually feel when I was with him? I simply can't remember feeling anything, not like Kory—*

She opened the SUV door, slid inside, and gazed at the rearview mirror. Instead of her reflection, she saw Kory leaning against the door as she drove away from the lodge. Her heart leapt as she remembered the mountain, his body pressed against hers—that one moment. *It was different, jarring. Something stirred inside, a light, an awareness. So unlike Russ.*

She pushed the thought aside. *I don't want to think about it. I'm starting over, putting the past in the past. I need to get back to business.*

Leila was next on the list. *Do I really want to do this? Will anything I say change her back-stabbing heart?*

Closure. Exactly what she wanted. Confronting Leila would shut the door on the whole ugly thing.

Leila's fitness club was convenient for Ricki, close by, clean and friendly. Two years ago, the two women hit it off, immediately. They fell into an after-workout routine, a glass of wine and salad at a local bistro down the street. One day Russ showed up. The three hung out laughing, cutting up, just like fast friends. From then on, Russ made sure he joined them. She never questioned why. Little did she know what would happen behind her back.

Did I even care? It went on for so long. Did I see it and push it aside, ignoring the betrayal by the two people closest to me? Well, I sure couldn't ignore it after I found them in bed together.

She pulled up in front of the club. Leila always had a good work ethic. She loved her business, loved looking good, and fed off the gushing compliments thrown at her every day. Certain, she'd be there, Ricki headed for the door.

When she walked in, Leila was behind the counter flirting with one of the young body builders. When she saw Ricki, fear flickered on her face.

"Hi, Leila. I'm back in town and thought I'd come by and tell you personally what a scum bucket you are. What you don't know is you did me a huge favor."

"Ricki! I didn't know you were back. It's all over town what happened, what Russ did. I'm so very sorry."

She laughed. "No, you're not. The only thing you think about is yourself. You don't care who you hurt. Well, none of it matters anymore. My eyes are wide open. I don't have time for people like you. You and Russ deserve each other."

"But, I..." Leila came out from behind the counter, hands outstretched, eyes pleading.

Ricki came toward her, but instead of an embrace, she laid a resounding slap across the face of the woman who betrayed her. "I've been wanting to do that for a long time, you backstabbing bitch!"

The young man who flirted with Leila backed away, eyes wide.

She turned without giving Leila a chance to respond, laughing as she sputtered behind her, calling after her.

It was quite liberating to confront Leila. Her step was lighter, her mood lifted, because she knew nothing the woman had to say mattered, at all.

Back at the hotel, she studied the memo Captain Riley gave her. She inhaled deeply, let it out, and pulled out her cell phone.

A small town, the smaller the better. A chance for peace and healing, it's what I want.

A new town, new people, everything she needed to start over and put everything, even Kory, out of her mind. Lesson learned, time to move on.

CHAPTER
Twenty-Three

Kory watched Ricki's silver SUV until it was out of sight. Even after it turned the bend and disappeared, he remained leaned against the door jamb, kicking himself for letting her go without saying goodbye. Truth is, he tried to avoid her at every turn all day.

I'm a coward. So, my heart got broken. No reason to end it like a jerk.

"She's gone, huh?" Byron stood behind him, peering over Kory's shoulder.

"Yep, she's gone. Soon, they'll all be gone and it'll be the three of us. You, me, and Wolf."

"I sure did like her. Easy to talk to. Real concerned about my schoolin'. Hope she comes back one day."

"I wouldn't count on it, champ. Now about your schooling. Isn't it time for you to do your computer work?"

Byron gave him a wry smile. "I was just about to start. Wolf sent me to fetch you."

"Well, off you go, then. Where is the ole coot?"

"In his office with a stack of papers, scratching his head. He hates paperwork. I bet he's going to pass it off on you." Byron giggled and scurried out of Kory's reach.

He lowered his voice so the boy wouldn't hear. "He's one good kid." Kory liked Byron, treated him like a kid brother. "It was good of Wolf to take him on. Handled the parents well, too. Wolf might be rough around the edges, but he's got a huge heart."

He went to find his boss.

Wolf's large frame leaned back in his chair as he squinted at an invoice. "About time you showed up. Are you through mooning over Miss Sheridan?"

"I wasn't mooning over her. Just watching her leave. I didn't have a chance to say goodbye." He plopped into a chair by the desk.

"Didn't have a chance, my foot. You avoided her like the plague. I got eyes, you know. Chicken if you ask me."

"Well, I didn't ask, so can we just change the subject? Why did you want to see me?"

"It's the couples retreat. I still need another couple to mentor the group."

Kory stood up. "Well, in case you haven't noticed, I'm not a couple. You'll have to look elsewhere."

"Sit down, you clown. I *know* you're not a couple, but I was thinkin' you could supervise it anyway."

Kory remained standing. "No way."

"Okay, well, I thought I'd ask. The classes might be of interest to you. Some quality life coaches will be here. Thought you'd sit it on a few sessions."

"Nope. I've got other responsibilities to keep me busy. Got two more trail boss trainees coming in a few days. I'll have my hands full with them. Kyle's coming back next season, but Steve isn't. Got a job in the city for more money. You really need to up the wages, Wolf. Can't keep good help."

Wolf scowled. "Let me take care of business my way. You take care of your part and we'll all get along fine." He pointed to the door. "You got so much to do, you better get to it. Stop lollygagging around."

"I'm going. Just remember, *you* sent for me."

"Kory."

"What now?"

"I'm bettin' she'll be back."

He didn't answer, just closed the door behind him.

Kory set about assembling the paperwork for the new trainees. There were background checks, drug tests, all kinds of hoops these guys had to go through before approval. Wolf's training scenario for the newbies covered almost every problem the leaders would face. All this was classroom, textbook. The real test would come before the season opened. Kory would take them out on their first runs to test them in real world situations.

He paused at the thought. *Real world situations.* Nothing prepared him for what happened with Russ Desmond. *I need to talk to Wolf about it. We need to implement a plan, just in case.*

"Knock, knock. Are you busy, Kory?"

Buzz and Rebecca stood in the doorway, holding hands and smiling.

"No, not at all. What can I do for you? Are you ready to leave?"

"Yes, the car is packed. Buzz took a bus here, so I'm giving him a lift." She glanced at the floor. "Well, more than a lift. I'm taking him home with me for the winter. There's a little diner there. He's a good cook. Think I can get him on."

"Well, well. What good news! So, you two are an item now, huh?

I think it's wonderful. From what I've seen of him, you couldn't ask for a better guy, Rebecca."

"We're going to see how it goes, taking it slow. There's a one room apartment over the diner. It's been empty for a while. I know the owner, so…"

"Good idea. I hope it works for you guys. You deserve it." He punched Buzz's shoulder lightly. "Good man, Buzz."

"Thanks, Kory. Appreciate it."

"Well, we'll be going. Didn't want to leave without saying goodbye. And Kory?"

"Look, if you're going to tell me she'll be back, save your breath. We weren't as lucky as you two. It didn't work, can't work. It's best to leave it alone."

Rebecca shook her head. "Not what I wanted to say. You need to understand how confused she is. This thing with Russ has her doubting any decisions she makes. Look, my phone number is in the register book. And, so is hers. If you can't bring yourself to call her, then call me. I plan on keeping up with her, she's a good friend. If you ever want to know how she's doing, give me a call. She'll figure it out, but it has to be her way."

All he could do was nod.

"We're out of here. Take care, Kory."

He watched them go with a twinge of envy. *Why is it so easy for some and so difficult for the rest of us?*

CHAPTER Twenty-Four

"Glad to have you aboard, Miss Sheridan. Captain Riley spoke very highly of you. We're short-handed since the chief's retired, so your willingness to come to a small town is welcome. Most want jobs closer to the big city, think there's more chance of promotion. It's rare we get one like you. Small town living isn't for everyone." Captain Maddox smiled and shook her hand.

Ricki returned the smile and shook hands with excitement. "Well, the big city isn't for me. I found it out the hard way. I grew up in a small town and I really want to get back to my roots. This is very exciting for me. I'm anxious to get going."

"Please sit down. Coffee?"

She settled into the chair opposite his desk. "Yes, sounds good."

As he poured, he glanced over his shoulder. "Found a place to live, yet?"

"No, I have an appointment with the lone real estate agent here this afternoon."

He handed her the cup. "Not a lot of choices around here, but Ms. Ames will find you suitable lodgings. Are you comfortable at the motel?"

"Yes, perfectly fine, thanks."

"Why don't you come for dinner tonight. Noreen loves to cook. She always likes to greet the new officers."

"Well, if you're sure."

"Absolutely. I'll call her right now."

She liked Captain Maddox. A man of about fifty, silver hair, fit, pleasant green eyes. The fact he had a wife was even better. No single men, no potential dates. It was all business for her.

They discussed the schedule, what was expected of her, the jurisdiction, and when she would meet the sheriff. She noted he kept small talk to a minimum for which she was grateful. No talk of family, husband, children, nothing of a personal nature. Maybe Captain Riley had filled him in. At any rate, she'd work hard, focus on her job, and alleviate any doubts the new captain might have about her ability.

At two o'clock, she met Ms. Ames at the town square. A perky, middle-aged woman who took her job very seriously.

"Now, I have three places I want to show you. I thought we'd start here in town. There's a small apartment over the department store. Very nice and I am sure Mr. Cory would love knowing he had a law officer watching over the place."

Ricki jumped at the name. "Did you say Kory?"

"Yes, he owns the department store. Didn't you notice his name on the front? Cory's Mercantile."

At a glance, she saw the name in faded letters. "Oh, yes, I see it now. No, I'd rather not live over the department store. Don't you have anything on the outskirts of town?"

Ms. Ames frowned. "Well, Mr. Cory will be sorely disappointed you didn't, at least, look at the apartment." She waved her hand in dismissal. "Never mind. If you want more privacy, I have just the place for you. There's a cottage out by the county line. It's pretty far out, very secluded, spotty cell phone service. Care to see it?"

"Sounds perfect. Let's go."

Two days later, she watched the moving van pull into the driveway and sighed with relief. She hired a professional service to pack up her belongings and bring them out. It was a relief to know she would never set foot in her old apartment again.

The cottage on the edge of town was a little rundown, but with a little paint and some furniture, it would serve the purpose. Besides, she planned on working as many hours as she could. Saturate her mind with the job—and forget.

The community embraced her and she was a regular at Captain Maddox's house for dinner. She hit it off with Noreen, drawn in by her radiant smile, vivid blues eyes, and festive personality. Everyone who met her was instantly a friend for life.

The sheriff greeted her cordially and it wasn't long before she fell into the rhythm of the job. She worked with the captain for about a week, then he cut her loose on solo runs, satisfied she could handle it.

At the end of the first week, she didn't have time to think about Kory. Everything was new and exciting. She was glad to fill her days with learning the ropes.

To her chagrin, however, as she became comfortable with the routine, she found the new-found solitude allowed more time for idle thoughts. Kory drifted into her mind as she staked out a poacher in the middle of the woods. She didn't want to think about him, but was powerless to stop the random thoughts, his dark eyes, the way he ran his fingers through his wavy, black hair, the way he looked at her.

Why can't I get him out of my mind?

The lack of internet and cell phone service allowed a lot of time to think, as well. No one to call for an idle chat, a chance to enjoy nature in peace and quiet. There was a small pond behind her place and she enjoyed watching the deer come down to drink. A large downed tree provided a great place to sit and watch them without them spotting her. She spent a lot time drinking coffee from a thermos, huddled in her parka, letting her mind heal.

One night, while she sat on the front porch, the cell rang and made her jump.

"Hello?"

"Ricki? Is it you? It's Rebecca."

"Oh, my goodness, it's so good to hear from you." Ricki replied.

"I've been calling, but it goes to voice mail. Are you okay? Where are you?"

She laughed. "I'm in a little town called Murphy, about seventy-five miles from Lakeview. I asked for a transfer and got it. Service is spotty out here. You're lucky you caught me on the porch."

They chatted for a few minutes as Rebecca enlightened her on Buzz and his job at the diner.

"I'm so happy it worked out. You and Buzz need to come to Murphy, sometime. See where I'm living. You'd love it." The signal was fading. She was afraid it would be lost.

"I'm going to hang up now," Rebecca said, "But, I wanted to ask if you've heard from Kory."

Ricki sighed into the receiver. "No. I haven't heard from him."

"I know it's not my business, but he's in love with you. I talked to him before we left. Don't let him wait too long before you decide," Rebecca warned.

Her heart pounded. "Decide? Decide what? He made it very clear he didn't want to see me on the day I left. And besides, I love it here. The people are wonderful and my job is exciting. This is where

I belong."

"Byron told me he stood in the doorway and watched you leave. His pride got in the way. Stop being so stubborn. So, you made a mistake with Russ. Haven't we all made those same mistakes? Get over yourself and admit it. You're in love with him, too. I saw it in your eyes when you talked about him. Hell, even Buzz can see it."

"Oh, Rebecca, you're ..."

The signal went dead.

She stomped back in the house and let the screen door bang shut. "Why can't people leave well enough alone? Byron? Wolf? Rebecca? Even Buzz!"

The refrigerator rattled as she jerked open the door and grabbed a beer. She flipped the top open with a violent yank and plopped down in the kitchen chair.

"They can all just mind their own business. I'm happy here. I don't need Kory—or anyone."

Noreen came through the office door in a cheery mood. Ricki smiled at her new friend.

"What brings you to the station this early? Your husband is in a meeting. New dress? Green becomes you." Ricki pulled out a chair and motioned for her to sit.

"Yes, one of the new shipments at the Mercantile. Isn't it divine?" She twirled and settled herself in the chair. "The most exciting news. I've been petitioning the city to hold a picnic for the law enforcement. It's approved. We can start planning right away." The paper bobbed up and down as she waved it in the air.

"Whoa, I'm not going to be on any planning committee. I'm far too busy, and we have only three of us so-called *law enforcement*."

"Oh, I didn't mean you, in particular, dear. I think I'll hop over to Ms. Ames. I know she'll be excited about it."

"Good idea."

"Dinner tonight, Ricki? I've been wanting to talk to you about something."

"Sure, if it's not about the committee."

Noreen laughed. "No, no. Nothing like that. See you tonight. Regular time."

Noreen Maddox *was* a good cook. Ricki felt a little guilty because she never offered to return the favor. She justified her lack of social grace by telling herself it was too far for them to drive for a little dinner.

"Wonderful, as usual. I'm stuffed."

Captain Maddox pushed his chair back and made his excuses. "Got some paperwork to tend to. I'll leave you ladies to it."

After he'd gone, Noreen pulled her to the sofa and plopped down beside her. "Now, there's something I want to ask you."

"Okay, shoot."

"There's a new man in town. He's opening a café. Lord knows we need another one. Anyway, he's single. I want to introduce you to him."

Ricki stood, abruptly. "No. I don't want to meet anyone."

"Ricki, dear, sit down."

She stood her ground, refusing to budge.

Noreen clucked her tongue. "Okay. I see. Who is he?"

Ricki stammered, "What? What do you mean who is he?"

"I've been wondering why you moved way out here. Now, I know. You're running away from someone." She pulled Ricki's arm forcing her to sit down. "I swear, I tried and tried to get it out of Roger, but he's the most tight-lipped man I've ever known."

"Get what out of Rog…Captain Maddox? He doesn't know anything about me."

"Never mind. Tell me all about him. What's his name?"
She held her breath and stared at Noreen.
Noreen stared back. "Well?"
"K—Kory."
"I knew it! Now tell me all about him."

CHAPTER Twenty-Five

On the morning drive to work, Ricki mulled over the advice Noreen gave her. It didn't take much coaxing for her to get the whole story about Kory. The captain's wife was the most open soul she'd met in a long time and her sincerity overwhelmed her.

After she spilled her heart, Noreen revealed the love story between her and the captain. How she almost missed her chance, almost lost him because of her pride. She came from a family of breeding. Old money. He was a civil servant. The family didn't approve, thought she should marry on a higher plane. She almost let them dissuade her. A year passed. Roger became engaged to someone else. It was old Mr. Cory who talked to her one day. He'd let the love of his life slip away, and now, he was married to his department store, alone and bitter. For some reason, he was compelled to encourage Noreen to fight for her man.

There was no mistaking the love between the captain and Noreen. The advice she gave Ricki was the same old Mr. Cory shared with his friend so many years ago. Fight for what you want.

But how? He wouldn't even talk to me before I left.

Captain Maddox greeted her with a cheery voice the next morning. "Lunch is on me today."

"Lunch? I just had breakfast. What's the occasion?"

"Grand opening at the new café. Half price for law enforcement."

She laughed. "Oh, your generosity is epic!"

"Hey, I could make you pay your *own* way."

"Touche! Really though, what a nice thing for the owner to do."

"He's a nice guy." He winked. "Nice looking, too."

"Okay, Captain. Let's not go there."

"Sorry, just pointing it out. Anyway, seems like he's making a success of it. Don't be late."

"I'll be there."

She started to leave when he called her back.

"There's an envelope on your desk. Looks important, you might want to look at it before you go."

The return address was from the Lakeview PD. Her heart pounded as she tore it open. It was a letter informing her of Russ's trial date. She knew the day would come, understood she'd have to testify, but wasn't prepared for the physical reaction, stomach wrench and cold sweat.

"Bad news?" Captain Maddox asked.

"It's the trial date." She'd shared her ordeal with the Maddox's as their friendship grew. She thought it only fair. They all knew this day would come.

"Ah, when is it?"

"Two months from now."

"Noreen and I can come with you, if you need us."

"You don't know how much I appreciate the offer, but this is something I need to do on my own. Face my demons, trust myself, again. You know the drill."

He smiled. "I knew what you'd say. The offer stands if you change your mind."

The day progressed routinely. In between calls, she let her mind wander, tried to imagine what the trial would be like, how it would feel to see Russ again. She shook her head. "Not looking forward to it."

By eleven fifteen, her morning checkpoints were finished. She headed back to town.

"Hope the food is good, I'm starving."

Several cars lined the front of the little café, so she parked across the street. She spotted the captain's truck and Noreen's car.

"Good. Glad they beat me here. Makes it less awkward."

A little bell tinkled merrily when she opened the door. She looked around and saw Roger and Noreen in a booth at the end of the room.

They waved her over.

"Hey, you two." She started toward her friends, but stopped in her tracks. In the booth by the door, a man sat with his back to her. Something familiar triggered her memory. The long, shaggy hair streaked with gray, the broad shoulders—.

"Wolf?"

The man looked around. "Miss Sheridan? Well, what a sight for sore eyes. How are you?"

Before she could answer, a young man jumped up from the other side of the booth.

"Miss Ricki! Gosh, I never expected to see you again." He ran down the short aisle and threw his arms around her.

"Oh, well, Byron—." He almost knocked her off her feet. He jumped back. "I'm sorry. I just got so excited."

"It's all right, Byron. It's wonderful to see you, too. What in the world are you two doing here?"

"It was Wolf's idea."

She looked at Wolf. "Well?"

Instead of an answer, he turned to look at Captain Maddox. "Ask him."

The captain's already ruddy cheeks deepened in color.

Noreen smiled. "Come sit down. I'll tell you all about it."

After a glance around the room to make sure no other surprises awaited, she sat down beside Noreen. "What's this all about?"

Noreen put an arm around her shoulders. "It's all quite innocent, Ricki. Wolf and Roger are long-time friends. They grew up together in Lakeview. He came to ask a favor."

"A favor? So, this doesn't involve me?"

"Well, it didn't, at first."

She looked from Captain Maddox to Wolf. "What do you mean?"

The owner of the café interrupted. "Ah, I see we're all here." He presented his hand. "I'm Curt Noland, owner of this fine establishment. Don't believe I've had the pleasure."

His handshake was strong, matching his physique. Bright blue eyes, a killer smile, and one dimple on his left cheek completed her initial assessment.

"Hello, I'm Ricki Sheridan. Nice to meet you. Sorry I haven't made it in here before this." She nodded toward her boss. "He keeps me pretty busy."

"So I've heard. Well, no matter. The town wanted to get you all together and thank you for what you do around here."

"All three of us, huh?"

"Yep. Small town hospitality." He stepped back and raised his voice over the clatter. "Our law enforcement team has arrived. Let's give them a round of applause."

The place erupted with clapping, cheering, and general hoopla.

Ricki, the captain, and the sheriff, who sat with his wife in a booth across from them, all stood and tipped their hats.

The sheriff took the lead after the noise settled down. "Thanks to all of you for your continued support. We couldn't do our jobs without you."

Short and sweet, he sat down. Another round of applause resounded through the room until it trickled to a stop. The normal clatter picked up again as everyone resumed their meal.

"Well, I have a kitchen to run. Every Tuesday, at noon, is half price for all of you, so keep it in mind."

They all said 'thank you'.

Ricki turned back to Noreen. "Now, what's all this about, this so-called favor?"

Noreen explained, "Wolf came to ask me and Roger to host the yearly couples retreat this year. We've done it before, but can't this year. The grandkids are coming for a week or two and I can't turn down the opportunity to see them."

Ricki's heart dropped hard. *The couples retreat!* She'd forgotten about it. Kory asked her to be a part of the staff, but she couldn't trust herself to be around him when she wasn't sure how she felt.

"Oh, I see. The retreat. I bet you guys are great at it. Too bad, but grandkids take priority, for sure. Small world." She wanted a change of subject, didn't want the conversation to continue, didn't want Kory's name to come up. "Isn't the waitress going to take our order?"

Maddox motioned for the young waitress and she came with pad and pencil at the ready.

As everyone gave their order, Ricki's heart continued to beat erratically, like a bingo ball in a cage, assuming there was a hidden agenda to this meeting. One she would not care for, at all.

While they waited on their food, Wolf and Roger talked about high school. Byron beamed with pride when he told her about his good grades. Noreen and the sheriff's wife talked about the upcoming picnic planned for the community. No more was said about the retreat. She relaxed, just a little.

The food arrived and most of the conversation halted for a few minutes, but not for long.

Wolf kept his eyes on the large, double-decker hamburger in front of him. "Ricki, I can't for the life of me find anyone to oversee this couples retreat. Now, I know you said you didn't want to stay there at the lodge, but I'm desperate. I have people coming. I need an organizer."

She stopped in mid-bite. "Wolf, it may have escaped your notice, but I'm the game warden here. I have a job, a nice place to live. My hands are full. Besides, I'm not a couple."

Wolf muttered under his breath.

"What did you say?"

He spoke louder, "Kory said the same thing."

Her heart tumbled at the mention of his name.

"You asked Kory?"

"Yeah, thought he could benefit from some of the sessions. Fact is, you could, too."

Byron decided to jump in. "I think it's a good idea. I could help you, Miss Ricki!"

She shook her head at the excited teen. "No, Byron. I'm too busy here."

Her appetite disappeared. She stood up. "I just remembered, I told old Mr. Sherman I'd check on the fence at the corner of his property. His dog keeps getting out. His arthritis won't allow him to walk the property. I better get going. Thanks for the lunch, Captain. Nice to see you Wolf, Byron."

She went to the counter, thanked Curt Noland, and headed out the front door, eager to get far away.

A coincidence, my foot.

CHAPTER Twenty-Six

KORY STOPPED KYLE HALF WAY DOWN THE HALL TO THE office. "Has anyone seen Wolf? And where's Byron? I haven't seen either one all day."

Kyle shrugged. "Haven't seen them. Heard something about a jaunt to Murphy to celebrate Byron's semester grades. Field trip or something."

"Murphy? What's to celebrate in a little town like Murphy?"

Kyle shrugged again. "No clue." He passed Kory and went on his way.

The phone rang in Wolf's office. He stood still trying to decide if he should answer it or not. After the fifth ring, he hurried in and picked up the handset.

"Hello? Yes, this is Wolf's Den Lodge. The couples retreat? Yes, I think we still have room."

He listened to the would-be client while searching for a scrap of paper to write down their name and phone number. A small tablet sat on top of a ledger. He rummaged through the desk drawer for a pencil.

"Yes, I've got it. Well, the organizer isn't here, now, but as soon as he returns, I'll have him give you a call. Pardon? Oh, the speakers? Honestly, I don't have a schedule in front of me. I'm not sure who the speakers are. I do know the classes are excellent, however."

After he hung up, he looked around for any sign of a schedule. "Where in the world would Wolf put it? Maybe it's posted in the lobby."

No one was behind the check-in desk. His frustration mounted. He grumbled out loud. "It's not like him to leave without telling me. Who's running the show around here? He could have left Byron, at least. He's just a kid, but he knows the ropes."

The search yielded nothing.

He continued to mutter, "Did he cancel the retreat? Maybe he couldn't get enough instructors or maybe there weren't enough clients. He should have told me."

Kyle came out of the dining room chugging a carton of orange juice.

"Did Wolf tell you anything about the retreat? Is it still on?" Kory asked.

Kyle swiped the back of his hand across his mouth. "Never mentioned it to me. I ain't got nothing to do with it."

Kory shook his head. "Well, I'll tell you one thing. I'm not going to answer the phone again. He needs to get his butt back here."

"I noticed the message light blinking on the front desk phone. He's got people calling. Probably about the retreat. It's in two weeks, ain't it?"

"Yeah, I hope he's ready. Oh well, not my business. I've got enough to do getting ready for the trainees. You coming?"

The two men headed for the equipment storage building to sort out the gear.

"Hey Kyle, why don't you start without me. I want to check the annex where they have the meetings. Maybe there's a schedule there."

"I'm on it, boss."

A few minutes later, he opened the door to the meeting room and looked around. Nothing was set up. The chairs were stacked against the wall and the tables broken down in the corner. "Well, there's still two weeks to get ready."

He saw nothing resembling an itinerary. One lone chair sat open in a corner. He sat down and addressed the empty room. "Wish I could have talked Ricki into staying. I think we would be great together with our experience, and all." He took a breath. "But—it is what it is, and I'm not doing it alone. It would be awkward. Oh well."

He headed back to help Kyle and tried to put Ricki out of his mind.

"Find anything?" Kyle asked.

"Nope. Nothing is ready in there, but it's not my problem. We have two guys coming this afternoon for some training. We need to get this gear together."

"Just so you know, you and Ricki would be great at the couple's retreat. I heard you asked her."

"Yeah, well, she turned me down, so drop it."

"Don't get too touchy. She liked you all right. If Desmond hadn't shown up, you two might have made it."

Kory jerked too hard on one of the older pack's strap and it broke. "Shut up, Kyle. We don't have time to analyze my love life."

"Or lack of one," Kyle whispered.

CHAPTER Twenty-Seven

OLD MR. SHERMAN GRINNED LIKE A POSSUM WHEN SHE knocked on his door. "Well, howdy. You said you'd come by and dag blame it, you did. You gonna look at the fence?"

She laughed, "I always do what I say, Mr. Sherman. Yes, I'll go look at it. Is your dog here?"

"Yes, I put him inside. Afraid something will happen to him. He's not the brightest log in the wood pile." He stepped out on the porch and pointed to the east fence. "It's all the way down in the corner and where he's getting' out. The old legs just won't carry me that far anymore."

"Shouldn't be hard to find. I'll be back in a little while."

He turned to go inside. "Just made some sweet tea. You come back up here after you fix it and get you a glass."

"Sounds good. Won't be long."

The fence was old, but still sturdy. She figured either the dog dug a hole to climb out of or something in the woods did. At any rate, the old dog was all the man had left. It would devastate him if anything happened to it.

She made sure to check the fence all the way down. Sherman said it was in the corner, but you can't be too careful. Might be other spots too.

This was a part of her job she really enjoyed. Helping out, making a difference in someone's life.

Everything looked good until she got to the corner. He was right. This is where the dog made his escape. The corner post was rotten and broken off, leaving a soft spot for the dog to dig.

The shovel she'd brought along wasn't going to fix it. It needed a new post.

Back at the house, she sat on the porch with Mr. Sherman and enjoyed a glass of tea while she explained what had to be done. "I'm going back to town, get a new post and a bag of concrete. We'll get you all fixed up. I'll check the rest of the corner posts before I go to make sure everything is okay. You got an old wheel barrow around here?"

"Sure do, but a little thing like you can't do the job. I can't afford to pay anyone."

"You underestimate me, Mr. Sherman. I grew up in the country. I know my way around a fence post."

"Well, if you're sure. There's an old wheel barrow in the shed. Should be good enough for what you need."

"Good, I'll be back in an hour or so."

On the ride to town, she clicked off some of the tools she'd need to fix the fence. Logan's Hardware should carry everything.

She parked in front of the store and got out of her truck.

"We meet again, Ricki," Wolf and Byron stood by the old lodge pick-up.

"Oh, hello again. You two still here? Not much to do in Murphy. I figured you'd seen the sights and were heading back home." The knot in her stomach tightened.

"Stretched our visit with Roger and Noreen a bit. Hoped I'd run into you before we left."

"Look, I have to get some concrete and get back out to Mr. Sherman's before it gets dark. I'd like to stay and chat, but I'm pressed for time."

"Puttin' in a fence post all by yourself?"

"Done it before."

"Why don't I send Byron here to help you. I really need to ask Roger something else. You can drop him back at the station when you're done."

Byron beamed. "Can I, Miss Ricki? Please?"

She didn't like the way this was going. *Why can't they just leave?*

Byron was a nice kid. He did do her many favors. She couldn't stand to zap his enthusiasm. *Wolf was probably counting on it.*

"Okay, but we need to hurry."

He helped her load the truck and they headed back to Sherman's place. Wolf was long gone.

Byron chattered on about his grades, how Wolf was giving him more responsibility, how his parents loved how he'd grown up, and she listened patiently.

She interrupted him. "Byron, why are you and Wolf really here?"

He stammered, "What? Why because Captain Maddox and Wolf are old friends. He comes down here quite often. I met them last year when they came to do the couples retreat. Mrs. Noreen is super nice."

"Yes, she is. So, there was no other reason Wolf came down here?"

"None I know of, why?"

"Oh nothing."

She introduced Byron to Mr. Sherman and headed to the shed for more tools.

It was pleasant working with the eager young man. He'd dug post holes before, so he was a big help.

"Miss Ricki, can I ask you a question?"

"Sure."

"Why don't you like Mr. Kory?"

Stunned, she dropped the shovel. "Who said I didn't like him?"

"He did."

"What? Why would he say such a thing?"

"Because you didn't say goodbye."

She stumbled for words. "I, he, we…"

"He's a great guy. I can tell he really likes you."

"Byron, this is complicated. I do like Kory. Very much. It's just…"

"You already have a boyfriend? Mr. Desmond?"

Byron's sweet, innocent face took on a quizzical look. It was clear the boy didn't know much about girls. Probably never had a girlfriend. How could she explain it to him?

"Oh, no, Russ isn't my boyfriend. He's in big trouble for what he did. I made a huge mistake when I dated him. He was dishonest and had very bad judgement." She tossed the shovel into the wheelbarrow. "We're finished. We need to get you back to Wolf."

"But, you know so much about everything! How come you couldn't see he was bad?"

"I keep asking myself why, every day."

"And, you don't see Kory is a good guy?"

She let her breath out. "Yes, I know Kory is a good man."

"Then, why aren't you nice to him? He didn't hurt you."

They arrived at Mr. Sherman's doorstep. "That should do it, Mr. Sherman. All fixed. I checked the other posts and the corner is the only one compromised. You should be able to let your dog out now."

"Thank you so much. Old Howler will be happy not to be trapped inside! Got time for another glass of tea?"

"Not this time. Gotta get this young man back to town."

"Much obliged Officer Sheridan. Don't know how to repay you."

"No need, just take care of Howler."

They didn't talk much on the way back to town.

Byron broke the silence. "You didn't answer my question."

She glanced at him. "What question?"

"Why you don't like Mr. Kory."

"Byron, I do like him. It's not so simple. It's me. I don't trust myself to know what's best right now."

"But, how are you going to know."

"Know what?"

"How are you going to know if Kory is good for you if you're not around him?"

The truck rolled to a stop in front of the station. "Good grief, you sound like Roger and Noreen."

"Well, it's true. You should come back. Hang out. See if you like each other."

"Come on, Wolf is waiting inside."

Roger greeted them when they got inside. "How did it go? Get ole Sherman fixed up?"

"Yes, fence is fixed, he can let his dog out. Byron was quite a big help."

"Good job, young man. Look me up when you're ready to become a game warden."

"Really, Mr. Maddox? Awesome."

She looked around the office. "Where's Wolf?"

Roger didn't answer. He went to the refrigerator and pulled out a soda. "How about a soda for your hard afternoon's work, Byron?"

A queasy feeling settled in her stomach. "Captain, I asked you where Wolf is."

"Wolf? Oh, he's on his way back to the lodge."

"What? But, he left Byron. Is he coming back?"

"Nope."

"What's going on? Why didn't he take Byron?"

Roger handed the soda to the boy.

Byron popped the top just as the captain answered.

"Because you're taking him back."

CHAPTER Twenty-Eight

"You're kidding, right?" Ricki blinked at Captain Maddox.

He turned his back and poured a cup of coffee. "I'm afraid not. Wolf had an emergency. Had to get back. I assured him we'd get Byron a ride back to the lodge."

"And, you volunteered me? This smells like a conspiracy. Well, I'm not going."

His voice was terse, but he didn't turn around. "You might be bordering on insubordination, Officer Sheridan."

Byron stepped in front of her. "Look, I can take the bus back. There's always a run in the evening between Lakeview and Murphy. It's no problem."

Headquarters sat across the street from the bus terminal.

Roger pointed out the window still holding the coffee pot. "Left five minutes ago."

"Oh. Well, I'll call my dad. He won't mind."

She edged Byron aside gently, moved he would try to save her from trouble. "Wait, I'll take you. I wasn't expecting this, but it's okay. We'll go in the company truck. It'll be a treat for you." To Roger she asked, "Was this your idea or Wolf's?"

Maddox turned. "Look, no one is conspiring against you. Your shift is over. You know Byron. Thought it would be better if someone he knew took him home."

"Of course, I get it. Sorry, it sounded a little bit like a scheme to get me back to Wolf's Den."

Maddox is a fair man. Not the type to engage in plots and intrigues. His feelings are hurt. I feel like a fool. Should have known better. He'd always treated her with respect and dignity since the day she arrived. She had no right to accuse him of something like matchmaking. Once again, she jumped to a conclusion. *Wish I could do a rewind. I've made it all about me. More proof my judgement is way off.*

"Roger, I mean, Captain. I apologize. It was such a surprise to see Wolf. Guess I'm still sensitive. Come on, Byron. I bet you're hungry. How about a hamburger over at the diner before we set off?"

"Could I try their tacos? I had a hamburger at lunch."

She laughed. "Sure, anything you want."

⁘

Byron munched on his tacos. Ricki sipped coffee.

Curt Noland stopped by to greet them. "Ah, glad you made it back to see us so soon."

"Well, I'm taking him back to Lakeview and you know teenagers. Always hungry."

"Very nice to have you. Hope we see much more of you in here. Best food in town." His blue eyes crackled with mischief with the statement.

"Pretty much the *only* food in town," she laughed.

He struck a pose of fake indignation, one hand on his wounded heart. "You did *not* have to point it out, Miss Sheridan."

"So sorry! Please, call me Ricki. Everyone does."

His warm smile complimented his friendly eyes. "All right, Ricki it is."

Byron gulped the last bite of his food and swallowed hard. "I'm finished. Let's go. It'll be dark soon."

"Slow down, young man. We don't want you choking on the cuisine. Might give me a bad reputation." Curt glanced around the restaurant with a false sense of drama, as if someone lurked, ready to pounce on a bit of bad news.

She liked his sense of humor, his friendly personality. He wasn't bad to look at either.

"I didn't choke. Come on, Ricki. Let's go."

"Byron, it's not like you to be rude. Are you feeling bad?"

"No, I'm just ready to go."

"Okay, okay. Let me pay the bill and we'll get on the road."

"Why don't you settle up when you get back. Sounds like he's in a hurry," Curt offered.

"Well, if you're sure. I should be back before you close."

Curt nodded and picked up the empty plate.

"Thanks, Curt. Let's go, Byron."

Back in the truck, she let a mile or so pass in silence.

"What happened back there, Byron?"

He stared straight ahead. "What do you mean?"

"Why were you rude? What's the big rush?"

He continued to stare out the window, but didn't say anything.

"Byron, I'm waiting. What's going on?"

He glanced at her, but looked away. "Nothing."

"Oh, it's something all right. Spill it."

He shifted around in his seat and looked at her. "It's Mr. Noland. I don't like him."

Small, delicate flakes of snow fell, hitting the windshield and melting immediately. She kept her eyes on the road. "Why? He was nothing but kind to you. I think he has a great sense of humor."

"He flirts with you."

She laughed. "He wasn't flirting, he was being friendly."

"Same thing. He likes you."

"And, why does it bother you?"

"Because."

She persisted. "Because why?"

"Because you should be with Mr. Kory."

They rode in silence for a while. She couldn't answer him, didn't know how to process Byron's perception of the situation. He had his heart set on her and Kory getting together. How do you explain to a young man of sixteen the complexities of the heart?

"Byron, it's not so simple. After what happened on the mountain, I need time to find out exactly how I feel about relationships. I got it so wrong the first time."

"Seems simple enough to me."

She glanced at him. His jaw was set like stone, his eyes stared straight ahead, his body was rigid, hands clenched. *Why does this mean so much to him?*

"Well, I'm listening. If you can explain how you feel, I'll surely try to see your point of view."

He relaxed a little, glanced at her, but returned to staring out the windshield. "I see the way he looks at you. And, your eyes light up every time you see *him*. It doesn't take a rocket scientist to see how you feel about each other."

"Yes, I like him very much, but like I said, it's complicated."

"What's so hard about it? You're fighting it when you don't need to."

"Byron, why is this so important to you? I see how upset you are."

He swiped his eyes quickly. "I had a girlfriend once."

"You did? Wonderful. Tell me what happened."

As they rode along, he told the story of a girl named Lauri. She was beautiful, funny, and she actually talked to him. He wanted to ask her to the school dance. He didn't. Another boy ended up asking her and she accepted. They ended up being boyfriend and girlfriend. He lost his chance.

"I see. She wasn't really your girlfriend, then?"

"She was supposed to be. I did everything wrong. I took it all for granted. I waited too long."

By now, they were getting close to the lodge. She had to deal with this, make him feel better.

"You're right. Sometimes, we think we have it in the bag, then something comes along and pulls the rug out from under us. So, I'll tell you what I'm going to do. I'll make sure Curt Noland doesn't get anywhere close to me until I figure out this thing with Kory. Will it make you feel better?"

He sighed. "Yes, I just know you and Kory are supposed to be together." He looked at her intently. "Don't screw it up."

She laughed out loud. "Byron, you are one wise young man. I'm proud to have you as a friend."

"Besides Wolf, Kory is my best friend, and now you are, too. Don't do what I did and wait too long. Your chance to be together could slip away in a second."

"You're very young, Byron. I bet a special girl is right around the corner waiting for you. And, thank you. I will think about what you said."

The rest of the trip they talked about the lodge, his job, his parents, but she couldn't help but wonder at the wisdom and insight of this young man. *He's so serious, so caring. Some young lady will be mighty lucky to have him.*

While they talked, she imagined Kory's face in front of her. Handsome, smoky brown eyes, his square jaw and broad smile. Byron managed to stir up those feelings again. She was pushing them down, losing herself in work, and a new beginning. But Byron's sincere plea made her stop and think. *Am I throwing something good away? Am I getting in my own way?*

As the elevation grew, so did the snowfall.

Glad snow tires are standard on the company truck.

The road curved around a long bend. She knew the lodge would come into view in less than a minute. *How am I going to handle seeing him? What will I say? Maybe it's better to just drop Byron off and leave, not take a chance.*

Her intentions ground to a halt when she pulled into the parking lot.

The open door of Wolf's Den Lodge illuminated the silhouette of a man leaned against the doorjamb.

Kory.

CHAPTER Twenty-Nine

BYRON JUMPED OUT OF THE TRUCK AND RAN UP THE STEPS. "Mr. Kory! Look who's here."

The snow fell faster now, the flakes larger, obscuring her vision, but the form in the doorway was unmistakable.

Why did it have to be him?

She remained behind the wheel and watched the two talking. Byron pointing in her direction, animated, and earnest. Kory nodded and gestured for him to go inside.

The boy hesitated, but did as he was told.

For a few seconds, neither of them moved. Finally, Kory walked toward the truck.

He motioned for her to roll down the window. "Hello, Ricki. Do you plan on sitting here all night? Why don't you come in and have a cup of coffee?"

"Hello, Kory. Nice to see you. I really should start back. The snow is falling heavier, the roads will be more dangerous at night. Thanks, though."

"I hate to break it to you, but you won't be able to return tonight. You'll have to stay here."

"Why? I had no trouble on the way up here."

He grabbed the door handle and opened it. "Road's blocked. Big tree came down, several cars piled up. It's going to be a while before they clear it. I wanted to catch you, so I waited in the doorway. Wolf called Captain Maddox to see when you left. We figured you were way past it when it happened. Wolf's on the phone with Maddox, right now. Come on, it's cold."

Reluctant, she slid out of the truck. "But, I can't stay here tonight. My job..., but how did you know about the tree?"

"The park service keeps us informed because of our guests."

The universe is conspiring against me. I wasn't ready to see him, much less spend the night at the lodge.

Together, they trudged through the fresh snow, bumping shoulders as they hurried along. Each touch sent shockwaves through her. She stole a glance at him and noticed his set jaw, the way he kept his eyes on the doorway, but he didn't move away from her.

Inside, they stamped their feet on the large mat before stepping on the wood floor.

"Let me take your jacket. Go on over by the fire. I'll get the coffee." He reached for the coat.

Unable to control the situation, she shed the jacket and handed it to him. "Thanks."

The warmth of the fire and the cozy lodge brought back the memories of her stay here over a month ago, of Kory, of what they shared in the beginning. The visions surrounded her like a warm blanket. For a moment, she yielded, let the scenes dance in front of her. It felt right. *Maybe Byron has a point. I should take a second look at this. But is it too late for Kory?*

Wolf's voice brought her back to the present. "Really sorry about this Miss Sheridan. The storm blew in early and is worse than expected. Wasn't supposed to come in until tomorrow morning. I'm so glad you made it through before the tree came down."

She rubbed her hands over the fire. "I'm glad too. What I don't understand is why you left him there. What was the emergency? The captain said you didn't plan it, but it sure felt like it."

"Crisis with the retreat. My main speaker cancelled."

Kory came back with the coffee. "What Ricki needs now is something hot. Are you hungry? Cook prepared some food. Told him you and the boy were coming in. Byron's in there, right now, wolfing down a roast beef sandwich."

They all laughed.

"He's always hungry. Yes, a little food would be nice." She glanced out the front window. "Look at it snow. I had no idea this was supposed to happen tonight. I should have kept Byron in Murphy. I have a spare bedroom. Or the captain and Noreen could have kept him. It looks really dangerous out there."

"The weather service was off by a few hours. It happens sometimes. Was supposed to come in tomorrow morning," Wolf said.

In the kitchen, Byron was finishing the last of his sandwich. "Hi Miss Ricki. Man, Cook makes the best roast beef sandwiches. Are you gonna have one?"

"As a matter of fact, I am."

"Here, sit by me." He pulled out a chair.

She accepted his offer and looked around. "Should I go in and make my own? I hate to bother anyone."

Cook, who looked more like a lumberjack with his big burly arms and shaggy beard, hurried out of the kitchen. "No need. I made an extra one, just in case. Anyone else need a sandwich?"

Wolf and Kory shook their heads.

"I better get back on the phone and try to secure a speaker. Why don't you make sure Ricki gets a room and settles in?"

"Sure thing, boss."

After he left, Ricki turned to Byron. "Did Wolf really rush back here because of the retreat, Byron? Do you know anything about this?"

"They don't tell me much. Say I get too excited." He laughed.

"You don't say. You do have a tendency for the dramatic."

He lowered his voice, "I'm really glad you're staying."

"Didn't have much choice. Just hope I can get out of here in the morning."

"Well, it's the weekend. Why don't you just hang with us?"

Kory came back with a key in his hand. "Pretty much the pick of the crop tonight. Any room you want. I gave you one with a view this time. If it's not satisfactory, let me know. Plenty more to pick from."

"I'm sure it's fine."

He sat down across from her. "The snow is beautiful tonight. Just enough light to see it falling. Very peaceful."

His eyes softened, his jaw wasn't set so firmly. The kindness shone in his eyes like a beacon showing her the way home. She wanted to believe there was something special between them, wanted to let herself fall into the depths of his eyes and the warmth of his arms. Loving him would be so easy, but uncertainty kept jerking her back from free-falling over the edge.

The moment dissolved as Byron stood up, the sound of his chair on the floor like a buzz saw run amok.

"Better go check in with Wolf. Haven't secured all the doors tonight. It's my job."

"Goodnight, Bryon," she said.

"Goodnight, Miss Ricki."

She watched him leave, then turned her gaze to the window. "I better get some sleep. I hope to get out of here in the morning."

It was odd to be alone with Kory. The connection they shared vibrated the air. She knew he felt it, too. The urge to reach out and take his hand, throw caution to the wind, and ask if she could have another chance almost overwhelmed her.

"Don't leave, Ricki. Stay. Stay and work with me," he whispered.

Her eyes misted. She turned slowly and met his gaze. "Kory, it was wrong of me to leave like I did. I was confused, even unhinged after what happened. I was in a dark place, doubting everything. I'm not sure I'm ready yet, but I want you to know, it has nothing to do with you. I've thought of our time on the mountain over and over. The first moment you kissed me. Something happened. It turned me upside down, jarred loose emotions I've kept hidden inside for a long time. I must explore those issues. Make sure what I'm feeling is true."

"Some of it was my fault. I rushed you, then I was angry because you didn't fall immediately into my arms. I was hurt. I avoided you at every turn, let you leave without saying goodbye. Like you, I keep going back to the moment I kissed you." He took her hand. "It was right, Ricki. You know it was."

"I..."

"Kory, I have to talk to you." Wolf blustered through the doorway.

Slowly, she pulled her hand out of Kory's grasp and looked at Wolf. "What's wrong?"

"What is it, boss? You're out of breath." Kory stood and hurried to Wolf.

"I'll tell you in the hallway. Come with me."

Kory followed him out the door.

Alone in the empty dining room, she didn't feel alarm. The lodge was always in a state of disarray. Wolf thrived in chaos. Refused to bow to convention. The moments alone gave her time to think about what Kory said. It would be easy to give in to the rush of emotion, but it's what kept getting her in trouble. *No, I'm going to take my time. I won't rush...*

Kory came through the doorway. Wolf followed.

She stood. "Something's wrong. What is it?"

Wolf looked at Kory. "Maybe we should wait until morning."

"What is going on? Is something wrong back in Murphy?"

Kory spoke up. "She has a right to know."

"Know what? One of you please tell me."

Kory took her hand and gently pulled her into the chair. "It's Russ. He's made bail."

CHAPTER Thirty

R**ICKI FOCUSED ON KORY'S FACE. SHE HEARD WHAT HE SAID,** but it didn't quite register in her brain. "Bail?" she asked. Her gaze drifted to Wolf, as if needing confirmation.

Wolf answered quietly, "Yes, yesterday."

She shifted to Kory. "But, how? He's up on attempted murder charges."

Wolf moved a chair from the table and sat beside Kory. "Remember his friend, Miles Parsons? He pulled some strings, got him out. Nice to have friends in high places, I guess."

"Miles," she whispered. "But, I got a notice today. There's a trial date set. How did you find out he made bail?"

"Officer Kemp called while I was sorting out the speaker for the retreat. He thought we should know," Wolf answered.

Kory tightened his grip on her hand. "We received the same notification about the trial. My guess is, he's long gone, maybe skipped the country, but there's always a chance—."

"A chance for what?"

"He'll come looking for you. Revenge is a powerful motivator."

She stood, jerked her hand from his grasp, anger flooding her body. The flush of it made her lightheaded. "He tried to kill you. Tried to kill us!"

Kory rose, as well. "Ricki, he's a sick man. A sociopath. He doesn't understand right and wrong. Don't you see? It's all about *him*."

Wolf agreed, "I hate to admit it, but Kory is right. I think he'll come after you."

She pushed the chair aside and walked toward the door. "He doesn't know where I am. He probably thinks I'm back in Dallas. No one there will give him information."

Kory took a step back, but his voice was firm, "He's a detective. You, of all people, understand he knows how to find people. It's public record, anyway. It won't be hard for him to discover you took a job in Murphy."

Her anger subsided as fast as it arrived. His freedom wasn't something she thought about. Russ was in jail. There would be a trial, and with the amount of witnesses, he'd be convicted and go to prison. Over and done. She bound it up in a neat little package and put it aside. *Miles Parsons. It never once occurred to me.*

She looked at Kory, suddenly exhausted. "You're right. He's not going to stick around with the amount of evidence against him. He'll skip. It's how he operates. He never takes responsibility. It's always someone else's fault. I'll be sure to fill the Captain in on the situation. We'll take extra precautions." She sighed, ready for the sanctuary of her room. "I'm bushed. Think I'll turn in. Thanks for giving me the news."

"Ricki, I think you should consider staying at Wolf's Den. You'll be safer here until we find out where he's gone. We can protect you here."

"Protect me? We have law enforcement in Murphy. You have no

protection at the lodge. How do you think you can protect me better than Captain Maddox and the sheriff? What makes you think *I* need protection?" The hair-trigger temper flared, again. The need to prove she could take care of herself.

Kory sat down. "Simple geography. Too much area to cover in Murphy and the surrounding county. You're out there alone. They couldn't help you if he showed up."

The defensiveness refused to subside. "I can take care of myself."

Wolf spoke in a low, but resolute voice. "We're family here, Ricki. You are part of it, now. All our campers become part of this place. We take care of our own." He pushed the chair back and stood. "It pains me you think so lowly of us. All we want is for you to be safe. You can be a bit of a hothead. Spewin' words out before you've heard all that's to be said. Go on back tomorrow, if you feel it's best. I'll call Maddox and let him know about the situation. I happen to agree with Kory, though. You'd be safer here."

Surprised Wolf spoke so passionately, she tried to rein in her annoyance. "I'm sorry. Maybe I did pop off too quickly. I've always had to prove myself because I'm a woman. Gets my hackles up. Yes, I get defensive. I apologize to both of you, but my decision stands. I'm heading back tomorrow. Thanks for the offer."

They didn't stop her, but she felt their eyes boring into her ridged back as she left the room. *Well, they can think what they want. I'm not afraid of Russ, anymore. I know he's out, now. I'll be prepared.*

After a warm bath, she brushed her unruly curls in front of the mirror and tried to discern where Russ would show up first. A knock startled her. She donned her robe and answered the door.

It was Wolf. "Captain Maddox is on the phone. Wants to talk to you. You can take it in my office."

"You called him?"

"I said I would, didn't I? He has a right to know someone might be stalkin' his officers. Puts the whole town at risk."

She knew he was right. *Should have called him myself.*

"Let me throw my jeans on. I'll be right down."

Wolf gave a curt nod and headed down the hall.

It only took a second to don her tee-shirt and jeans and pad barefoot down the stairs. No one was in the office. The handset lay on its side atop Wolf's oversized desk.

"Hello?"

Maddox greeted her. She listened while he stated all the reasons she should stay at the lodge for the time being.

"But, Captain, who will take my shift, check on my territory? I can't stay here forever," she complained.

Her heart sank when he offered new information. Russ hadn't surfaced anywhere. Maddox agreed to work together with the Lakeview PD to keep an eye out for him. In the meantime, she was more valuable at the lodge. Russ was sure to seek vengeance on Kory, as well as her. Both offices wanted an officer at the lodge, in case he showed up. She was their choice.

"Are you sure? I mean, they could easily send an officer from Lakeview to check out the area up here. I don't want to leave you and the sheriff in a bind."

He assured her all would be well with him and the sheriff. Everyone was on high alert. With three locations and other area towns notified, it was a matter of vigilance.

"How long will I have to stay up here?"

She hung up the phone and sat down in Wolf's chair staring into space. "This isn't at all what I planned."

"What isn't?" Kory popped his head inside the doorway.

"Oh, it was Maddox. He wants me to stay up here for a few days in case Russ comes up here."

He entered the room and sat down across from her. "Well, I for one, am glad he made the decision. You still mad?"

"Bewildered. It all happened so fast. I just realized I have no clothes, nothing. I planned on going back tonight."

"We can take care of it in the morning. Head into Lakeview, talk to the police, gather some clothes and necessities. When we get back, you can tell us your plan of action. I wonder if we should send Byron home to his parents? We've got me and Wolf, you, Kyle and Buck. The others went home for the winter."

The chair's springs complained when she stood up. "That's just it. We have more than enough able bodied men to watch this place. Maddox and the sheriff are the only two in Murphy. It's probably the first place he'll look. I don't want them in danger."

Kory stood, as well. "Look, the lodge is secluded, away from the beaten path. We need more eyes out here. I'll see everyone is armed. He's not just coming after you, Ricki. He wants his revenge on me, too. Better we have more fire power here."

"I guess you're right. About Byron. It's up to his parents. We need to notify them of the danger. Guess we should explain it to him before we call his parents."

Together, they walked out of the office, matching steps, shoulder to shoulder, putting a plan in place. Something about him beside her restored her confidence. Normally, she worked alone, relied on her instincts, but more and more, she wondered if the loner life style was more of a defense, or a testament to her stubbornness.

They found Wolf in the dining room with a cup of coffee.

"Well, what's the verdict?" he asked.

Kory answered, "Well, Maddox said he was contacted by the Lakeview PD."

She continued, "He wants me to stay. Russ has gone underground. No one can locate him. They think he'll try to go to Murphy."

"They also think he'll come here." Kory finished. "The captain said he wants her here. Figure he'll go to Murphy first, they can apprehend him there and be done with it."

Wolf rubbed his beard, but didn't say anything.

"We were wondering about Byron. Should we let his parents know? They might not want him in harm's way," she offered.

"Yes, I'll call them. He won't like it much, but then, he doesn't have a choice."

"Kory mentioned Buck and Kyle are still here. With me and Kory, we've got four to take turns at watch. Sound okay to you?"

Wolf nodded. "Sounds fine. You don't want me to take a turn? Am I too old, now?"

Kory and Ricki laughed.

"You've got the retreat to deal with. It's in two weeks. I'm hoping we get this thing dealt with before then. The trial is a month away. He could be anywhere. The sooner he shows himself, the better," Kory said.

"Yeah, I don't want trouble during the retreat. Don't need the publicity."

"Wolf, I really am sorry for…"

"Not your fault, Ricki. You did exactly what I want people to do. Come here for rest and relaxation, a new experience, something to jar them out of their comfort zone. I'm not blamin' you, girl. In all these years, we've never had anything like this happen. I guess it was bound to, though. Don't you worry none. At least, you are here to help us deal with it, now."

"Thanks, Wolf. I'll do my best," she whispered.

"Better go tell, Byron. You two devise the schedule and post it. I'll see it's followed."

After he left, Kory pulled out a chair. "Want to decide who takes the first watch?"

She sat down. "We can talk to Byron in a bit. We need to get Buck and Kyle in here. They might balk at taking a turn, decide to go home for the winter."

"Those two? Hell no. They love excitement. I'll round them up. Want another cup of coffee while you're waiting?"

"Sure, but, I'll get it. I know my way."

The hour was late. She didn't expect anyone to be in the kitchen, but Cook was there, pen and pencil in hand, checking the cupboards.

"You're here mighty late. I was coming after some coffee. Hope

I'm not disturbing you."

Cook smiled. "No, not at all. Making my list for the trip to Lakeview in the morning. Still gotta feed this crew, ya know."

The coffee was cold, so she set about making a new pot.

"I've got an idea. Kory and I are going to Lakeview tomorrow. We can pick up what you need. My boss in Murphy ordered me to stay here for a few days. I didn't bring any clothes.

"Yeah? Well, cool. Sure, I'd love to have some extra time to myself. You sure you don't mind?"

"Not at all. No sense in you making an extra trip."

"Boss, giving you a little R&R?"

"No, it's business."

"Have anything to do with the incident on the mountain a month ago?"

"I guess you heard about it."

He laughed. "I hear everything. We don't get much excitement around here, so it was big news." He pulled the chef's hat off his head and held it to his chest. "But, I'm ever so relieved you're okay, Miss Sheridan. Wouldn't wish it on anyone."

"Call me Ricki. Like Wolf says, we're all family here."

Kory's voice drifted through the closed door. "Where's the coffee?"

"Coming," she called.

She grabbed four mugs and headed for the dining room. "Coffee was cold. I made a new pot. Hey Kyle, Buck."

They all nodded and sat down.

The coffee finished, she carried the mugs out to the men.

"I guess Kory filled you in. We're taking precautions. Need to have a twenty-four- hour watch going. It's not likely Russ will make it this far once he finds out where I work. We're confident my boss and the sheriff will apprehend him in Murphy. In case they don't, he'll probably end up here."

"We can't give you a gun, Kyle, because of your priors, but we'll make sure you're covered all the time. Buck, you'll get a rifle. I think three shifts will work for now. Kyle and Buck, you'll work together between midnight and dawn. Between us we have sat phones and walkie talkies to keep in touch. I'll take the evening shift until midnight, Kory can do the day shift. Work for everyone?"

"Can't have a gun, huh?" Kyle frowned.

"Yeah, can't break the rules. It's why I'm pairing you and Buck. He'll have the gun. You'll have the eyes. If I know Russ, he'll use the cover of darkness." She turned to Kory. "Thoughts?"

"I'd rather take the evening shift. You shouldn't be out there after dark."

"Why? Because I'm a woman?" The old defensive reaction rose to the surface.

He sighed deeply. "No, because you said it yourself. He'll strike when it's dark. If he comes this far. I'd rather be the one to confront him."

She frowned. "Sorry. Still defensive, I guess. Okay, I'll take the day shift. We have enough communication devices for everyone? I want you to buzz each of us if you see anything, even if we're asleep."

Kory looked at the clock above the kitchen door. "It's nearly midnight. I guess it means Kyle and Buck. Any complaints about taking the first shift?"

"Nope. I need a thermos of coffee, though. It's cold out there. What about you Kyle? We can discuss our strategy in the kitchen," Buck said.

"I'm right behind ya. Still think I should have a gun," he mumbled as he followed Buck.

"Don't worry, little buddy. I've got your back."

The kitchen door closed behind them.

Kory finished off his coffee. "The sat phone and walkie talkies are in Wolf's office. Want to come with me to get them? We need to find Byron next."

"Sure."

Side by side, she marveled at the easy rhythm they fell into as they walked. Her shoulder brushed his and a small smile played across her lips. *It's so easy to be with him. Natural, comfortable. I wish it were me and Kory out there on the late evening shift.*

She blushed at the thoughts swirling around in her head. Only an hour ago, she was hopping mad at the suggestion of staying on here, unsure of her emotions toward him, but the more they were together, the more the attraction grew.

I wonder if he feels it, too?

"Are you afraid he'll catch us off-guard, Ricki?" he asked. A mischievous twinkle danced in his dark eyes.

She wanted to get lost in those eyes. "No. I'm not. I plan on staying vigilant." She paused. "It feels good to be working with you."

His smile lit up his face like the noonday sun. "Music to my ears, Ricki. I won't say anything else, though. I don't want to jinx it."

They stopped outside of Wolf's door.

"Wait, I know the tone. Sounds like he's upset with someone," Kory said.

Ricki followed Kory inside the office.

Wolf scowled into the phone. "He was here an hour ago, Mr. Johansson. Never said a word to me about leaving. You sure he's not there?" He paused, listening. "I see. I'll call the Lakeview PD. You let me know if he shows up there."

When he hung up, Kory asked, "What's up, boss? Was it Byron's father?"

"Yes, Byron's missing."

CHAPTER Thirty-One

"MISSING? I THOUGHT HE WENT ON TO HIS ROOM. We were about to go talk to him," Ricki said.

"So did I. His room is empty. I thought I should be the one to talk to him about going home for a few days, but he wasn't there. I've looked everywhere." Wolf scratched his head. "Man! Of all times to pull a stunt."

Ricki didn't like what she was hearing. Generally, he was a level-headed kid, followed the rules. He wouldn't jeopardize his friendship with Wolf, and the opportunity he gave him, if something wasn't terribly wrong. "I saw him by the registration desk. Said he was heading to his room, but needed a pencil or something. I didn't see him go upstairs. Do you suppose he hung around, maybe overheard us talking about sending him home?"

"Could be, but it's not like him to take off without telling someone. He knows he can always talk to me about anything. I don't get it." Wolf shook his head. "Maybe—."

Kory spoke up. "We'll organize a search. Kyle and Buck are already on patrol, maybe they saw something."

She voiced what they all were probably thinking. "It's too soon for Russ to show up here. He only got out yesterday. I personally think he'd head for Dallas first. Do you really think he'd come here?"

"Who knows what the lunatic would do?" Wolf spat.

"We can't take any chances. The search starts now." Kory turned for the door. "You coming, Ricki?"

Hesitant, she looked at Wolf. "Are you all right? You look pale."

He glanced up. "If anything happens to the boy, I'll…"

"We'll find him, Wolf. Do you need me to stay here with you?"

"No, no. Go on with Kory. The more eyes on this, the better. I'm okay. Just report back every half hour. Everyone have the walkie talkies?"

"Yes, everyone has one and a gun, except Kyle," Kory said.

"Okay, well, don't waste any more time. Find him."

Ricki glanced back at the blustery lodge owner on her way out. *He really loves the kid. It's nice to see a softer side of him.*

Halfway down the hall, Wolf called them back. "I just remembered something. My old cabin is about a mile from here. It's the first cabin I ever built. I took Byron and his dad there one time. Taught them to tie lures. It was a good bonding experience for the two of them. Told them the story of how I came to this place. There's firewood, a few cans of beans. I'd look there first."

"The old run down shack you call a fishing cabin? I haven't been there in a while, but I remember it was rickety, almost falling down. Do really think he remembers the way up there?" Kory asked.

A wounded look flashed across Wolf's face. "I've done some work on it. It's not so bad. Byron and his dad made a few trips up there, just the two of them. So yes, I figure the kid knows the way."

"I use to go up there a lot to fish, but haven't made the trip in a while. Did you fix the old bunk?"

"Well, I propped it up. Nobody spends the night there, anymore. Just go up for a day of fishing. It'll do."

"Okay, we'll start there."

"Let me know immediately if you see or hear anything. Byron is priority," Kory told Buck. "But, don't leave the this place unprotected. Go out a little way, but make sure you can see the lodge. Ricki and I are going to head for Wolf's old cabin. It's a pretty good bet he headed there."

"Got it," Buck said. "I'll let Kyle know. You guys be careful. Russ is a sly one. This could be his doing."

Kory nodded. "The thought crossed my mind. Hopefully, it's just a kid who doesn't want to go back to his parents."

Buck turned around and pulled out his walkie talkie.

Kory shrugged a small knapsack onto his back. "Come on, Ricki. We have to hike up there. The trail isn't wide enough for an ATV or snow mobile. No one goes up there anymore. If he hiked up the trail, his tracks should still be visible."

Armed with parkas, guns, walkie talkies, flashlights, and a satellite phone they trudged through the snow until they found the beginning of the overgrown path.

Sometimes, they walked side-by-side, but most of the time they gave way to single file. The trail widened, as they went along and looked like deer used it as a game trail. Snow fell, but the path was still evident.

Ricki watched the snowflakes thicken. "It's really coming down. Can we find our way back?" she asked.

Kory brushed the snow from his parka. "I know this trail like the back of my hand. Wolf told me about it, but never showed me where it was. Being the stubborn cuss I am, it became a challenge. I was determined to find it, and I did. He never knew I went up there.

I still do, occasionally, to soak in the ambience, but it's been awhile. He goes there, too, although he won't admit it. I see the evidence, the missing cans of beans, a recent fire. Maybe it's a reminder of tougher times and how he beat the odds. Wolf keeps to himself a lot, doesn't talk about his past much. Maybe he goes there to think.

"Wolf's quite a guy," she whispered.

He didn't reply, but tenderly reached for her hand. She didn't pull away. Even through the heavy gloves, the vibration of his desire pulsed through. They walked together, hand in hand, not speaking until the path narrowed.

The effort to hike through the snow, along with the uphill climb slowed any conversation.

Finally, Kory turned to her. "It should be around this bend."

Sure enough, as they rounded the corner, a hand-hewn log cabin came into view through a veil of snow.

"Do you see any light?"

Kory shook his head. "No, but the tracks lead right to the door."

The weather worn door wouldn't budge as they tried to push it open.

"Funny, never had trouble with it before. It's a good sign, though. Could be locked from the inside."

"Maybe the boy is in there," she said, excitedly.

Heavy oil cloth curtains made it impossible to see into the cabin.

"If he is, the fire is out. There's no smoke coming from the chimney. He could freeze to death. There's a window back here I can get through. I'll check it out. Wait here, in case he tries to bolt out the front door."

The view around the cabin was pitch black. All the flashlight picked up was the snow coming down in sheets.

Kory called from behind the cabin. "He's in here. Hurry."

She followed his footprints around the side of the cabin assisted by the flashlight.

He pounded on the window until it shattered. "He's wrapped up in a sleeping bag. I hope we're in time."

Together, they cleared the glass and Kory hoisted himself up and through the window. She pulled herself up and followed him through the small opening.

Byron's head was covered. He lay by the cold ashes of the wood stove.

"Wake up, Byron." Kory shook him.

The boy didn't respond.

"You keep working on him. I'll start a fire," she said.

Kory kept shaking him and tried to find a pulse. "Outside the front door. The wood is under a tarp on the porch."

She hurried to unlatch the door.

The wood clattered to the floor beside the stove. She grabbed the kindling from the basket, grabbed a long match from a shelf, and rushed to get a fire going.

He continued to talk to Byron, shook him, rubbed his hands, until finally a moan broke the tension.

"Mr. Kory?" his voice was barely audible.

"Yes, it's me, kid. You're almost frozen. Can you sit up?"

"I don't know," he murmured.

By now, the fire caught and a blaze roared inside the stove. She kept the metal door open hoping the warmth would get to Byron quicker.

Kory picked him up and moved him closer to the fire.

She saw a blanket on an old bunk, hurried over to retrieve it and covered the broken window. It didn't help much, but at least, it kept the snow from blowing in.

"Keep rubbing his hands. There's a lantern on the table."

Byron gave her a weak smile as she knelt beside him. "I'm sorry, Miss Ricki. Guess I didn't think this through."

"Never mind. The important thing is we found you in time."

The lantern illuminated the rugged cabin. It looked like it hadn't been used in a while. It was dusty, empty beer cans were piled in a box next to the door, cupboard doors hung open.

"Not my cup of tea for a get-a-way."

Kory laughed. "Yep, pretty rough, but in the spring, it's teaming with wildlife. There's a pond out back, full of fish. When you're up here fishing, a man doesn't think about housecleaning."

She decided to ignore his philosophy. "Feeling better, Byron? He needs something hot in his stomach to warm him up."

Kory found the coffee tin and a can of beans. "Will this do?"

"Perfect."

The cabin wasn't warm and cozy but, it wasn't freezing anymore. The lantern gave an illusion of warmth, too.

Coffee made, she poured Byron a cup.

He looked at her and wrinkled his nose. "I don't like coffee."

"Don't see as you have much choice. Drink up," Kory declared.

While she warmed the beans in a battered aluminum pot, she looked at Kory. "We need to let everyone know he's safe."

"Right. I'll get the message out. Problem is, *we* can't get out tonight. We'll have to stay here. He's too weak to make the trek out."

"I agree. We'll just have to make do."

He stepped outside with the sat phone to alert Wolf and the others.

While he was gone, she asked, "Why did you come up here? This isn't like you, Byron."

He took small sips of the coffee and averted his eyes. "I...I heard you and Mr. Kory talking. You wanted to send me home to my parents because of Russ. My place is here, now. Didn't want all of you to treat me like a kid."

"I see. You're right. We should have talked to you first, but everything happened so fast. Russ is a very dangerous man. We thought it wise to get you out of the cross fire."

"I can handle myself as good as the others."

"You proved yourself back in Murphy, for sure. I should have stuck up for you. I apologize. I'll make the case for you to stay at the lodge when we get back."

He looked up with adoring eyes. "You will? Then, I can stay?"

"The last word is Wolf and your parents. I'll make a case for you to stay. It's all I can promise." The beans smelled good as she stirred the pot. "Time for something to eat."

Kory stamped his feet, knocking the snow from his boots before he stepped inside. "Got ahold of Wolf. He's calling Byron's parents. He was greatly relieved we found him. I told him we'd make the hike back in the morning."

"Any word about Russ?"

"No, all's quiet, right now."

She handed a plate to Kory. "Here, have a plate of beans before Byron scarf's them all up."

Byron shoveled spoonsful into his mouth. "Didn't realize I was so hungry."

Kory took the battered tin, but didn't eat. "He might need this more than me."

Together, they watched the boy's color slowly return.

"Amazing what a little hot coffee and beans can do for you," Kory remarked. "We have about five hours before daylight. We need to find a place to bed down. I'll keep the fire going. I think there's another can of beans we can have for breakfast."

She scoured the cabin for blankets and a clean place to lay down. The bunk didn't look too inviting and only one other blanket was found. No way was she going to lay on the dirty floor. The best bet was to circle the fire. The blanket could act as a little insulation.

Kory came back in with an armful of wood. He spied the blanket on the floor. "Is this our bed?"

"There's nothing else. We need to stay close by the fire. If we sit close together we should be able to stay warm. Our parkas will insulate us. Byron has the sleeping bag.

"Good idea." He piled the wood next to the stove, stoked up the fire, and took his place next to Byron. Ricki sat on the other side of the boy.

Byron ate every mouthful of beans. The fire and a full stomach made him drowsy. He nodded off, leaning against her shoulder.

As he fell deeper into sleep, she eased his head into her lap, stroked his hair, and whispered, "You had us very frightened. I'm so grateful we found you."

Kory moved around to her other side, took her hand, and looked into her eyes. "If I had to be stranded with anyone, I couldn't think of any other two people I'd choose."

The three huddled closely in front of the fire, warm, safe, and together.

CHAPTER Thirty-Two

RICKI DIDN'T KNOW WHEN SHE FELL ASLEEP, BUT AWOKE with light penetrating the thin blanket over the broken window. Byron still slept in her lap, but Kory was gone.

She looked around.

The old, rickety table was cleared off, dusted, and adorned with three battered tin plates and a steaming pot of beans.

Kory handed her a cup of coffee. "You might need this. It took me two tries to pry myself off the floor."

"When did I fall asleep? We were talking and I don't remember anything else."

"You nodded off just as you were telling me how strong and brave I am."

She laughed. "Yeah, right."

Byron stirred.

She moved his head to the sleeping bag. It *did* take two tries before she could stand up.

"Kory watched her with a smile, but his voice was serious. "We better get moving. I hope the kid is strong enough to walk. I don't want to carry him out."

"A little of the coffee and a few more beans, and I predict he'll be right as rain," she said.

They sipped coffee at the table giving Byron a little more time to sleep.

"Those beans sure smell good." She hovered over the pot.

"By all means, have some. You deserve it after cradling the boy in your lap all night." He scooped a large spoonful onto her plate.

"Only if you'll join me." She watched him prepare the plates, warmed by his caring spirit. "Kory," her voice soft and full of emotion.

"Yes?"

"I really enjoyed last night. All of us by the fire. It was nice."

He held the serving spoon in mid-air and met her gaze. "It *was* nice. *Very* nice."

She saw the compassion in his eyes, but there was something else, too. Love? It was impossible to look away. The seconds stretched on and she wondered what he saw in *her* eyes, because her heart was overflowing. *Can a person fall in love in one moment?*

Byron sat up and yawned. "Is there anything to eat? I'm starved!"

The spell dissolved, but Ricki knew something changed.

They talked of the trek home while consuming the meager breakfast.

"I hope we can make good time. I have two trainees coming in today."

Ricki chimed in. "I need to take over for Buck and Kyle. Since we haven't heard anything, I'm guessing all was quiet during the night. I need to check in with Captain Maddox, too, see if he's seen anything of Russ."

THAT ONE *Moment*

The hike back to the lodge went smoothly in the daylight. The snow still drifted down, but not as heavy as the night before. They kept single file to keep Byron between them, so he wouldn't be tempted to sneak off.

Kory knew the trail even though the new snow covered their previous tracks.

Byron kept trying to wangle a guarantee he could stay on at the lodge.

Kory told him to save his breath and keep walking.

Ricki didn't recognize anything until they came to the clearing behind the lodge.

She hoped Buck or Kyle appeared before they got closer. A little reassurance all was well would be welcome, but no one was in sight.

She whispered loudly, "Kory, stay back in the trees. I don't like this."

"What's the matter?" he asked.

"It's too quiet. One of the guys should be on this side of the lodge. I don't see either one. Something isn't right." She pulled Byron back inside the safety of the trees.

Kory joined her. "You may be right. I feel it, too. Something's off."

She continued to gaze at the lodge. "What do you suggest we do?"

"We better not use the walkie talkie. If Russ made it this far, well, it might alert him we're back. I don't want to put anyone else in danger. I could try to sneak in, see what's going on, but he might be watching for us." He knelt in the snow and scratched his forehead.

"Let me go, Kory. I know Russ, how his mind works. It's me he wants."

"No way. I'm not letting you go in alone. You know he won't stop until he gets us both."

Byron tugged at Kory's sleeve. "I have an idea."

"Look, this is complicated, Byron. Ricki and I need to come up with a plan." He looked at the boy and smiled. "Thanks, though, but we've got this."

"Wait, let's hear it, because, right now, I've got nothing," she said.

The boy beamed at her.

Kory looked from one to the other, then turned his attention to the lodge. "Okay, shoot."

"You know where the trail branches out about a half mile back, goes behind the outbuildings?"

"Yes, what of it?" Kory asked.

"Wolf let me park an old snowmobile behind the building. Said I could work on it in my spare time, 'til I got it running."

Kory turned to look at him. "Are you telling me you got it going?"

His smile got bigger. "Yep. Sure did. I can hike back there, get the snowmobile and head to town, get the police." He looked at them, his head swiveling back and forth like a weather vane in a storm.

"No way will I let you go out there alone," he said.

"Wait." Ricki grabbed his arm. "Byron's idea is a good one. We can wait until we see what's going on. Either way, he'll be out of harm's way."

Kory shook his head. "It's risky."

"You have a gun. We have the fire power. They don't know when to expect us with all this snow. It could buy us some time."

Ricki continued to search the lodge for any signs of life.

Kory looked from Byron to the lodge and the trail behind them. "Okay. Let's do this. But, Byron, you need to be quiet as you can until you start it up, then you need to stomp on it and get out of here, pronto. Got it?" Kory explained.

"I got it." He turned to go.

"Wait," Ricki said. She pulled out the sat phone and handed it to Byron. "Take this. Kory's got the walkie talkie. When you can, call the PD."

He nodded and took the device.

They stood together in the shelter of the trees and watched him go.

"Not sure this was a good idea," Kory said.

"It's the only one we've got. Either Buck or Kyle should have showed, by now, if they stayed on their shift. It's too quiet."

Twenty minutes passed with no sound or movement.

Kory frowned. "He should have made it by now. I didn't hear an engine."

Ricki slipped her hand into his. "All this snow might muffle the sound. At any rate, he's safe and away from here. It's what we wanted in the first place."

"I suppose. We need to find out what's going on in the lodge."

"I've been thinking, let's call Wolf on the walkie talkie. If he answers, you can tell by his voice if something is wrong. We'll tell him the snow is too deep, it's bogging us down. All we need is to hear his voice," Ricki offered.

"It might work. Wolf can't hide much from me. It's worth a try."

Kory mused, "They should be expecting us. It's strange Wolf hasn't called *us*."

"I was thinking the same thing," Ricki said.

"Ready?"

She nodded. "Give it a go."

The device crackled, then stopped when a voice came on the line. "Wolf, is that you?"

CHAPTER Thirty-Three

Ricki moved closer to Kory to listen.

He spoke into the walkie talkie again. "Wolf, can you hear me?"

He released the button, but the voice didn't respond.

"Something's not right," she said. "He would answer if he could."

"I agree."

He tried again. "Wolf, Wolf. This is Kory, can you hear me?"

Ricki's heart pounded. *Why haven't we heard from anyone? Russ wouldn't come here first. He wouldn't take the chance of being caught. Please Wolf, answer!*

"Try Buck," she suggested.

He pressed the button again. "Buck, come in. This is Kory. Do you receive?"

A voice clear and strong, and immediately recognizable came on. "Why hello, Mr. Littleton. I'm sorry, but Wolf and Buck can't answer you. They're kind of tied up, at the moment."

"Russ," she shouted. "What have you done? Don't you dare hurt innocent people. If it's me you want, I'll surrender to you if you let the others go."

Russ's demonic laughter echoed through the snow-covered trees, a stark contrast between good and evil. "Nice try, Ricki. No one goes anywhere, but I will promise you their bodies if you don't show up soon. Who lives, who dies, well, it's up to you. Oh, and your lover boy Kory needs to accompany you. The first body will be thrown out into the snow in twenty minutes. Better not waste any more time."

Kory sucked in his breath. "Twenty minutes. We need to do something."

Ricki's mind reeled. "He'll kill *us* if we show up. He'll kill *them* if we don't. We have no choice."

"Ready?" Kory asked.

She grabbed his arm. "He might shoot us on sight if we rush out there. We need a plan of action."

Crouched behind the tree line, they discussed the options.

"I can go alone. Buy some time. Tell him you twisted an ankle. It's worth a try," Kory offered.

"I don't know—." She tugged his sleeve. "Look, someone is outside. They have a rifle."

He squinted toward the lodge. "It's Cook. Why is he carrying a gun? I've never seen him with one before."

"He heard everything yesterday, all the plans. Do you think…?" she answered.

They watched as Cook shouldered the rifle and shaded his eyes toward the line of trees.

"He's looking for us," Kory stated.

"Could he be trying to warn us?" she asked.

"Look, he's talking into a device. Who's he talking to?"

"It doesn't matter. Russ is calling the shots from inside. We're running out of time, Kory. There's no other option. We should go now. It's the only way to save the others."

They stood up together.

"I just hope Byron got through and is safe. We did the right thing sending him," Ricki said.

Kory agreed. "We can only pray he made it. I should go a few steps in front of you. If he shoots, you'll have a chance to get away."

"Maybe we should spread out. You go right, I'll go left. If we walk out together he'll have to aim at one or the other of us. It'll give one of us a chance to get a shot off."

He nodded. "Good idea. Let's wait to see if Cook goes back inside."

The minute ticked by.

At the last second, the gun-toting chef stepped back inside the door.

The walkie-talkie cracked and Russ's voice came on. "Times almost up. Which one do you want me to throw out first?"

Kory answered, "We're coming in now."

They walked in opposite directions inside the tree line.

After several yards, they stopped.

Kory nodded at her; together they stepped into the clearing.

She braced for the impact of a bullet, but none came.

Ricki would take the door to the kitchen.

Kory intended to enter by way of the sunroom door.

As she got close, the screen door opened. Cook stepped out pointing a rifle directly at her. "Get inside."

She looked at Kory, knowing Russ was probably stationed in the sunroom.

He put his hand on the door handle and stepped inside.

A shot rang out.

Adrenaline kicked in. She rushed the cook, planted her knee in his groin, and swiveled around to jab an elbow to his face. In the confusion, he dropped the rifle. She kicked it away from him, drew her own gun, and pushed him against the wall.

"Now, you scumbag, where are the others?" she growled, one forearm across his throat.

"Please, please, don't shoot me!" Cook pleaded. He trembled as she pressed harder. "I'll tell you, I'll tell you."

As much as she wanted to know if Kory was still alive, she knew the fate of the others rested with her. She had to get to them.

She pressed harder. "Start talking."

"They're tied up in a room upstairs."

"Let's go," she released his throat and pushed him forward. "I said go!"

He hesitated, but took a step toward the door. "I'm sorry Miss Sheridan. I have kids; he threatened my family."

"You tipped him off?"

"Yes, he called. Wanted to know if you were here. I didn't answer him, at first. He sounded crazed. Said he'd kill my family, and then me."

Ricki shoved him forward. "He'll probably kill you anyway."

⁂

The staircase to the guest rooms was through the dining hall. Once through the door, they had to cross the great hall. The stairs were just past the registration desk.

It could be a trap. Corner me upstairs. But, I have no choice. If I run to Kory, Russ will shoot me. I must find the others.

She opened the dining room door a crack and peeked out. It looked clear. *I have to try, it's my only chance.*

"Let's go," she whispered.

He hung back. "Please, he's out there and armed."

She shoved him. "Then he'll shoot you first."

They were halfway across the room when Russ stepped out from behind the sunroom door. "Aren't you even a little bit concerned about your boyfriend, Ricki? It's not like you to leave anyone behind."

The smirk on his face curdled her stomach. She wasn't going to play into his hands, instead, she focused on his gun. "Where are the others, Russ? What have you done with them?"

"They're safe enough, for now." He looked at Cook. "Good work, my man. She fell for it."

Cook turned and wrenched the gun from her hand. "Stupid broad." He sauntered over to Russ. "Thought she could outsmart us. We showed her."

She let Cook take the gun without a struggle. "Where's Kory?"

"You don't have to worry about him. He'll keep. Now, let's go upstairs." He waved the gun toward the stairs.

He hasn't mentioned Byron. I can only pray the boy made it out undetected and is safe.

She led the way upstairs with Russ behind her. Cook took up the rear. At the top of the stairs, Russ pointed down the hall. "Last room on the left, darling."

At the door, she stopped to face him. "You better not have hurt them."

His eyes glittered like a madman's, his laugh, maniacal. "See for yourself." He pushed the door open.

She stifled a scream. Side by side and face down, Wolf and Buck lay in a pool of blood.

Kyle was missing.

CHAPTER Thirty-Four

Russ stuck the gun in her back. "Let's go. Nothing you can do for them."

She turned around. "You didn't have to kill them."

"Why, my dear. Have you turned soft? Compassion doesn't become you. Head downstairs. You're coming with me."

She concentrated on each step on the way down. *He still hasn't mentioned Kyle. Does he even know about him? Or is he involved in this, too? So much I don't know, yet.*

The unknown variables kept her calm. Kory could still be alive. Kyle, too. The hope Byron made it to town gave her the will to keep Russ engaged, hopeful he'd make a mistake. Time was the only thing she had on her side.

Russ shoved her through the kitchen door and toward a chair. "Sit down."

She did what he asked.

"Cook, bring some coffee. My darling fiancé and I must talk. You've been a very bad, girl, Ricki. You shouldn't have left me. Nobody leaves Russ Desmond. You cost me my job, I had to spend weeks in the hole they call a jail while you simply picked up with your life. You thought you could hide from me."

Cook brought the coffee.

Russ shoved a cup toward her. "Go ahead and drink up." He looked at Cook. "Go keep watch on the front. I don't want any stragglers coming in."

She picked up the coffee cup and took a sip, hands shaking, not with fear, but rage. "You've lost your sense of reality This is wrong, Russ. Turn yourself in. You're a cop. You broke the law. There are consequences."

He laughed. "Not if I get out of the country. I can start over anywhere. You, on the other hand, don't get off so easy. You belong to me. You have to pay for what you did."

"I don't belong to you, Russ. You cheated on me. I left you. You said you needed a different kind of woman. We are over. Can't we just leave it there?"

"No, we can't. You're coming with me. Did you think I would let you off so easy?"

"We'd never make it out of the country together. They'd look for us."

"You're just buying time. I know the tactic. It won't work. Finish your coffee. We need to go."

Her mind raced to find something, anything to stall him. "Could I have some to coffee to go? This is cold."

He frowned, but hesitated. "Can't leave you here. Let's go to the kitchen."

Physically, she couldn't overpower him, she knew, but maybe there was some way to get him to turn his back. If she could escape out the back door, she might have a chance.

It's worth a try.

An idea formed. She stood up slowly and grabbed her knee. "Crap, my knee popped out. The deep snow must have taken a toll on it." She rubbed it.

He watched her, gave her a few seconds, then nudged her forward.

She limped, trying to slow him down. *I have to buy every second I can. I only have a couple of chances. If Kyle eluded Russ, he might be around somewhere, waiting. And, if Byron made it to town, help might be coming. If only I knew Kory's still alive.*

He stepped around her and pushed open the kitchen door. "There's gotta be a thermos around here, somewhere. Find it. We'll make a fresh pot and get out of here."

Acutely aware of the gun trained on her back, she rustled through the cupboards. *I hope I don't find one.*

The kitchen was huge, cupboards lined the walls, both above and below. She took her time.

Russ got impatient. "Let me look. You make the coffee."

She limped to the stove and fumbled with the coffee filter, dumped out the coffee, doing everything in slow motion.

"Ah, there it is." Russ pulled out a thermos.

Her heart dropped. It was a matter of minutes before he'd force her out the door and into his vehicle.

Another idea formed. Before she slipped the pot into the coffee maker, she let it slip from her grasp. It crashed to the floor and shattered glass everywhere.

Russ swore and slapped her across the face. He looked around. "There, over on the other counter. Another pot. Get it."

Her hand flew to her face as she stumbled against the counter. *Crap. Another pot.*

"Stop stalling. You dropped it on purpose. Next time, I'll shoot you."

Time was running out. She stretched his patience as far as it would go. Now, his anger would explode if she tried anything else.

She did as he said.

It only took a few minutes to finish.

"The coffee is done. Fill the thermos," he ordered.

"Let's go." He motioned her to the backdoor.

She remembered to limp.

"Open it," Russ growled.

The door swung open. The barrel of the gun settled against the middle of her back.

"Don't try anything stupid, Ricki."

He forced her down the steps and followed close behind.

At the bottom step, she heard a thud and loud grunt. The gun clattered to the ground.

She spun around. "Byron!"

His face was pale, his hand shook, and the pistol he held fell to the ground.

She scooped it up and held it on the unconscious Russ. There was no time to question him about how he got there.

"Get some rope. We need to tie him up. Cook is in on this. He's out front with a gun."

"There's rope in the shed. I'll get it." He hurried to the small tool shed at the side of the lodge.

Her hand shook as she trained the weapon on Russ. *Please God, don't let him come to.*

Byron came back with enough rope to hog tie a steer. They tied Russ's hands behind his back.

"Here, I found some duct tape, too. We can muzzle him."

She grinned, despite the situation. "Good man, Byron." She tore a piece off and took special pleasure in securing it over Russ's mouth. Together, they dragged him into the kitchen and stuffed him in the pantry.

She looked at Byron. "We've need to disarm Cook. You hide in the shed, I'll circle around front and try to take him by surprise."

A familiar voice startled her. "I've got a better idea."

She swiveled. "Kory!" In one glance, she took in the blood-stained clothes and the gun trained on the cowering cook's head.

Byron grinned from ear to ear.

"You knew about this?" she asked the young man.

"Yep. Knew it all the time. I found Kory on the floor of the equipment building. Guess ole Russ thought he was dead, but he only hit him in the shoulder."

Bewildered, she asked, "What about him?" She pointed to Cook.

"Mr. Kory got the drop on him with my help. I distracted him when he looked away."

Focus returned as she took in Kory's bloody shirt.

"Byron, tie up Cook and make sure you duct tape *his* mouth, too." She looked at Kory. "We need to bind up your wound, stop the bleeding."

Kory smiled. "Whoa, hold on. The kid got some clean rags in the shop. It's all doctored up, for now. The cops will be here in a few minutes."

Her attention turned to Byron, who was busy tying Cook's hands. "The police? So, you got through?"

"Yes, the ATV sputtered out on me about half way." A sheepish look crossed his face. "Forgot to put gas in it. But, I had the sat phone, so I called. He said he'd dispatch his officers right away. They should be here any minute."

"I can't believe this. Your quick thinking saved the day, Byron." Unfortunately, there was bad news to impart to these two and she didn't know how to break it. "Byron, Kory, I have something very bad to tell you."

Byron glanced at Kory, then back at her.

Kory placed his hand on Byron's shoulder.

Her heart melted at Kory's compassion and kindness to this boy. Her next words would devastate them. "It's Wolf and Buck. They…"

"Where are they?" Kory asked.

"Upstairs," she whispered. "Last room on the right."

Before she could stop him, he bounded up the steps and was gone.

Byron looked at her with pleading eyes. "They're not..."

"I don't know. There was blood everywhere."

The teen left Cook on the ground and raced after Kory.

A window opened above and Kory yelled down. "They're still alive. We need help up here."

She couldn't drag Cook alone. Instead, she checked his restraint and left him on the ground.

The pounding in her chest resumed. Hope glimmered once more.

Oh, please stay alive!

CHAPTER Thirty-Five

SIRENS SCREAMED OUTSIDE THE MAIN DOOR AS SHE RACED for the stairs. She stopped, looked up at the landing, and shifted her focus. *Better to intercept the police.*

Carefully, she opened the door a crack. Three patrol cars lined up in front of the lodge, weapons drawn.

She ran back to the dining room and jerked a white tablecloth from one of the tables. Through the crack in the door, she waved it outside. "It's me, Ricki Sheridan."

"Open the door slowly, with your hands up!"

She recognized the officer's voice and did as he directed. "It's me, Kemp! The scene is secure. You can come in."

"Miss Sheridan? Are you okay?"

"Yes, but we need help. Two men are down and need medical attention."

Kemp nodded at one of his men. "You take the upstairs." He

nodded at the other officer. "Make sure the area is totally secure. Keep your weapon at the ready. Ms. Sheridan, tell me what went down."

The first officer raced upstairs as directed.

"Where are the shooters? Any victims?" Kemp asked.

"As far as I can tell, two men are shot, one man is missing. Kory was hit in the shoulder, but is mobile. He's with Byron and the injured men upstairs. Byron ambushed Russ, knocked him out. He's tied up in the pantry. Kory and the boy got the jump on the other one. He's behind the lodge tied up."

Kemp's mouth flickered a smile. "Sounds like it's all handled. Nice work. What about the missing man?"

"Yes, Kyle. He was supposed to be keeping watch with Buck, one of the men who was shot. We can't find him," Ricki stated.

The third officer appeared with Cook on his feet, still bound. "Found this one behind the lodge."

"There's one still missing. Man named Kyle. We need to recon the area, see if we can find him," Kemp directed. "I'll take charge of this one."

The officer nodded and left Cook in Kemp's custody.

"You say Russ is in the pantry?"

"Yes."

Kemp shoved Cook into the back seat of the car.

"Can you watch this one while I retrieve him?"

"Of course." Even though Cook was tied up she didn't take her eyes off him.

The officer returned with Russ, still bound and duct taped, and glaring at her. He secured him in the second squad car.

"Is it all right if I see about Wolf and Buck?" she asked.

"Certainly, these two aren't going anywhere," he said.

She turned and hurried inside.

Kory was coming down the stairs. "An ambulance is on its way."

"How bad is it?"

"Wolf's hurt bad, but we've got the bleeding under control. Buck was grazed in the head. I think he'll be okay."

She shook her head. "There was so much blood. I thought for sure they were dead."

"It was pretty gruesome up there. Both are talking, though. It's a good sign."

"You better sit down, Kory. You've lost blood." She steered him to the leather sofa by the fireplace. "Byron still up there?"

"Yes, couldn't get him to leave Wolf's side."

"I hear a siren. Must be the ambulance." She grabbed his hand. "They're going to be all right, Kory. I know they will. I want you to go in the ambulance, too. You need medical attention. I'll stay with Byron, call his parents, help where I can. The police will be here for a while. Kyle is missing. One of the officers is checking the grounds."

He tried to shake his head.

She stopped him. "I won't hear any nonsense. You're going to the hospital. End of discussion."

He sank back into the soft couch. "I'm too tired to argue."

"Any idea where Kyle might be?"

"Kyle? No, no one has mentioned Kyle. I hope they find him."

The ambulance stopped in front of the lodge, red and white lights splashing color through the windows like a kaleidoscope.

Four men burst through the door carrying rescue boards. She pointed to the stairs. "Top left."

They nodded and hurried up.

Ten minutes later, a parade of characters made their way down. Two medics carried Buck with the officer holding an IV bag over him. Next was Wolf. The other two medics managed him with Byron holding the IV.

Byron's ashen face nearly killed her. He looked so incredibly sad. The man who mentored him was in grave danger.

"Come on, Kory. Your turn." She helped him up.

They made their way to the ambulance and she kissed him on the forehead before they closed the doors. "I'll see you at the hospital.

I've got to wait until Byron's parents get here. I need to help look for Kyle, too."

He nodded and squeezed her hand. "Thank you."

"I should go with Wolf, he needs me," Byron cried.

She held him back. "No, he's in good hands. We need you here. We'll go as soon as we can."

Anguish tortured his voice. "But, I don't want to leave him alone. How can you leave Mr. Kory? You don't care!"

Firm, but softly, she tried to impress on him what was necessary in this situation. "This is the tough part, Byron. We're law enforcement. There's a job to do."

He turned to her. "Law enforcement?"

"Yes, you said it's what you wanted to do. Well, here's your chance. There's one man missing. We need to find him. Will you help?"

The ambulance driver shut the back doors and headed for the front.

She stood with Byron as they drove off, sirens and lights blazing. It broke her heart to let Kory go without her, but she was needed here.

Kemp questioned Russ. She motioned for him to step behind the other car out of earshot.

"We still have a man missing. Kyle is somewhere in the area. He might be shot, bleeding. We need to find him. I can take the lodge."

Kemp frowned. "Yes, we need to find him alive." He looked at Byron. "You up to doing a little recon?"

Byron's large, round eyes didn't blink. All he could do was nod.

"Take the perimeter near the tree line," Kemp said. "Go slow, look closely."

"Yes, sir."

She started in the great room and continued through Wolf's office, the bathrooms, kitchen, and dining room with no luck. The thought of looking through the upstairs rooms where she found Wolf and Buck sickened her. What if Kyle met the same fate?

Halfway up the stairs, Kemp rushed inside. "We found him."

Relieved, she hurried out the door on the officer's heels.

Byron knelt in the brush beside the equipment shed.

"It's Kyle?" she asked.

"Yes, he's alive. Tied up, but alive," Byron smiled. He finished loosening the bonds.

Kyle sat up, rubbing the top of his head.

Ricki took a knee beside the wounded man. "What happened to you? Are you shot?"

"No." He patted both hands over his chest as if he might have missed something. "Someone jumped me early this morning, hit me over my noggin." Gingerly, he massaged the knot on his head. "Damn, I think they cracked my skull. Hurts like crazy."

"Did you see who it was?"

"Well, I heard a rustling in the brush, but when I poked my head closer, I saw an arm with a skull and cross bones tattoo." He stopped and looked confused. "Dadgum, I think it was Cook. He's the only one I know with blood dripping from the skull. But, why would he knock me out?"

She sat back on her heels. "Long story. I'm glad you are okay. Nasty bump on the head. You need to go to the hospital and have it checked out. Shouldn't fool with head injuries. Byron, go tell the other officers we found him."

The boy nodded and headed for the back of the lodge.

After he'd gone, she told Kyle what happened to Wolf, Buck, and Kory. "The boy is all messed up over this. I didn't want him to hear it explained again. You're lucky they didn't shoot you, too."

"Are they gonna live?"

"I hope so, Kyle."

Kemp helped Kyle to his feet. "We'll take him to the hospital in the squad car. I'll leave one officer here. It's a crime scene, we need to collect all the evidence we can. Can I give you two a lift somewhere?"

Ricki shook her head. "I'm going to wait here with the boy. Call his parents to come get him. I've got the truck, I'll head to the hospital as soon as Byron is secured."

Kemp smiled proudly as the boy rejoined them. "This one here is a natural. Sure could use another like him on the force. Good job, son."

Byron shook his hand and beamed. "Wow, two job offers. Game Warden and Police Officer."

The two policemen left with their charges. The third one awaited his boss's orders.

"Time to call your folks, Byron," she said.

"Do we have to? I want to go to the hospital."

"Your parents need to make the decision."

The officer had dispatch call Byron's parents.

"Let's wait in my truck. We don't want to go back inside the lodge until its cleared."

The truck's heater didn't take long to heat up. Warm and safe, she finally sighed a breath of relief. "Byron, you are an absolute hero. Without your quick thinking, I'm not sure any of us would be alive."

He flashed a crooked smile. "It's amazing what you can do when you have to. Do you think Officer Kemp was serious?"

"He was absolutely serious. You have all the right instincts. Study hard, finish your schooling. You have plenty of time to decide which direction you want to go."

She kept the conversation on training and the police academy to keep him from dwelling on Wolf's injuries and all the chaos this day dished out.

Twenty minutes later a car turned off the blacktop road.

She turned and pointed toward the road. "Here come your parents."

CHAPTER
Thirty-Six

Ricki got back in the truck as Byron's parents drove off. They promised to take him to the hospital to check on Wolf, but the boy would remain with them until the lodge was cleared. At first, he wasn't too pleased about it, but when she told them about his heroics he beamed and took up the story, chattering about the whole incident. His father's face beamed with pride.

He has a whole new respect for his son, now. I think they will support him all the way.

The longing to rush to the hospital overwhelmed her, but there was one more thing she had to do. Call Captain Maddox.

She still had the sat phone, so she pulled it out. After she relayed the story and the news Russ was again in custody, she sighed and said, "I'll grab a bite to eat on my way. Should be there in an hour if the roads allow."

Captain Maddox would have none of it. "Wolf's my dear friend.

I want you to go to the hospital, check on him, and report back to me. I'm sure the police have more questions for you, too. You know the drill. I don't want you back here until they say so."

Relief washed over her like a refreshing shower. Duty was priority most times, but she desperately wanted to see Kory and make sure Wolf and Buck were out of danger.

"Thank you, Captain," she whispered.

She got out of the truck and found the lone officer. "Do you need me to stay? Help you with this?"

"No, Officer Bradley is on his way. I figure you're pretty anxious to get to the hospital, so head on out."

"Okay, if you're sure."

He nodded and continued tying off the police tape.

The truck hummed down the road, giving her time to reflect on the last twenty-four hours. She was wrong about where Russ would show up, which led her to believe his primary target was Kory, after all. Even with all the danger and chaos, her mind went back to the cabin, the cold night huddled together against the freezing night. Working together to keep Byron safe and warm.

It was so natural, a moment I'll never forget. Holding hands, talking into the night, sharing a common goal.

She envisioned working with him high in the mountains, shouldering the load together.

We make a good team. Except when I lose my temper. I'll really have to work on it.

Her stomach growled as she passed the little Lakeview diner about a block from the hospital, but hunger was the last thing on her mind. She wanted to see Kory.

At the front desk, a young receptionist directed her to Kory's room.

It was a small hospital. She hoped they wouldn't have to airlift Wolf to a bigger hospital if his injuries were serious. *I hope he's strong enough to fight this.*

Kory's room was the last one the right.

She stood outside the curtain. "Knock, knock. Are you awake?"

"Ricki," the voice called. "Come in."

The light in his eyes made her heart leap. New bandages adorned his shoulder, his color was good, and his brilliant smiled dazzled her. Errant black curls made him look like a little boy at the sight of a new puppy.

"Well, you look better than when I saw you last." She smiled.

"I feel right as rain now you're here."

Her smile faded. "Any news about Wolf or Buck? What about Kyle?"

"Wolf's in surgery. They found Kyle?" he asked.

She related to him how Byron's found him. "He should be here in the hospital for his head wound."

"Barb keeps me informed about Wolf, I'll ask her."

Her eyebrows raised. "Barb? Should I be jealous?"

"Are you?"

Heat rushed to her face, not in a fit of temper this time, but an urgency to stake her claim. She went to his side and took his hand. "Yes, I'm jealous of any woman who pays attention to you. I'm done fighting it. I want to be the woman in your life."

A tear welled in his eye. "You don't know how long I've yearned to hear those words. Are you sure, Ricki?" He winked at her and put his hand to his shoulder. "Don't mess with the injured guy, I might have a relapse."

Her smile only grew larger. "Oh, a funny man, huh? Well, you know what? I hope your shoulder takes a long time to heal so I can show you how serious I am."

His laugh was like music to her, but his light-hearted mood faded to a serious tone. "Does it mean you're going to come to work at the lodge?"

The old, familiar doubt snaked inside her brain and threatened to derail the joy she allowed herself to feel. "I haven't got that far, yet.

It wouldn't be right to leave Captain Maddox short-handed. Fact is, I love my job there. I would really hate to leave it."

"I get it, but how is this relationship going to work with you in Murphy and me up here? Or am I pushing you too soon?"

She leaned forward, shrugging off the shadow of indecision. "We don't have to think about it, right now. Maddox gave me a few days leave to keep an eye on Wolf and the rest of you. He wants to make sure his old chum has everything he needs."

"A few days? What great news. The doc said I can get out of here this evening."

"Well, where will you go? The lodge is a crime scene. They're not going to let you back in there for a day or two. Maybe you should stay in the hospital."

Kory knit his brows. "Well…"

A nurse slid the curtain back and entered. Her round, jovial face lit up the room. "Hello, dearie. How's the shoulder? Your color has improved greatly. Might it be because of this gorgeous creature holding your hand?"

His grin returned. "I believe it has everything to do with it. This is Ricki Sheridan, game warden in Murphy. Ricki, this is Nurse Barb."

"Thanks for taking such good care of him, Nurse Barb."

"Oh, please, just call me Barb. Everyone does."

Kory asked, "Do you have any news about Wolf?"

While she tightened the blankets around him, she also checked the bandage. "Yes, I do. He's out of surgery, in recovery, and doing very well. The bullet missed his vital organs. You should be able to see him in an hour or so."

He squeezed Ricki's hand. "Did you hear? He's going to be fine. And Buck?"

Barb came around to the end of the bed and moved the curtain aside. "They'll keep him overnight to watch him. Head wounds can be tricky." She moved to leave.

"Wait, there's another man. Brought in after Wolf and Buck.

Name's Kyle. Any word on him?"

She nodded. "Yes, same thing. Ugly head wound. He's staying, too. Looks like you're the only one getting out of here tonight." She cast Ricki a look. "You driving him? He can't leave on his own."

"Yes, he's in my custody."

Barb beamed. "Well, looks like you couldn't be in better hands. However, you're not leaving until after lunch. We need to get vitals, again."

"Yes, ma'am." He gave a swift salute.

After the friendly nurse left, she turned back to the dilemma at hand. "Where are you going to go?"

Before he answered, a young voice inquired outside the curtain. "Mr. Kory? Are you in there?"

Ricki jumped up and drew back the curtain. "Byron! Come in. Kory is doing great."

The boy stepped in and stood in front of Kory's bed. "I came to see Wolf, but they said he's in recovery. He had surgery. Did you know?"

Kory answered, "Yes, they told us we can see him soon." He looked past Byron. The Johannson's stood in the hall. "Please come in. Thank you for bringing him here. You've got quite a boy here."

"Thank you," Mr. Johannson answered. "We think so, too. How are you, Kory? They told us you were shot."

"Right as rain. Bullet went clean through."

"Glad to hear it. We won't bother you. The nurse told us where you were. Byron, here, wouldn't take no for an answer."

Kory looked at the young man. "Wolf's going to be just fine. You know what a tough old bird he is. Don't you worry."

Byron nodded.

As the Johannson's turned to go, Barb blocked their way. "Excuse me folks, I have news about Wolf."

213

CHAPTER Thirty-Seven

Byron spoke first, "Is he okay? Is anything wrong?"

Barb turned to him. "He's fine. In fact, he's asking for you, young man."

"He is?"

"Yes, if you'll come with me, I'll take you to him. The rest of you can see him in a bit."

Ricki's eyes filled with tears. "He sure does care about the boy."

Byron's father agreed, "Don't know what we would have done without Wolf. He put him on the straight and narrow. I'm mighty grateful. We'd best be going. After he sees Wolf, we'll head on home. Not sure when everything will get back to normal at the lodge, so we'll keep him with us until it all levels out."

She shook hands with both of them. "Probably only a couple of days. I imagine Wolf will remain in the hospital for a while, but Kory and Buck will be back to run the place. They'll need Byron."

Mrs. Johannson spoke quietly, "It'll be good for him to keep busy. Blessings to you Kory. And you, Miss Sheridan. Thanks for all you did for our boy."

The room was quiet after they left. She sat beside Kory, not speaking, just holding his hand. The horrific events at the lodge changed everything between them, put it all in perspective. The path to love was clear as a summer blue sky, now. She wanted Kory, wanted the dream, to experience true love for the first time. Negative thoughts tried to crowd in, throw her off course, but she'd declared her love and meant to hold steady. Her job in Murphy, the commitment to her boss, logistical obstacles threatened to bar her way and muddy the water, but she shook them off. *One problem at a time. I'm not giving up this time.*

A short while later, Barb returned. "The Johannson's have gone home. Wolf is asking for you two."

Ricki helped Kory get to his feet. "Can you walk down the hall or do you need a wheelchair?"

"I'm not about to let Wolf see me in a wheelchair. I'll make it just fine."

Barb's jovial face took on a stern look. "Now, mind you, only a few minutes. He needs his rest. Lordy, he's a cantankerous man. Hasn't changed a bit. Wouldn't take no for an answer. He wants to lay eyes on you himself."

They entered his room almost on tip toes. Wolf lay with his eyes closed in the darkened room, his skin ashen.

Kory whispered, "Wolf? You just gonna lay there, man? There's work to be done."

Wolf's eyes flew open. In a raspy voice, he asked, "Kory. You okay, boy? Byron said you was shot."

"I'm fine. They're letting me out of here. Guess Russ has poor aim. How you doin', boss?"

"Could be better. Not as spry as I used to be. Gonna take me a little time."

"Well, don't you worry about anything. As soon as the police say so, Buck and I will be taking care of what needs to be done. You just heal up."

"Buck? He shot him. He's alive?"

"Yes, head wound, but he'll be fine. Kyle, too. Knocked him in the head, but he's a tough buzzard like you. Everybody made it and the bastard is behind bars. For good this time."

Wolf smiled weakly. "Ricki?"

"Right here, Wolf. Fine and dandy. Don't worry."

"You got him."

"Couldn't have done it without Byron. He's the hero of the day."

Wolf tried to turn his head to look at her. "I want to hear it all…"

"Oh no," Barb interrupted. "You need to rest and these fine folks need to find a place to stay."

"Can't go back to the lodge?" Wolf whispered and tried to sit up.

Kory rested a hand on Wolf's shoulder and eased him back on the pillow. "Not for a couple of days. Police have to clear the area."

Wolf's voice weakened. "Stay with Martha."

"Martha?" Kory asked.

"Buford," he whispered. "Tell her I sent you."

"Okay, enough. He needs rest." Barb pushed them out the door.

Kory continued to walk toward his room. "I've never heard about a Martha Buford before. Maybe it's in the phone book, or someone at the desk can tell us. Not sure I want to stay with a perfect stranger. Maybe the little motel has a room."

Ricki started to answer, but stopped when Barb caught up with them.

"Martha Buford's house is on the edge of town. She's a celebrity around here. Known for her hospitality. Warm-hearted, charitable. A true lady. I'll give you the address. You really can't miss it. It's a quaint little place. And I guarantee if you mention Wolf's name, she'll be glad to take you in." She gave them an exaggerated wink. "They were an item back in the day."

A few hours later, they were settled in Ricki's truck following the directions Barb gave them.

"Buck looked good. Kyle seemed a bit squeamish. I hope a good night's sleep will set them right again," Kory said.

"Yes, all of this could have been so much worse. For Russ to shoot all three of you and no one died—. Do you think he actually *meant* to kill you or is he just sloppy? I guess I'll never know."

"Who knows what was in his mind? The idea he wanted to take you out of the country proves to me he didn't want murder on his hands. Maybe it's why he didn't kill us. Would he have killed *you*? We might not find out for sure."

Ricki didn't respond, just rode in silence thinking about what might have happened. "Never heard Wolf mention this Martha person, not since I've known him."

Ricki turned into a narrow driveway, "Guess we'll find out. Here we are."

It looked like all the lights in the house were on through the beautiful lace curtains in the windows. Classical music drifted through the air, a mellow piano. She thought it was Bach, but couldn't be sure. *How can I ask a perfect stranger for a room?* She almost lost her nerve. Poised to knock, she stopped and looked back at Kory.

He shrugged.

She went back to the truck. "Surely, there's a motel in town. I'm not sure I can ask a stranger for a bed. What do you think?"

Before he could answer, the door opened and an elegant, older woman appeared in the door. "May I help you, young lady?"

Kory encouraged her, "Go on, at least talk to her. After all, we're sitting in her driveway."

She walked forward. "Hello, my name is Ricki Sheridan. I'm the game warden in Murphy. My friend in the truck is Kory Littleton.

Wolf sent us."

The woman's face was smooth, with only a hint of a wrinkle at the corner of her eyes. The 1940's dress and erect bearing spoke to elegance and grace. The light-colored hair tucked neatly at the nape of her neck only added to the timeless persona.

Ricki felt like she'd travelled back in time.

The woman looked past her to the truck. "Wolf? Is he with you?"

"No, you see he's in the hospital."

The woman gasped, "In the hospital?"

"There's been a shooting at Wolf's Lodge."

The woman paled and swayed slightly. "Wolf's Lodge? Wolf—is he…?"

Ricki reached out to steady her. "Maybe you should sit down. He was shot, but is recovering. Just out of surgery."

Martha declined. "No, I'm fine."

"I'm sorry to bring you this news. I gather you know him well."

The color flooded back to her face. "Well, yes. We're old friends."

Ricki kept her hand lightly on Martha's arm. "I see. Wolf is the one who told us about you. Said you might take us in for the night."

"Where are my manners. Please, come in." Martha turned to open the door.

"Let me get my friend."

She helped Kory out of the truck.

The door swung wide and Martha ushered them in. "There's a small room with a bed next to the parlor. I use it sometimes when I don't feel like climbing the stairs. You are welcome to stay in there."

Together, the women helped him into the room and settled him on the bed.

"I serve dinner at six, but I'll bring yours to you." She was gracious and concerned.

"No need. I can go out and bring us something. Thank you."

"I won't hear of it. Tonight, dinner will be a little late, but I will be serving." Martha left and came back with towels and an extra blanket.

"You and your husband should be comfortable in here."

"Oh, he's not my husband, we're not married."

"My lands, the way you two look at each other, it's clear to me you're a couple. Maybe you *should* be married. Anyway, it's a big bed, and by the look of him, he won't be sowing any wild oats for a few days." When she smiled, charm oozed from her person.

Ricki laughed and wanted to smack the smug look off Kory's face. "Okay, okay. Why do I feel ganged up on?"

Ricki changed the subject. "Have you known Wolf long?"

Martha looked away, sadness shadowed her face. "Wolf and I go way back. We were an item—once."

"I've not known him long. He's quite a man."

"Yes, he is. Now, *this* young man needs to rest. I'd like to go to the hospital to see my old friend before visiting hours are over. Do you mind? I'll be back to serve dinner."

"Certainly, Ms. Buford."

She smiled. "Please, call me Martha."

When she left, Ricki fluffed Kory's pillows, put up the towels, and spread the folded blanket at the foot of the bed.

The few chores done, she sat in the chair, suddenly shy.

"Ole Wolf," Kory said. "Sneaky old man. Who would've thought he could attract a beautiful woman like Martha?"

"Her skin is like porcelain. She's so elegant and refined. Wonder what went wrong?"

"I don't expect Wolf to ever tell. We'll have to get it out of *her*."

They talked a bit, but she urged him to sleep.

He insisted she stretch out beside him.

That's how Martha found them. Lying close together holding hands.

For two days, they basked in the radiance of Martha's home. During the day, they spent time with Wolf, Buck, and Kyle. Afterward, they retreated to the oasis of Martha's home, talking, sharing, and enjoying each other's companionship. At night, they lay side by side, the distance between them narrowing, until holding hands wasn't quite enough. They kissed, melting into one another, savoring the growing flame of desire.

On the last evening, Ricki sat on the veranda with Martha drinking a cup of hot tea. The night air was very cold, but each had a quilt wrapped around their shoulders and the warm liquid kept the cold at bay.

"What happened, Martha?" she asked.

"What do you mean, dear?"

"Between you and Wolf? Why aren't you together? It's clear you care about each other," Ricki probed.

Martha set the cup on the small table next to her chair. "I ask myself the same question all the time. What *did* happen? In the end, it seems so inconsequential. We spent years apart, devoid of the companionship humans need to survive in this world. I grew up in a different world. Everything had its place. Proper and orderly. If you know Wolf, you also see the bluster. Acts before he thinks, thrives on chaos. However, I was prideful. I wanted him to conform to my way of life. *He* wanted me to come with him to the lodge."

Ricki studied her face. "You loved him, didn't you?"

Martha stared into the night. Sadness filled her eyes. "Loved him? Ricki, I love him still. I remember the moment we met. That one moment. Magical, a sign from above, but I fought it. He wasn't exactly what I had in mind to wed. We dated for a few years, but it always came down to lifestyle. It all seems so silly now. What I remember is his kiss…" Her voice trailed off.

Ricki let her savor the memory.

Finally, Martha came back to the present and looked lovingly at her. "You've had a moment with Kory, haven't you, dear. I can see it."

It wasn't a question, it was a statement. Everyone could see it.

Wolf, Byron, Buck. Even Martha, who she just met.

So, why did I fight it?

"Don't make the same mistake, Ricki. In the end, *things* don't matter. They can't keep you warm at night. Pride was my downfall. If I could do it over, I would, but it's too late for me. Don't end up alone with nothing but memories."

She reached for Martha's hand. "It's not too late for you and Wolf. The love is still there, stronger than ever. He's recovering much faster because of your visits. The two of you belong together. Go and take your moment back."

Tears filled Martha's eyes and she faced Ricki. "I will, if you will, dear."

CHAPTER Thirty-Eight

On the third day, Officer Kemp called. All was clear, they could return to the lodge.

Ricki didn't bring up the unspoken question. Was she going back to Murphy or staying with him at the lodge? The physical attraction between them was undeniable, but an emotional bond overshadowed desire. *Maybe* because they were forced to put sexual eagerness aside in the wake of Kory's injury. *Maybe* because of their combined failures of the past. What blossomed in its place was a friendship, a connection much deeper than lust. In a way, the gunshot wound gave them time to explore areas most couples overlook in the heat of passion.

The old defensive chains, insecurity, wariness, suspicion, skepticism, all the tools they used to hold the other at arm's length, fell away. Self-preservation took a back seat as they regained the ability to trust.

And, Ricki's hair-trigger temper was nowhere to be found.

Martha hugged them both when they left. "You two are meant for each other. Don't let anything keep you apart. Love like yours is rare. Hang on to it with all your might." Her eyes shimmered with a faraway look. "See you come back here and visit me. I've grown quite fond of you both."

They made a last visit to see Wolf.

True to form, his cranky nature dominated the entire room. He barked out his agitation. "The retreat is in two weeks and nothing is ready. Those consarned doctors say I can't leave for another week. How can I get everything ready layin' here in this dad blame bed? Can't they see? I ain't no layabout."

Kory spoke in a soothing tone, "We've got this, boss. Simmer down. Kyle's out there cleaning up the place, already. Buck's seeing to the kitchen and finding another cook. Byron's taking the reservations. Who says the place can't run without you?"

Wolf grumbled under his breath.

"Besides, I'm headed out there, myself. I'll make sure the place runs like a top."

Wolf looked at Ricki. "What about her?"

Instead of answering the question, she evaded. "Want to tell us a little bit about Martha? We know she's been coming up here every day to see you."

He frowned. "None of your business. Why don't you two get out of here and make yourselves useful."

Laughing, they bid him goodbye.

The only sound during the ride to the lodge was the noise of the highway, the tires humming a rhythm neither wanted to disturb. The heavy silence speaking to what should be said and the decision *she* must make.

Ricki knew he wanted an answer. *Staying or going? Which would it be?*

How could she answer him when she simply didn't know? Torn

between wanting him and the responsibility of her job, she let the silence take over.

Byron greeted them before they could get out of the truck with Buck right behind him.

The seasoned trail boss bear-hugged Kory. "Glad to have you back and in one piece. We've got a few bumps in the road needin' your attention. I just ain't got a knack for this kind of work. Byron's got all he can handle with the phone ringin' off the wall."

She watched them walk toward the lodge, Buck filling in the details, Kory listening intently.

Byron hung back. "You coming in, Miss Ricki?"

Reluctant to tear her eyes off Kory, she turned slowly. "Well, maybe for a minute. I need to call my captain. Tell him I'm on my way back."

The boy hung his head. "Sure hoped you'd stay."

"Well, we all have responsibilities. I have mine back in Murphy. I need to get back to them, now everyone is safe and sound."

Inside the lodge, she went to Wolf's office to use the phone in private. Byron had cleaned the small space from top to bottom until it gleamed. She laughed. *Wolf's gonna hate this. He likes his chaos.*

She dialed the captain's number, but hung up when Kory poked his head through the doorway.

"Can we talk?" he asked.

"Sure."

"Are you going back to Murphy?"

She sighed. "I don't see as I have a choice. My job is there. They need me."

Kory leaned toward her. "Don't. They can find someone else. *I need you. Ricki, I love you.*"

Martha Buford's words rushed back at her. *Go and take your moment.*

She looked at him, his eyes moist with emotion, cheeks flushed, hair tousled, yearning with his whole body to make her stay.

When she started to speak, he stopped her. "I heard you and Martha last night on the porch when she told you to take your moment." He reached for her hands folded on the desk. "Let's not be Wolf and Martha. I want to grab life by the horns and live it with you. I don't want to waste time on petty differences. You love me. I know you do. I knew the minute I kissed you on the mountain, that one moment, it was crystal clear. We were supposed to find each other."

Tears filled her eyes until he became a blur. They brimmed over and fell on her cheeks. Her mind went back to the kiss. Even though she fought it, tried to run away from it, made excuses at every turn— she knew it, too.

She spoke softly, "Something special is happening between us, Kory. I don't deny it and why I hope you can understand. I need to go back to Murphy, for a while. I have responsibilities there. You know as well as I, we aren't the kind of people to ditch our jobs at the spur of the moment. I love my job as much as you love yours. You've got your hands full with the retreat. I've left my boss short-handed. Let's take a step back and see what happens."

"Ah, the voice of reason," he said. "Why does it feel so wrong, when I know you are right?"

A smile played on her lips, even though tears coursed down her cheeks. "Are you admitting I'm right for a change?"

He reached over and wiped the tears away from her wet cheeks with his thumb. "You know, I think I am." He straightened. "We'll do it your way this time, Freckles. Go back to Murphy. Do what you have to do. But, I want you to take this with you, as a reminder."

He took her hands and gently pulled her to her feet, searched her face, and whispered, "You're so beautiful."

Afraid to breathe, she let him have the moment as she drank in his rugged handsomeness, the tousled hair, his puppy-dog eyes. His arms wound around her waist. She burned his touch into her memory.

He leaned in, took her mouth gently at first, tasting,

exploring. Just like on the mountain, he pressed into her, the kiss explosive—hungry.

Unable to talk or even breathe, Ricki pulled away.

When the erratic beat of her heart slowed, her voice returned, barely audible. "I could never forget something like that, Kory. You make it hard to leave."

"Then, don't," he chided.

"Not fair."

He stepped back and turned toward the door. "Please, come back to me."

And then, he was gone.

CHAPTER Thirty-Nine

THE TASTE OF RICKI'S LIPS STILL TINGLED ON HIS. KORY yearned for her to change her mind, find him, and throw herself into his arms. Soft pale skin, sprinkled with those adorable freckles, the tip of her dainty nose, those luscious lips were burned in his mind. He trembled at the restrained passion vibrating through her body. *Can I withstand the onslaught once it's power is unleashed?*

But, she was right. Neither of them were the type to throw away something they worked toward for so long. The journey must lead them back to each other with no regrets.

The decision to rip away from her embrace took a physical force he didn't know he possessed. *I can't force her. This time I'm going to get it right.*

He headed toward the convention room; the nerve center for the retreat. Benches graced each side of the doorway. He chose the one on the right, closed his eyes, turned his face toward the sun, and soaked in its warmth.

"It won't be long before the sunshine disappears for clouds and snow. Better take advantage of it," he mused aloud, and compared the heat of those rays to the fire of their kiss.

Something blocked the light.

"What are you mumbling about?" Kyle stood, arms akimbo, in front of him.

Kory opened his eyes. "Nothing, just enjoying a moment in the sun."

"I brought these two newbies to help with readying the convention room. They both have strong backs. Don't want to do anything to hurt the old gunshot wound."

He looked around Kyle and stood. "Hello, my name's Kory Littleton. We sure could use a couple more hands."

The two men smiled and shook his hand.

"Alright, Kyle. You know the ropes, get 'em started."

"You got it." He glanced at the new guys. "In here. We need to make sure it's ship shape before the guests arrive.

Reluctant to give up his spot in the sun, he reclaimed the bench, the interruption unable to disperse the power of emotion coursing through him. *Does she realize what we found? Will she decide to stay or step back, give in to the doubt and fear of the past?*

He stood up. "I want to see her, one more time."

The great room of the lodge was empty. Byron was behind the desk.

"Where is she?" he asked.

Byron nodded toward the door, sadness in his eyes.

Kory hurried forward and flung open the door, only to see the back end of her truck disappear down the black top road.

Too late! All I have now is the image of her face and the kiss. He prayed it was enough to hold him.

Ricki wanted nothing more than to follow Kory out the door and throw herself in his arms with a promise to stay. Unfortunately, an intense sense of duty pulled at her. The folks in Murphy, who welcomed her so freely, deserved better.

She lectured herself as she drove down the road. "Captain Maddox took a chance on me. I must prove to him I'm the kind of person who keeps their word. What kind of an example would I be to Byron if I just quit and indulged in an impulse?"

However, another voice argued deep inside. *What about Wolf and Martha? Look where practicality got them. Bitter and alone. Is it what I want? Why can't I have it all?*

The warring factions continued to plague her mile after mile. It didn't help when Kory's face floated in and out of her mind as the road stretched ahead. Nor did the memory of the kiss.

Early afternoon found her pulling into Murphy proper. Captain Maddox's truck sat in front of the café. She parked alongside.

The little bell chimed her arrival.

Maddox sat with his back to her, alone, head slightly bowed.

"Care to buy a girl a cup of coffee, Captain?" she asked.

Her boss looked up and smiled. "Welcome back, Sheridan. We were beginning to wonder if you'd come back. Here, slide in."

He motioned for the waitress to bring a cup of coffee.

Curt took the coffee pot from the young hostess. "Glad to see you back, Ricki. We heard about all the fuss up there. Everyone okay?" The café owner filled the cups, a concerned look on his face.

"Hello, Curt. Yes, everyone's on the mend. Wolf is still in the hospital, but he has a good nurse." She looked at Maddox.

The captain winked at her. "Yes, Martha is a jewel. Never did figure how he let her slip away."

"I have a feeling he won't this time," she said.

"Glad to hear it," Curt said.

"I owe you for the meal a few days ago. Never thought I wouldn't be back. So sorry." She fished in her jacket pocket for her wallet.

Curt waved his hand. "No, no. It's on me. Wouldn't dream of taking your money."

"Well, thanks. I really appreciate it."

A customer entered and smiled at her. "Got another hungry one. Maybe we can talk later?"

"Sure, later," she said.

She turned her attention to Maddox. "What's the scoop around here? Everything quiet?"

"Yeah, yeah. No big problems," he answered.

"Noreen okay?"

"Yeah, fine."

"Then, what is it? Something's on your mind. Care to share?" she asked.

"Nah, maybe later. I want you to go out and check on old Mr. Sherman. No one's been out there. Figure its time. How about dinner with me and Noreen tonight? Been a while. She's been asking about you."

"Sounds good. Thanks for the coffee, I'll head out to check on Sherman right now. See you tonight."

Before she pushed through the café door, she glanced at Maddox. His head was bowed, once more, over his coffee.

Something isn't right. Maybe Noreen can tell me.

Mr. Sherman beamed at the sight of her truck.

She rolled down the window to say hello.

"You did a right fine job on the fence, Ms. Sheridan. Howler has stayed put. Much obliged."

"Glad to do it. We're here to protect all animals, even old Howler here." She stepped out of the truck, patted the dog's head and roughed his chin. "If you need anything else, you know where to find me."

The old man shook her hand vigorously. "Right kind of ya. You come by for a glass of tea anytime. Don't need to be nothin' wrong for you to come for a visit."

"I'll be sure and take you up on the offer anytime I'm out this way."

They visited about the weather, the coming winter, and the dog.

She smiled and waved as she got in the truck.

Nice old man. Glad to make his days a little brighter.

She checked on a few more spots before heading back to town.

I'm looking forward to seeing Noreen. She might give me a clue as to what is eating her husband.

After a change of clothes and a vigorous hair brushing, she headed to the Maddox house.

"Ricki! I'm so glad Roger invited you. Why, I've been beside myself with worry. All the shooting and such. Why, you'd think it was the wild west around these parts. Come in. I want to hear all about it." Noreen ushered her inside, prattling on while she took her coat and gloves.

"Everyone is fine. Wolf is still in the hospital, but recovering nicely," she answered.

"Come in the kitchen with me. You can help with the ice in the glasses," Noreen suggested.

"Where's the captain?"

"Oh, he'll be along."

Ricki thought she saw a shadow cross her friend's face. "Everything okay? He looked a little down when I saw him earlier."

"It's business. He'll tell you all about it."

The table was set, the food was ready, but Captain Maddox still wasn't home.

"Noreen, I get the feeling something's up. What is it?"

"Everything is fine. I want to hear about your handsome Kory and, of course, Wolf. How is he doing?"

"Kory is healing fast and Wolf…well, I need to ask. Did you know about Martha Buford?" Ricki asked.

Noreen's smile brightened. "Why yes. The four of us used to do all kinds of fun activities together. Those two were meant for each other."

"Why didn't they stay together?"

"Stubbornness. Couldn't, or should I say, wouldn't compromise. Silly pride, both of them." She shook her head. "When I think of all the wasted years…" Her voice trailed off.

The front door opened.

Maddox came in and smiled when he saw Ricki. "Oh good. You made it."

Dinner was filled with small talk, mostly about the incident at the lodge, Wolf and Martha, Russ Desmond's fate, and how Byron saved the day.

"The boy has potential, for sure," Maddox said.

Ricki looked from one to the other, noting neither would make eye contact with her. "Why don't you tell me what's going on, you two?"

Noreen looked at her husband.

The captain looked at his plate. "Well, something's come up. I need to make a decision and I'll be darned which way I should go."

"Well, maybe I can help. Tell me what it is," she offered.

He looked up. "Well, it's about the sheriff. Or should I say his son."

"The sheriff's son? Is the boy all right?"

Maddox waved his hand. "Oh sure, sure. He's fine. The problem is, he isn't a boy. He's a young man."

"Get himself in some trouble?"

"No, just the opposite. He just graduated from the academy."

Ricki smiled. "Well, the sheriff must be proud."

"He is."

"So, what's the problem?"

Noreen poured her another cup of coffee, then served the captain.

Maddox stirred sugar into the cup and avoided looking at her. "Sheriff wants him to come here to work."

No one said anything for a moment.

Ricki broke the silence. "Here?"

"Yes, here. Problem is, there's not room in the budget for another game warden."

Ricki laid her fork down. "You mean…?"

He nodded. "I have to make a choice. You or the sheriff's son."

"And, if you don't choose the sheriff's son it won't set well between you?"

"Sorta the way it is." He looked her straight in the eye. "I like you Ricki. Your work is impeccable. I don't know what I'm getting with this greenhorn boy. I'm between a rock and a hard place."

Noreen cleared the plates away without a word.

Maddox continued to stir his coffee.

Ricki sat silent.

CHAPTER Forty

A WEEK LATER, WOLF WAS FINALLY RELEASED FROM THE hospital. He grumbled about his clean office, barked orders around like he'd never left, and generally made life miserable for everyone.

Byron was back at the registration desk annoying Wolf with his constant whistling. The boy showed his happiness with enthusiasm since his mentor was back behind the helm.

Reservations were full. The convention center was in order, the guest rooms sparkled, and the grounds looked like something out of a garden magazine. Everything was in place—but the speakers.

"I have to do everything myself. You'd think as long as you've been here, Kory, you could scrape up a couple of speakers for this thing," Wolf complained.

"I called everyone I know. Even tried the numbers you gave me. No luck," Kory answered.

"Well, there's only one more thing to do."

"What?"

"I'm gonna call Martha. She's done it before. Was quite a big success. I figure she'll do it, if only for the opportunity to fuss over me."

Kory laughed. "Great idea. Why didn't I think of it?"

Wolf huffed. "Well, get out of here so I can call her. Don't need any eavesdropping from you."

Kory grinned as he headed for the shed. *Ole Wolf still has a hankering for the woman. Maybe this time they'll hook up for good.*

He promised Byron he'd hike out with a gas can and bring the old snowmobile back. The boy said he'd meet him at the shop.

The door was open and Byron stood just inside. "Are we going now, Mr. Kory?"

"Yep. If we don't go now, we might not get a chance after the retreat starts. You ready?"

"Should I tell Wolf where I'm going?"

"No, I told Kyle to watch the desk. I don't think you want to disturb Wolf right now. He's on an important mission."

Byron looked quizzically at him. "Mission?"

"Never mind. Let's go."

The boy knew exactly the direction to head and Kory let him take the lead. He was proud of the strong young man he'd become.

The snow was deep and hard to walk through, but an hour later, they found the machine right where Byron said they would. It took a bit of priming and fiddling, but they got the old snowmobile running and safely back to the lodge.

Together, they walked with their arms around each other's shoulders to the lodge, laughing and bragging on their prowess.

Wolf greeted them with a scowl on his face. "Where have you two been?"

"Out rescuing the old snowmobile. You know, the one that saved your butt from being killed?" Kory laughed.

Wolf *never* blushed, but Kory thought he saw just a hint of color.

The old man's voice softened, "Oh, I forgot it got left out there. If I haven't said thank you, then I'm saying it now, Byron. You saved everyone here. You got good instincts. Proud of ya."

The boy beamed. "Thanks, Wolf."

Wolf's voice went back to its former brusque tone. "Now, get your butt up to suite 19 and put it right. Miss Martha is coming for the retreat and I want it spotless."

"I'm on it. You can count on me." Byron scurried past Wolf.

Kory smiled widely at his boss.

"What are you grinning about?" Wolf asked.

"So, she's coming? Good for you. Now see you don't chase her off before she gets started good."

"Why don't you mind your own business?"

"Why don't you admit you're sweet on her?"

Wolf glared, turned, and went back inside.

He thought about Martha coming and sighed. *It will bring back the memories of our time at her house. Ricki lying next to me, those sweet kisses while I healed.*

He followed the narrow path to the convention room. Kyle said it was ready, but he wanted to make a final inspection. Inside, the tables were in line, covered with pristine white cloths, chairs aligned perfectly, and small candle arrangements adding color. A podium graced the front of the room.

The new cook gave him a menu of the meals to be served, refreshments, drinks, etc. Everything was in order. *Amazing they had pulled it off after what happened.*

He let himself dream for a minute. Envisioning Ricki beside him at the front podium, talking about new found love, decisions to be made, compromises to address, unloading baggage from past relationships. *I bet we could have put together a hell of a program.*

THAT ONE *Moment*

Martha Buford arrived the next day.

Kory embraced her warmly. "It's so good to see you, Martha."

"You look the picture of health, Kory. I'm so glad to know you recovered completely." She whispered in his ear. "I miss you and Ricki. You brought a ray of sunshine into my life."

"Those few days with you mean everything to me," Kory said. "A chance to heal, a chance to get to know Ricki better."

She smiled. "Yes, dear. It was providence, I dare say."

"It's good of you to help Wolf out like this. I'm sure you're the better of any speakers we could have booked."

"Ah, you flatter me, young man."

"Have you heard from her? She went back to Murphy, you know. Her job. I hope I can get down to see her after this retreat is over."

"Yes, I *have* heard from Ricki."

He blinked. "You have? Well, you are one step ahead of me. I haven't. They must be keeping her very busy."

"Must be," she said.

Something in the way she replied, something about the twinkle in her eye, made Kory hold her gaze a moment longer.

"Will you help me with my bags?" she asked.

"Of course, Martha. Anything for you."

"Oh, and you might want to hang around and help with those bags, too." Martha pointed to the road.

"What bags...?" his voice trailed off.

Coming around the corner was a grey SUV.

"Ricki?"

Martha laughed, softly, 'Yes, my boy. It's her."

Kory hurried to open Ricki's door and pulled her into his arms. "Ricki," he cried hoarsely."

"Yes, Kory. It's me, and this time, I'm here to stay."

Epilogue

Ricki and Kory united forces along with Martha Buford and presented a most enlightening couples retreat. They even got Wolf involved.

Ricki settled in at the lodge and went to work with Kory as his survivalist partner.

She admitted being replaced in Murphy was the best thing that happened to her.

A mountaintop wedding is planned in the spring.

Byron finished his studies with honors and applied to the police academy.

The story of Wolf and Martha is begging to be told.

An Unlikely Arrangement

Chapter One

January 1929

THE VOICES CONTINUED … MUFFLED, NO MATTER HOW HARD her ear pressed against the thick, wooden door. *Did they say Kirby? Who is Mr. Kirby?* The crisp, winter wind shook the windowpanes, but the gooseflesh rippling on her young flesh was not a result of the cold. She pushed hard, away from the oak barrier. "You can't do this to me, Mother. I am seventeen, a grown woman. Let me out." Ruth Squire rattled the lock while her other fist pounded the heavy door. "Do you hear me?"

No answer; she didn't expect one. She was familiar with discipline, plenty of it, the consequence of a strong will and zeal for adventure, but never like this, locked inside the second-story bedroom. Ruth's hands fell to her side. Crazy from confinement, she paced, a lioness caught in a cage.

"What is she going to do to me this time? Even Father won't talk to me." The metal springs of the bed squawked in protest at her weight. Sprawled across the rumpled bedcover she stared at the only link to the outside world. The flicker of the gas street lamp outside the warbled glass window did nothing to soothe her.

Although…No, not the window, that is how I got in trouble in the first place.

Alone against the world, everyone gone—her best friend Ginny, Father, and worse, she had made an enemy of Mother. Instead of rage and exasperation, her mother remained calm, determined—even sinister. "This side of her is something to fear, I believe."

The growl in her stomach intensified, and thirst ravaged her throat. *What time is it? Do they intend to keep me in here until morning with no food or drink?* A key rattled in the lock, and she jumped up as the door swung open.

Priscilla and Robert Squire entered bearing a white linen-covered tray. "You will eat now, Ruth. We'll talk after you have finished."

"I'm not hungry, take it away." Ruth's stomach lurched at the look on her father's face. His sad blue eyes showed no sign of the familiar, easy smile of assurance. Although he stood taller, he wilted beside his wife, a shadow of a man. One hand smoothed his peppered hair; the other jingled the change in his pocket.

The tray hit the nightstand with a bang. "There is no room for argument. I said eat." Mrs. Squire crossed her arms against an ample bosom.

Ruth looked to her father for help, but he only sighed, and took a seat in the chair across from her.

The warm aroma of cook's scones broke down any defiance, and her fists unclenched, although she continued to glare at both parents. She eased onto the side of the bed, hesitant, eyes on the enemy, and devoured the light, flaky scones, and warm tea in short order. The back of her hand swiped across her mouth, a move she knew Mother would abhor, and swallowed the last of the tea in one gulp.

"We have done our best to lead you on the right path. This was your last chance and now it's time for desperate measures," Mrs. Squire said.

"I wanted to have a little fun, Mother. All young people like to dance." The attempt to wiggle out of trouble would prove futile, but she tried anyway. "I'm not interested in the other children, or the fact you value fun over responsible behavior. You are not yet eighteen, and you will not spoil my plans to have you properly married one day with a family of your own."

Ruth tossed her short black hair and poked out her chin before she spoke. "Marriage? I want to have fun, go places, and see the world. I don't want to be like you."

The pop of the slap resounded through the room. Ruth reeled backwards, held her hand to one burning cheek, and blinked in horror.

Though not tall, Priscilla Squire stood strong and broad, a stout woman, in a dark blue, shapeless dress and sensible shoes. Long, streaked, gray hair pulled back into a bun and faded, lackluster brown eyes completed the severe look.

Father sunk lower in the chair and shuddered. Mother rubbed the palm of her hand and strode toward the door…Father slinking after her like a cowed puppy. "Come morning you will have the run of the house, although Sarah's duties tomorrow include sentry and keeper of the keys. Don't try to leave, Ruth. We have arrangements to make in the morning. Now sleep."

The perfunctory remarks stunned her. "Arrangements? What arrangements? Father, what is she talking about?"

The slam of the door and turn of the key sealed her fate. *Unless… Can I get a message to my friends, Danny or Ellen? They probably wonder why I didn't show tonight. Excitement made me careless. I'll try to call in the morning. Maybe one of them will come and help me escape.*

Exhaustion took over. She curled up on the bed and cried until an uneasy sleep overtook her weary body. The jangle of the key in the lock woke her at the murky, black hour before dawn. A slow, steady throb pulsated in her head. She sat up, tried to shake the sluggish daze from her brain, and waited. *Maybe I can talk to them now. Tell them I'm sorry. Surely, they will be reasonable this morning.*

No one entered. She slipped out of bed and tried the knob. The door opened at a touch. She quickly threw on a robe and ventured into the hallway. The stairs creaked and threatened to announce her cautious escape. A quick search of the house soon confirmed her parents' absence, but she found the little Irish maid alone in the laundry room. Sarah O'Brien administered her duties flawlessly and had ever since Ruth could remember. A fixture in the family, Ruth did not consider her a servant, but a long-standing friend and confidant.

"Good morning, Sarah. So, they're gone? This time it must be serious." She waited: Sarah didn't respond. "There's nothing to do but wait in my room, I guess. That's where I'll be if you need me."

The diminutive maid continued folding the linen napkins. "Breakfast's gettin' cold in the kitchen. It'll ruin afore long."

"I'm not hungry yet, and I cannot spend the day in my robe and slippers." She hurried up the stairs, slipped into the bedroom, and closed the door. It took only a moment to pull the cotton day dress over her head and kick off the satin slippers. She opened the door a crack to make sure Sarah had not followed, took a deep breath, and tiptoed down the hall to Mother's private sanctuary—a room forbidden to her. Once inside, her eyes adjusted to the dim light. "It smells of violets in here—such a feminine scent for my stodgy old mother. What a surprise. I wonder what else I will find. Ah, the window. Should I climb down the trellis?" In three strides, she reached the window. A quick tug of the sash and all hope dissolved. It would not budge. "Now what?" She glanced around. "I don't see the telephone anywhere, either."

Across the room, the clear glass knob on the closet door twinkled in invitation. "Naturally, the closet, a perfect hiding place." She stepped into the dark, cavern-like wardrobe. Before she found the light, the creak of a door opening frightened her. Footsteps echoed on the wooden floor.

"Ruthie Squire what in the name of everything holy are you doin'? Have you got a death wish, child? Your mum does not even let your papa in here. Come out this instant."

"All right, Sarah, I'm coming. Where did they go, by the way? They tell you everything."

"You know I cannot tell you. They would fire me for sure. Breakfast is awaitin'. Come down to the kitchen."

The temptation to trick Sarah, slam the door shut, and lock it crossed her mind. She studied the back of Sarah's head, haloed by short, blonde hair, and followed her down the stairs. It would not be fair to this woman, a friend for seventeen years. Mother would fire her. "You are right. She is a ruthless woman."

"Oh child, she's protectin' ya, is all."

"You can say what you want. You are not the one choked to death by her rules."

Sarah looked up from the bottom landing. "I live by them, too, girlie. Different ones, to be sure, but rules all the same, and they protect my job here. One day you will learn it for yourself."

"Are you going to lecture me all day or get my breakfast, Sarah O'Brien?"

"Thought you weren't hungry, girl. At any rate, your breakfast is already made, and I'll be thankin' ya to watch your tongue, or we will be addin' another crime to your long list."

"All right, all right, I'm coming."

After a quick breakfast, she thought again of the telephone, but the candlestick device continued to elude her. Mother kept constant guard on it. Father's office stayed locked. She was sure it was in the forbidden closet. Discouraged, one hand followed the smooth wood of the stair's banister back to her room. *How do I get inside Mother's room without Sarah knowing?* The afternoon passed slowly as she contemplated different scenarios of punishment until, exhausted, she plopped onto the vanity chair, grabbed her brush, and brooded over what loomed ahead of her. "Probably boarding school."

Her fingers dipped into a small pot of rouge, the one indulgence Mother allowed. "Maybe I will make myself up like a clown. They would kick me out of the stupid old boarding school right off." Her laughter filled the room. "If Mother wasn't such an old tyrant I would wear lip paint." She applied the correct amount on both cheeks, enough to give a rosy glow. "I look too young in this brown frock. Let me see…if I pull my hair back like so—yes, much better. I could pass for twenty instead of a mere seventeen."

"It is good to see you making use of your time, Ruthie."

The flimsy chair toppled as she jumped to her feet. "Mother, I didn't hear you come home."

"Prepare yourself for company. I will send Sarah up to help." Her mother's eyes narrowed—a clear warning.

"Please tell me…" Frozen, she watched her mother's ramrod straight back stiffen, but continue out of the room.

The maid appeared in the empty doorway. "Who is it, Sarah? Who is coming?"

Sarah entered the room, picked up the tortoise-shell hairbrush, and began grooming Ruth's hair. The housekeeper worked in silence, the brush rough against Ruth's scalp. The sound of horse's hooves on cobblestone and a high-pitched whinny interrupted the two women. Ruth escaped Sarah's grasp and peered through the upstairs window.

"Why is a horse-drawn milk truck parked in the alley? Sarah?" She looked over her shoulder, but the room was empty. *Sarah has turned traitor, too.* Drawn to the scene below, she peered at the sight below. "Why would a headmaster drive a milk wagon?"

The front door's brass knocker reverberated through the house. *My fate has arrived.* The voices enticed her into the hallway to listen.

"Please wait in the drawing room, Mr. Kirby. Our daughter will be down soon." Mother's voice sounded strangely light and friendly.

"Mr. Kirby?" She scurried back to the bedroom determined not to come out. A knock on the door startled her and she sat hard onto the bed, heart pounding.

Her mother swept into the room—all business. "Sarah has prepared the green dress. It is more suitable for receiving visitors. Change and be downstairs in fifteen minutes, not a moment longer."

"Who is Mr. Kirby?"

"If you want to find out you best hurry." Mrs. Squire left the room without further comment.

Alone, Ruth stared at the empty doorway. In the next instant,

Sarah appeared—the freshly brushed green satin in her hand. Neither woman spoke as the homespun cotton fell to the floor. Ruth stood woodenly as Sarah pulled the green dress over her head and fastened the intricate buttons.

After a final adjustment, Sarah gave a gentle push at the small of Ruth's back. "Come on, dearie. It's not as bad as all that. Go on now, I'm right behind ya."

Tears threatened to spill over the rims of her eyes as she moved forward on leaden legs.

The conversation in the parlor sounded polite, friendly. The familiar creak of the stairs announced her approach, and her parents turned in tandem to welcome her. The parlor was a favorite room. Ornate Cherrywood framed the forest green velvet sofa, a cozy place to curl up and read. Colorful flowered globes sat atop the twin oil lamps and each graced the matching end tables. Heavy, dark green drapes kept the warm afternoon sun at bay. In the corner on the settee, next to the glassed bookshelves, sat a man she thought looked too young to be a headmaster of anything, much less a school full of young women.

He stood and removed his hat, exposing sandy blond hair, bright blue eyes, a strong chin, and easy grin. "Ruth, please greet Mr. Peter Kirby. Mr. Kirby, this is our daughter, Ruth." Mother smiled. "Mr. Kirby has agreed to marry you. The ceremony will be next week in the family church."

ABOUT THE *Author*

Award Winning Author Patty Wiseman is a native of the Seattle, Washington area and attended The Wesleyan College in Bartlesville, Oklahoma. Northeast Texas is home, now, along with her husband Ron. She created the Vintage Mystery Series, The Velvet Shoe Collection set in the 1920's. Intrigue with a touch of romance fuel the stories of strong women who overcome obstacles and propel them into strength and triumph.

Her books include: *An Unlikely Arrangement* – won 2nd place in Forward National Literature Awards, *An Unlikely Beginning*, won 1st place in Texas Association of Authors in Romance, *An Unlikely Conclusion* – won 1st place in Texas Association of Authors in Romance, and her brand new book, *An Unlikely Deception* – Book Four of the series. She's also written a motivational book called *Success Your Way – Make a Wish, then Make a Plan*.

She is a member of the Texas Federation of Women's Clubs – Marshall Chapter, a Lifetime Member of the Worldwide Who's

Who for Professional Women, named VIP for 2013, a member East Texas Writers Association, a member of the Northeast Texas Writer's Organization, and Texas Association of Authors

Favorite quote "Find out who you are, then do it on purpose." ~ Dolly Parton

Website: www.pattywiseman.com

Facebook: www.facebook.com/PattyWisemanAuthor

Twitter: www.twitter.com/PattyWG

Email: patty_wiseman1966@yahoo.com

GooglePlus: www.plus.google.com/+PattyWisemanAuthor

BOOKS BY PATTY WISEMAN

The Velvet Shoe Collection

An Unlikely Arrangement
An Unlikely Beginning
An Unlikely Conclusion
An Unlikely Deception

Success Your Way

That One Moment

Made in the USA
Columbia, SC
11 November 2021